OLLIE'S NIGHTMARE

Book Three of Ollie's Heart

Mark Mortland

7th Street Dreams

DISCLAIMER

Ollie's Nightmare is a work of fiction intended for an adult audience. It explores themes of trauma, resilience, LGBTQIA love and relationships, erotic scenes, and the power of found family. While this story contains intense emotional moments and fictionalized legal conflicts, it remains true to its heart: a journey of love, healing, and self-discovery.

This book includes mature themes and adult situations, including past parental rejection, emotional distress, and legal struggles, but always with a focus on hope, support, and overcoming adversity. Readers sensitive to these topics should approach with care.

At its core, Ollie's Nightmare is about the strength it takes to reclaim your life, the love that makes healing possible, and the unbreakable bonds that form when people choose to stand by one another.

Table of Contents

CHAPTER 1: A NEW NIGHTMARE

I *feel* a noise - loud but unidentifiable - a deep, somehow animalistic rumble somewhere outside, making my Bronco shudder violently. My eyes shoot open, heart pounding. The air inside the car feels thick, suffocating, and wrong. I bolt upright. I'm instantly awake and ready to fight. I fling my car door open with a growl of my own: "Okay, assholes!" I shout, trying to sound braver than I feel. "Didn't you learn your lesson from last time?!"

The silence that answers my outburst is unnatural. It feels like the world is holding its breath, keeping its true nature secret from me. I step out with clenched fists, but... there's no one. The parking lot is empty, bathed in sickly, pale-yellow daylight. It's too bright, too sharp; the air itself radiates with wrongness. My chest tightens. I reflexively spin around, ready to defend myself, but there's only my Bronco in the middle of a desolate Walmart parking lot.

Wait. No! Damn. Why is it so bright? And why am I still here? I should have left by now; I should be lifting at my gym. My alarm - how did I miss my alarm? Panic claws at me as I realize I don't know where I am. I'm untethered, floating through this empty, wrong version of reality. The air is heavy, pressing against my skin. My brain is thick with confusion: I don't know what time it is. I don't know what day it is. I don't even know which Walmart this is.

I need something - anything - to feel normal again. I stumble toward the store entrance. The automatic doors slide open, but there's no greeter, no people - still no human sound. The fluorescent lights hum above me, casting long, sterile shadows on the empty aisles. My footsteps echo in the silence; every echo makes me feel more alone.

A wave of suffocating panic crashes over me. I'm hit with an overwhelming sense of abandonment and loss. My father. I need to find my father. Now.

"Dad!" My voice cracks, echoing through the emptiness. "Daaad!" I shout again, louder this time, my throat tightening as the word sounds more desperate. I don't even understand why I'm calling for him, but I have to. I have to find him. I run through the aisles, my feet pounding against the hard tile, my chest heaving as I push through this empty labyrinth.

Then I hear his voice. Cold. Distant. Behind me. "Stop shouting, Oliver."

I freeze, his uncaring voice chilling me to the bone. I whirl around, searching for the source, and spot a dark, shadowy figure at the end of the aisle. My heart leaps into my throat as I sprint toward him, but the lights flick off just as I reach him.

Everything plunges into darkness.

Still, his voice remains. "Stop calling me 'Dad.' You don't have a *father* anymore," he growls, sending another icy chill down my spine. His voice again cuts through the silence, each word sharper than the last. "You chose this. You're not my son. You're nothing." The words twist around me like a suffocating fog. I try to scream, but all that comes out is a choked, pathetic sob.

Suddenly, a cold, dead-feeling hand slaps across my face, and I'm falling, endlessly falling. Yet my father's words keep stabbing at me from the darkness, cruel and venomous. "It's your fault. You ruined everything. You disgust me."

I reach out, desperate to stop my fall, but there's only emptiness. I'm weightless, spiraling down into a bottomless pit of darkness. But the darkness is alive, pulsing with despair, wrapping around me and dragging me deeper into oblivion. I scream, but the sound is swallowed whole by the void.

Another strike comes from the darkness - the cold slap harder this time. Blinding pain from my nose overwhelms my senses, and I feel warm blood trickling over my lips. My father's voice returns louder, mocking me as if claiming victory with every syllable. "You're alone, Oliver. Alone forever."

My voice is only a ragged whisper, and my words fade into the shadows as my strength ebbs. I curl into myself, hugging my knees. The darkness is endless and crushing. I'm becoming nothing - an abandoned stray.

Until... From the depths of my crumbling sanity, a name surfaces: "Corey." I latch onto it like a final lifeline. "Corey!" I cry out, my voice breaking while the void swallows every echo. The abyss is merciless; there is no answer. I keep falling.

"Corey!" I shout again, clinging to the fragile hope the name gives me. I know he *must* be there. "Corey, find me..."

CHAPTER 2: SLEEPING WITH THE DADS

Concerned hands and soothing voices gently awoke me, melting away the cold weight of the nightmare with their warmth. At least I didn't throw any punches or elbows this time. I knew it was just a nightmare. Yet, even before I opened my eyes, tears came - hard. My old nightmare hadn't disappeared; it had simply changed form and was still part of me, a part I thought I had left behind.

When I opened my eyes to the dim light of my bedroom, Chris was standing near my waist, and Ted was kneeling beside my chest. Both were in "dad mode," desperately trying to pull me back to reality.

Ted took the lead. "Ollie, we're here. You're safe. It's okay. It's Ted and Chris, your dads."

Unlike before, when Corey first tried to wake me from a nightmare, and I bolted up with fists ready to fly, I didn't feel the urge to fight. I understood the reality that was still breaking my heart. Slowly, I sat up and let my new dads pull me into their embrace, where I sobbed, allowing my emotions to wash over me.

It was 3 am again - my old nightmare hour.

Once the tears slowed and I could form words, I apologized, as I always do. I looked into Ted's eyes. "Dad, um, Ted. I'm sorry..." I sniffed, "for waking you up. I guess I got a little too loud?"

Ted smiled, brushing it off. "Sport, I love it every time you call me 'Dad.' It's worth being woken up for." He pulled me closer, kissing the top of my blond curly-haired head. "I thought your nightmares were getting better. What happened? Do you remember what it was about? We heard you shouting 'Dad' right before the serious screaming and sobbing started until you finally just kept crying for Corey."

I looked down, avoiding his gaze. "I'm sorry. I usually handle it better, but this one... Um, this new nightmare is horrible. It's cruel. It hurts. It started happening when I'm here alone after spending weekends at Corey's house. I hoped it would just go away, but it's only getting worse."

I looked at my new dads and took a deep breath. "I wake up in my Bronco, parked in some random Walmart lot. I'm alone as if none of this" - I gestured to my wonderful room - "ever happened. And there's a shadowy figure of my father telling me how much he hates me for being gay. Then he slaps me, and I start crying for Corey to find me. It's really messed up. I'm sorry things got so out of control tonight. I just... I miss Corey. I miss him a lot by midweek. His absence is like a hole I can't fill. And my nightmare comes in through it." My eyes were watering again.

Chris, ever practical, asked, "So this only happens when you're here after your weekends with Corey? What about your other nightmare, the one about your car break-in? Does that still happen when you're with him?"

"Only maybe a couple of times since I've been with y'all. And I haven't punched him once." I smiled weakly. "He... holds me tight while I wake up, and it helps calm me down. I guess he knows a few tricks from being a nurse."

Ted placed a hand on my cheek, his voice at its softest. "Oliver... son. When we decided to have you live here instead of moving straight in with Corey, it was to help you adjust and decompress. We weren't trying to keep you away from him." He glanced at Chris, who nodded in agreement. "Ollie, if you're doing better with him - if you sleep better with your Norse God, maybe that's where you need to be."

I chuckled softly. "Did I call him a 'Norse God' in my sleep, or did he tell you?"

Chris grinned. "Oh, we have eyes and ears everywhere; we're dads." Then he hugged me. "Ollie, Corey doesn't tell us everything, but he's been making a case for you to move in with him. It's obvious how much he loves, cares about, and wants to keep you protected. And... well, we can see you need and love him too."

Ted chimed in. "Sport, you'll always have a home here, no matter what. But it looks like it's time for a change. If being with Corey helps avoid these nightmares, you should be with him. We can move your things this weekend if you want. As we said... Spoiler alert: Corey's already on board. And we promise not to list your room on Airbnb. Well, for at least a week." My new dad winked.

Their words sank in, and the weight of my nightmares seemed to lift. I chuckled, still sleepy. "That sounds amazing. I'll text Corey tomorrow." As they gave me a final hug and started to leave the room, a sudden rush of panic hit me. "Dads... would it be okay if I slept on the couch tonight?"

Chris paused and turned back to me, concern flashing across his face. "Of course, Ollie. But the couch isn't nearly as comfortable as your bed. Are you sure?"

I hesitated before explaining. "It's just... when I was a kid, after a bad dream, I always had to sleep somewhere else to stop it from returning. Usually, it was in my parents' room. I need to be somewhere different for the rest of the night."

Ted wrapped an arm around my shoulders. "No couch, Sport. Come on." He pulled me up into a walking hug, guiding me through the house toward their bedroom. "You can sleep with us tonight. It's okay."

I tried to protest weakly. "Dads... I, uh, always wake up with a..."

Chris laughed and gave me a playful nudge. He had finally tentatively started using Ted's nickname for me. "Sport, we've already seen you with a..." He winked and flashed me Corey's smirk. "Remember? You. Kissing Corey. Boxer briefs? Biker shorts? Trust me, there's nothing to be embarrassed about. Now, come on, we won't let anything hurt you anymore. Including your nightmares."

I followed them into their room and climbed into bed, immediately comforted by the familiar scent of Corey from Chris's side. It felt... right. I snuggled in, becoming Ted's big spoon while imagining that Chris' arms were Corey's wrapped around me from behind.

It would have been perfect if not for one big little thing: both snored. Loudly. Still, it was the most comforted I'd felt without Corey present in weeks. I might need to rethink sharing a bed with the dads on a school night again. It was going to be a very groggy Thursday.

CHAPTER 3: TEXTING

I started texting Corey as soon as Ted and I arrived at work, and I had replied to all my morning emails.

Ollie: *I kinda slept with the dads last night. But they snore. Way too much.*

Corey: *Um, what?! You can't just casually drop that without an emoji to explain* [Laughing Tears Face]

Ollie: [Angel Face] *Okay, here's the deal: I've started having a new nightmare that only happens when I'm away from you. After I wake up, I can't go back to sleep alone. I know it sounds pathetic. But, um. Can I start staying with you more? Like maybe all the time?*

Corey: *You already know the answer to that, pup. Of course!*

Ollie: *I know, but I'm scared I'll like it* too *much.*

Corey: *What do you mean by 'too much'?*

Ollie: *Corey... I already love you so much that it hurts to ever think about leaving. It's like my butterflies go wild when I'm with you. I'm the luckiest pup on the planet. But then I remember that I have to leave here* *in just over three months and go back to Michigan. And when I think about it, I can't even breathe.*

Corey: *Breathe, pup, my love, I know. But did you say butterflies?*

Ollie: *Yeah, the ones you give me just from being near you.*

Corey: *Ah, I get it. The same ones you give me* [Smiling Heart Face]

Ollie: *Wait! I give you butterflies too* [Exploding Head]

Corey: *You're smiling uncontrollably right now* [Smirking Face]

Ollie: [Smiling Eyes Face] *You already know me too well. Um, should we tell the dads that we found our song?*

Corey: *Let's hold onto that secret weapon for now. We might need it to convince them of something big later. Right now, they've already agreed we need more time together. Let's take this win and just be happy.*

Ollie: *Speaking of... They're cool with moving my stuff this weekend. Which is great, but Corey, I don't think I can take another nightmare like that.*

Corey: *I know pup. It's already Thursday. Just sleep with them again tonight if you need to, okay? You've got this. And I've got you tomorrow night. I love you, my Ollie.*

Ollie: *I love you too my* [Wolf Head]

CHAPTER 4: SCHOOLED

The spring co-op term officially ended tomorrow, and with the summer term starting on Monday, I was feeling a little sad about losing all my recently made co-op friends. Over the last couple of months - without working two jobs *and* finally having a real place to sleep - I'd been able to join all the company-planned co-op activities. As it turned out, I was part of a pretty awesome group. Since I was also staying for the summer term, I was looking forward to meeting new friends on Monday.

There were even two cute gay guys who both admitted they'd had crushes on me during those rare times I'd been able to hang out with everyone. They said they thought I was being "mysterious" with my unintentional aloofness. Thankfully, I'd become really close with them in just a short time. They were appropriately jealous when I told them about Corey. Not that I was bragging, I just loved finally being able to share my joy with others. Both of them were attending UT in Austin, and we made sure to exchange contact info and promised to stay in touch.

In other news, I somehow ended up taking over as the lead student for our co-op newsletter after the original lead had a surprise appendicitis. Poor girl. That's a rough way to end a term, but at least her family flew in to help her recover. I was secretly grateful she had their unconditionally loving support. I knew what it felt like when it didn't come. I even sent her a very personal "Get Well Soon" card. And! My take on the newsletter was a huge hit. I got a bunch of kudos, which only fueled Ted's claim that I was a "Super Co-op." If I can't make my real father proud, I'm damn sure gonna keep making my new dad proud.

Our final Friday was going to be a total blowout, with a big farewell party and a celebratory lunch, complete with fun awards. As Ted and I drove home, stuck in the usual rush hour traffic, I felt torn between excitement for tomorrow and dread about another potential nightmare tonight.

Ted, always able to read me like only a father could, cut through the silence. "Ollie, remember when I gave Corey grief for not simply asking what kind of music you like?"

I panicked for a second, almost blurting out how Corey and I had both woken up singing "No Rain" that Monday morning almost two months ago. But then I realized, hey, why should I be nervous about finishing our most important 'assignment' early? I shook it off, and Ted thankfully didn't notice.

"You're doing the same thing he did, overlooking the obvious," Ted continued. "Why don't you just text Corey right now and invite him over for dinner? Then ask him to stay with you tonight. You're cooking your amazing meatloaf, right? The one from your grandmother's secret recipe that has to sit overnight before you bake it? Trust me, you've already got Corey's heart, but great food is always the perfect way to keep it yours."

Ted flashed me his now signature fatherly look, which I loved just as much as Corey and Chris's sweet smirks.

Suddenly, all my stress melted away. "Thanks, Dad! That's perfect. Well, I was hoping to experiment on you and Chris before trying it on Corey, but it looked pretty good when I put it in the fridge last night. I'm sure y'all," Ted gave an approving nod at my use of 'y'all' - "will love it."

I pulled out my phone and texted Corey with the invitation. Our date was set.

****

Corey came over as soon as he got off work, right around the same time as Chris. Go figure, they both worked at the same clinic. It reminded me of my own routine with Ted, commuting together every morning and afternoon. It was one of those small comforts I realized I'd miss once I started living at Corey's place - or *our* place, as I should start calling it. But come Monday, for the first time in a while, I'd be driving to work alone. Just me and my beloved Bronco.

CHAPTER 5: A BOLD MEATLOAF

Corey entered our dads' kitchen and grinned, clearly impressed with my decision to tackle a meatloaf. "Ollie, it takes a brave man to make meatloaf for his family. I'm serious. Meatloaf is the most personal American meal you can cook."

He wasn't kidding, and his expression said as much. But I couldn't help chuckling anyway.

Seeing my reaction, Corey smiled. "Remember that armpit scent speech I gave you when we first met?" He looked at me grinning, because he understood there wasn't any way I couldn't. "Believe me pup, the same rules apply to meatloaf. Not everyone loves it, and even if they do, everyone has their own personal taste for it. You're really putting yourself out there with this. I'm impressed, and I know it's going to be absolutely awesome."

I can't believe I actually let myself pale again at the seriousness of his words, which, this time, only made Corey laugh. He grabbed me in a big, reassuring hug. "I hope you know you're already unconditionally loved by your dads, and, duh, by me." He booped my nose. "Perfect meatloaf or not." I just melted into his embrace.

To help calm my nerves, Corey worked with me on a couple classic sides while my potential masterpiece baked in the oven. We made homemade mashed potatoes and fresh green beans. Corey asked the dads if they wanted a salad, but they waved it off as soon as the aroma of baking meatloaf filled the house. Grinning, Chris said, "That meatloaf smells way too good to have to wait through a salad. And… As a doctor, don't tell anyone I said that."

I laughed, once again, loving the way Chris's smirk mirrored Corey's. At this point, they were practically the same.

The meal turned out perfect. I absolutely blew my new family away. My grandma would've been proud - well, if she'd still talk to me. The pièce de résistance? No one could figure out my secret topping until Ted finally gave up. "Ollie, I can't believe how amazing this is. Seriously. What's the sauce on top?"

I reveled in my moment, soaking in the praise. "Y'all should recognize it. It was the perfect match for my grandmother's recipe…" I teased them, watching their faces for any hints of recognition, then I dropped the bomb. "It's Whataburger spicy ketchup."

I couldn't help but laugh as the dads and Corey started clapping.

And Ted couldn't contain his happiness either, exactly what I hoped for. "Bravo, Sport! You're officially a Texan now. We couldn't be prouder."

I beamed, my chest full of pride, not just about the meal but for being able to make my family so happy. That's all I long to do. My final night at my dads' house was perfect. We all helped with the cleanup, laughing and sharing more Corey Stories. Some to his protests, most to my amazement and amused disbelief. Through both types, all I could think was: *this* is my wonderful family. How the heck did I get so lucky?

Eventually, our dads retired to their wing of the house with their usual evening drinks. Corey and I headed to our side, the promise of young love - and a few other things - hanging in the air.

CHAPTER 6: TURNING THE TABLES

Corey is my fantasy man and every time we're together, he becomes even more so. I can't resist him. The moment we got to our room AND shut the door; I enthusiastically tackled him. We tumbled onto the bed and landed with me on top. My arms pushing down on his broad chest, trying to playfully dominate his larger frame. He looked up at me, sweet and loving, but caught completely off guard by my mock attack. My day had started out with a horror, but it was ending on an incredible high.

"Hey pup! You're the one who just cooked us an amazing meal, shouldn't I be the one throwing you onto the bed to show my appreciation?"

"Corey, you always treat me so perfectly. Every night we're together, you're my ultimate lover and protector and I love you for it. But you're my man too. I just cooked a meal for our family. I proved I can take care of you, just like you take care of me. Now it's my turn to show you how much you mean to me."

His eyes softened, and I could feel his heart beating in his gaze as I continued.

"My wolf. I'm not challenging you. Why would I ever want to? But, Corey, tonight, can I make love to you? Just like with the meal, I want to give you the same pleasure you always give me. I think it would be the perfect way to end our time together in this room - your old bedroom. Plus... it's the final part of me I haven't shared with you, or anyone. Can I give you my last virginity?"

Corey's expression shifted to a mix of surprise and amusement. "Ollie, if you fuck as well as you deliver these unexpected confessions, I'm in for an amazing ride. Seriously, do you just have all these little speeches saved somewhere, all prepped and ready to go?"

I laughed. "Oh, hayal no! You know my inner monologue's writer is a noob. He's currently freaking out about pulling off a real sex scene. He's trying to steal inspiration from every incredible experience you've ever given me. Until he eventually gets enough confidence to coax me into doing things I'd never be brave enough to do on my own."

Corey gave me a teasing, yet sincere look. "So, are you sure you really want to top me? Because, you may not know everything yet. It's definitely about a lot more than just trying something different."

Still straddling his waist, I met his gaze, my heart steady. "Yes, my wolf, I'm sure. I want to give you the same feelings of love and security that you always give me. I want you to feel as cherished by me as I feel by you. Don't worry, if switching roles isn't something we ever do again, that's okay - but tonight... please let me try."

****

After a very intense look from Corey that I didn't fully understand, he gave me an affirming nod. I started simply, with a sweet, soft kiss and by slowly pulling his shirt up along his reclined torso. Following our usual rhythm, I immediately pressed my face into his exposed pits, drinking in his scent. It grounded me, as always, but I knew I couldn't stay in that moment forever. I had an assignment to complete, something to prove tonight. I needed him to feel my love.

Scenting my baby beard thoroughly, I moved in for a real kiss. Corey moaned as my beard brushed against his, our lips meeting with the electric connection we'd built over our weeks of being together. This time, though, I had *him* trapped with *his* pits exposed. And as I kissed him deeply, I controlled our motions and fed him the attention he deserved. His scent became more intoxicating to me than ever.

I pulled up and removed my shirt, offering him the opportunity to mix my musk with his. Corey reached up and cupped my cheek. He took my offer, pulled me close and pressed his face into my pit, inhaling deeply. The feeling of his nose nestled in my blond tuft still gave me goosebumps. Now, with both our scents mingling in our beards, we kissed again. This time more serious, more driven, more connected.

I wasn't rushing. Like Corey always allowed me to do, I wanted him to savor every moment. But it was time to move our intimate journey forward. Rising off the bed, I quickly removed my shorts and underwear, freeing my aching hardness. I looked down at Corey, hoping he was as ready as I was, and I wasn't disappointed. As I pulled his remaining clothes off, I saw that his body mirrored mine, eager and waiting.

But I still practiced restraint. This was about so much more than just our release. I moved back over Corey's dark blond furred chest and gave him a soft kiss, then I began my journey down his body. My lips traced his neck, his chest, his nipples - each kiss or lick, drawing soft coos and moans from him, encouraging me. Every reaction built my confidence. I was making him feel the way he'd made me feel so many times before. I love pleasing my man.

I slowly licked a path down his thick dark blond treasure trail, wetting it to his hard abs. When I reached his bush, I paused, inhaling the rich scent of him. This was a part of him I'd come to love almost as much as his pits. I moved to the source of his maleness and I kissed his leaking shaft, tasting him. Letting him be my favorite flavor once more.

I moved lower, taking his balls into my mouth, savoring the weight of them on my tongue. Tonight, I wasn't stopping here. I was determined to explore new ground.

Corey let out a soft moan. As I continued, he propped himself up on his left elbow, his other hand's fingers threading through my curls. "I love you pup. Seriously, how long have you been planning this? You're working my body on a whole new level. It's amazing. But be careful, if you keep this up, I won't last long. And if you want to top me tonight... well, you'd better slow down."

I looked up past his chest, meeting his eyes with a lusty smile, taking his words in as praise while knowing I had more new fun in mind. I kept moving lower, determined to reach his playing field that I'd never ventured onto before. His scent deepened, intensified, and I followed it to his most intimate spot. Gently, I lifted his legs, exposing him to me fully. I paused, and looked back into his eyes, asking for permission. "I love you, my wolf," I whispered, and he nodded, granting me access to his most intimate furry place.

I was suddenly overwhelmed. I now understood why Corey nearly wept when he had to shave my hole and taint during my test so long ago now. Looking at my new Promised Land, I was filled with lust and excitement. I had no power to stop myself, I pushed Corey's meaty thighs higher. Without hesitation, I leaned in and pressed a wet kiss onto his entrance; introducing my tongue to its new best friend. Corey let out a surprised gasp, followed by a deep, rumbling moan. "Damn, pup. You're... wow. You're making me feel things I've never felt before."

I smiled at his reaction, but his next words immediately reminded me of the promise he made the first time he made love to me. "Just... are you sure you can keep that enthusiasm under control when you're, you know, using something bigger than your tongue?"

I pulled up, looking into his eyes, letting him see the depth of my love. "Corey, I promise to give you the same gentle care you've always given me. I'd never rush or hurt you. I just... I didn't know it would feel like this. And I promise, just like you told me, you're the one in control. If my enthusiasm and inexperience make me forget that, tell me and we'll take a break." To make my intentions clear, I moved my index finger to rest on his furry pucker, making his hole twitch and his body shiver.

His smile lit up his face. "I love you so much, my pup. But, ah, I've got a confession. It's not going to ruin the moment, but it might change it."

I paused, but gently urged my index finger's first knuckle through his tight ring, waiting for him to continue. His body shivered under my touch while his face showed nothing but increased pleasure.

"Ollie... you're probably not going to believe this, but until right now, I had no idea how great getting rimmed, or penetrated with a finger, would feel. My pup. I've never done this before. You're my first. I've never wanted to be topped by anyone else. You're the only person I've ever trusted like this."

For a moment, I couldn't process his words. "What?" Not even realizing that my finger was now completely embedded in Corey's hole, nudging his prostate.

Corey moaned softly, laying his head back on the pillow, still smiling. "You heard me. Like our dads told you, I can't commit to someone I'm not completely in love with. You, Oliver Aaron Carson, are not only my first true love, but you're about to be my first top. And I want you to be my only."

I froze, my mind spinning, I gave Corey a new kind of deer-in-the-headlights look. Unsure how to proceed, I was trapped between elation and disbelief, confusion and celebration. But his calm, steady gaze freed me and pulled me back into the moment. My finger still breaching his entrance, a reminder of the trust between us. "Corey, I had no idea. I... don't know what to say."

"Look at that face! You still can't hide a single feeling, and that's just another reason why I love you so much. You don't have to say anything," Corey said warmly, his smile full of love. "Just know that I want this. With you. We'll figure it out together. It's our first journey of exploring something new together. And it's going to be perfect."

****

Corey did his best to lighten the mood, "Take my maidenhead Ollie, I've saved it just for you."

I wasn't quite ready to proceed, "You know... I still don't understand what that really means. I mean, I have an idea..."

"It's a phrase for virginity that I learned from the first porno I ever watched. It's apparently a classic, but it was just old and weird to me. And it was straight porn. Anyway, the main character kept claiming the 'maidenheads' of his supporting female cast until, in the end, they exacted their revenge on him by binding him and letting two of his male students take his. Sadly, that part was only implied, right before the end credits rolled. I was all 'Wait! This is finally getting good'."

We both chuckled, and that little release of tension reminded me of where my finger still was. With renewed focus, I resumed my exploration and was amazed to see Corey's expression melt into a look of pure bliss. His eyes rolled up and a contented moan escaped his slightly parted lips. I gently sawed my finger in and out, making sure to graze his prostate with each stroke.

Corey looked like he was in heaven. "I had no idea," he kept whispering, his voice full of awe. He now actively held his knees close to his chest, giving me the freedom to use my other hand to give him new pleasures. I wrapped it around his precum slicked cock and started slowly stroking him as I gently added a second finger to help open his hole. There was no protest. His body welcomed the intrusion, showing no signs of discomfort, only an ever-growing euphoria.

Seeing Corey's pleasure only fueled my own, pushing me up another rung of our ladder of mutual bliss.

Before adding a third finger, I realized I could now change positions. Free to move, I shifted so I could lick his nipples, savoring the feel of his skin under my tongue. My third finger, slick and ready, slid into him, and Corey's response mirrored my own from when he had done the same to me. His face softened into pure surrender as he whispered the words I'd been waiting for.

"Ollie, please make love to me now. I've never been more ready, or needed it more."

I beamed down at him, kissing him deeply. "I will, but... well, you knew what you were doing with me. I'm still kind of clueless here. How do you want me to start?"

Corey smiled, soft and reassuring. "Don't lose your confidence, pup. You're doing great. I'm all yours. But, since I've been on the other side of this, and at the risk of making a bad pun, I think we should start doggie style. It's the easiest way for a new top. And I promise to keep you informed on how I'm feeling. I know you're going to go slow.

You've got me."

With that, I slowly removed my fingers. Corey leaned up to kiss me one more time before rolling over and getting into position, his movements slow and seductive as he settled onto his hands and knees. "Remember this pup? 'Head down, ass up?'" While I couldn't see it, I knew he was smirking.

I giggled - once again - before I slapped his cheeks and joyfully realized that the slap-er gets just as much pleasure as the slap-ee. "Corey, my love, I promise to never demean you. I'll only ever honor you. Um, dang, wait, that was pretty cheesy, wasn't it?" I blushed.

Corey saved me, "See pup? It's not easy to say perfect lines when you're about to rock your lover's world."

Damn! I'm Corey's lover. I tried to contain my goofy smile. I focused and realized that I could only rely on what I'd desire if the situation were reversed. I directed Corey to move to the edge of the mattress, while I stood behind him and positioned myself. I pulled my foreskin back and let the tip of my cock kiss the entry to his being. I tried my best to emote as much caring and love as I could, while I slowly applied pressure and hoped to reassure him by simply placing my hand on the small of his back.

I popped through Corey's resistance almost too-easily. I nearly chuckled, as if I never honestly expected that this would ever actually happen. But

Corey's immediate gasp and my own suddenly over-whelmed senses instantly halted my effort. Corey's pleasure was my only concern, so I hung on his every word. "Damn pup! Give me a second. Please!!! Don't move. Remember, you're only about 3/4ths an inch smaller than I am, and nearly as thick." As always, he lightened the moment. "How did you manage to take me again?"

I chuckled but tried my best to remain focused. "I had a skilled lover for my first time; you're not so lucky. But Corey, I had no idea. I'm only a few inches in and the sensations are overwhelming. You're so warm, so tight. I could cum in seconds just thinking about the honor you're giving me." I wasn't prepared for how connected I felt to Corey at this most im-portant moment.

I remained *mostly* paused, trying to use Corey's trick when he first entered me. I just kept gently pressing into him as I seductively leaned over his back and started kissing across his shoulders. I wrapped an arm around his chest to reassure him as I slowly, inch by inch, continued to sink into him. As I bottomed out, I finally felt Corey's body relax under me so I reassured him, "You've taken all of me, my wolf, how do you feel?"

Corey strained to chuckle, "Um, is 'unexpected' a valid reply? I swear I had no idea how intense this would feel."

I remained as motionless as I could, but I knew

Corey was able to feel every involuntary pulse of my over stimulated cock. "Is 'unexpected' good or bad?"

"Damn! Both." I could see beads of sweat breaking out across his shoulders, I knew he was processing so many new feelings and emotions. "Believe me I had no idea how much pain a bottom has to endure, no matter how gentle his top may be. But honestly, that pain's already mostly gone and now I'm equally amazed to learn how much pleasure a bottom gets to experience. Pup, my love, please fuck me."

I began to move with slow, deliberate motions. Each thrust of my hips seemed to send a surge of electricity through both of us. I was absolutely euphoric from the tightness, the heat, the way Corey's body was embracing mine - it was intoxicating. I suddenly remembered Corey's prostate exam. And I angled my hips up slightly to make sure I was hitting his butt nut with every thrust. I was rewarded with a deep moan from my man, as he shuddered beneath me.

"God, Ollie," Corey groaned, his voice laced with surprise and pleasure. "I didn't... I didn't know it could feel like this."

I beamed; the sound of Corey's pleasure only fueled my motions. And as our intensity built, I felt a familiar pressure rapidly building in my core. We were already way too close to our mountain top. But, I didn't want it to end yet, and definitely not like this. I confronted myself with a new twist on my favorite conflicted command: *"Ollie*! Stop!" I slowly pulled out; my breath coming in ragged gasps. And I heard Corey's sweet protest in his question.

"Ollie?" He almost whimpered.

"Um, sorry. I was having a little too much fun. Ah, and I hope you were too. But I don't want to complete our new exploration together without being able to see your face."

Corey enthusiastically rolled onto his back with an approving smile. "My Ollie. I need to see you too."

My heart swelled at the sight of him beneath me. His eyes were filled with love and trust, and lust. I gently re-entered and a soft gasp escaped from both of us as I sank back into my man's warm, wet, tightness. Bonus! I could now kiss Corey while we coupled. My lips met his in a slow, tender kiss as I forced myself deep inside his soul. The world around us faded into the background.

"Are you okay?" I asked softly, remembering that this position initially caused me a lot of pain when Corey was on top.

Corey nodded; his eyes dark with desire, not discomfort. "More than okay," he breathed. "Keep going."

With that reassurance, I began to thrust again, our bodies falling into a perfect rhythm once more. I tried to keep each push slow and deliberate. I loved being able to see Corey's eyes. Our gazes locked; we began a wordless dialog. Corey's childhood bedroom filled with the soft sounds of our shared breaths, the erotic slap of skin against skin, and the quiet gasps of our mutual pleasure.

My own sweat began to bead on my shoulders and pecs. My droplets started falling onto Corey's forest of chest hair, mingling with his own. I couldn't resist any longer - I dove into Corey's neck, inhaling the scent of him, a mix of our sweat and combined masculinity. Our mutual scent once again sent a shiver down my spine. I kissed his inviting lips, then moved lower, once more burying my face in his pit, inhaling deeply as our bodies continued to move together.

Corey's moans grew louder, his body was suddenly arching up beneath mine. The friction between us intensified. Corey's hard cock, trapped between our bodies, was slick with his pre-cum. It rubbed against my abs with each thrust. I saw his eyes widen, with a look of awe and disbelief crossing my alpha's face.

He tried to eke out, "I've never... never let anyone do this," he gasped, his voice shaking with emotion. "But I - "

Before he could finish, Corey's body tensed, and he let out a long, guttural moan. I saw his cock pulse fiercely, releasing thick spurts between our bodies. I witnessed the waves of pleasure wrack his larger frame. I held him tightly, feeling each spasm, each shudder, and kissed him deeply, pouring every ounce of my love into our embrace.

The sensations were all too much, and I quickly followed Corey over the edge. My release surged from my balls and vented out through my soul. My body spasmed as I shot my essence deep inside my lover. The heat of our closeness threatened to overwhelm me as I rode out our waves of ecstasy.

As lucidity slowly returned, I kissed my Corey again, slower this time, savoring the taste of him as our bodies finally stilled. We collapsed together, breathing hard, our bodies still tangled in the aftermath of our shared rapture. I looked down to see Corey's eyes misty, as he looked up at me, his voice was soft and filled with emotion. "I've never felt this close to anyone before. And I've never felt so loved."

My heart was bursting. "Me neither, my wolf." I whispered, pressing a soft kiss into his lips. Right as my own tears of started streaming down my cheeks. "Me neither."

Lightening the moment was my responsibility this time. "Um, did I pass my test... Again?" Corey saw my mischievous grin and we both started our customary post-coital giggles while we basked in the beautiful afterglow.

CHAPTER 7: BRAGGING RIGHTS

"So... does this mean I'm the wolf now?" I teased as we reversed our positions from the first time Corey bred me. I loved the feeling of wrapping myself around his slightly bigger body, knowing he was still full of millions of little Ollies trying to make him pregnant with my puppies.

Corey chuckled, "Pup, do you really want to be?"

I laughed, "Oh, hayal no! I love being your pup. I need your loving dominance." I curiously lifted my head off his shoulder to meet his kind blue eyes. "But, um, you did really like that, right?"

"That's my boy." Corey gave me that warm, loving smile I couldn't get enough of. "But I've gotta admit, we may be a lot more 'vers' than I ever expected. I'm stuck somewhere between feeling stupid for never letting anyone do that to me before, and being absolutely grateful that I saved it for you. You were amazing, Ollie."

And yes, I was smiling uncontrollably again. "You've thoroughly taught me that my butt rules my world. I'll be 'face down, ass up' for you anytime. But I'm thrilled to know I can return the favor whenever you want. It was amazing, and honestly, a huge ego boost." I kissed his cheek. "But my wolf, I still like you on top of me most of the time."

He hugged into my shoulder and we drifted off into a blissful sleep. I didn't even remember that I was supposed to be worried about a repeat performance of my newest nightmare.

*****

We'd shifted our positions during the night, and I woke up in Corey's arms, happily being his little spoon - the place where I felt safest. My father's new nightmare didn't have a chance of disturbing our peaceful slumber. My inner monologue boldly declared that my nightmare was over.

My silent watch alarm went off, and I quietly slipped out of bed, leaving Corey in his deep, content slumber. I was a bit wistful as I made my final journey through the dads' house to the kitchen to greet Ted, who was also up and prepared for our day.

"Ollie, you know this is how the rest of our lives is going to go, right?" Ted said with my new favorite fatherly look. "We engineers have to get up early, while our doctor soul mates don't have to go into the office until nine."

I smiled and wrapped my arms around my new

dad. "I'm more than okay with that, especially after last night." I pulled back, meeting Ted's curious gaze.

"Really son? Are you offering me a bit of 'TMI'?"

"Ted - sshhh!" I giggled. "Corey let me be the 'top dog' last night. It was a first for both of us. I was scared out of my mind, but we made it through. And, well, it was... unreal. Absolutely amazing. This Friday couldn't get any better." I sighed contentedly, leaning against the counter as Ted gathered his keys and wallet.

"Pup," Ted said with a knowing wink, "so it was really a first for both of you? I always suspected that about Corey, but there was no way I'd ever ask." I let out a playful, incredulous sigh as we hugged and made our way to the car.

CHAPTER 8: SUPER CO-OP

Eventually, we made it through the morning rush hour battle and arrived at work. As promised, it was an incredibly fun Friday - laughter, camaraderie, joy, and a little sadness at saying goodbye to great friends. But then came a completely unexpected surprise: I was voted Outstanding Co-op Student of the Term by both managers and my peers. I was in no way prepared for that, and now everyone knows what an emotional crybaby a big 6'3" former wide receiver can be.

There were so many hugs and congratulations. It was the most perfect day I've ever had without Corey by my side. Of course, I texted him with constant updates. Turns out, I was the only one surprised. Both of the dads and Corey already knew. Looks like I need to up my covert intelligence gathering game...

The weekend only got better from there. We moved my meager belongings into Corey's house on Saturday morning and spent the rest of the day lounging by Corey's heated pool, with me proudly wearing my new speedos. Both dads blushed. I defended my innocence by pointing out that Corey had picked them out. In unison, both dads gleefully chanted, "You're grounded Corey." I laughed out loud while still being grateful for Corey's loving encouragement.

It was another perfect weekend. My life couldn't get any better. But all good things must come to an end, and Sunday night quickly became Monday morning. Even so, I was excited - I was about to meet all my new co-op classmates and get another opportunity to make new friends. I was absolutely pumped as I got up early, ready to drive myself to the office in my Bronco, starting this new chapter on my own.

Corey was barely awake when my excited face kissed his sleepy one goodbye, quietly slipping out of our house and heading off to start my new adventure.

****

At 9:30, Ted finally texted Corey.

Ted: *Corey, is Ollie okay? Did he have another nightmare last night?*

Corey: *No, in fact, I've never seen him so excited to leave for work. Definitely no nightmares. What's going on?*

Ted: *Ollie never showed up at work. He's not answering texts or his phone*

Corey stopped texting and immediately called Ted.

CHAPTER 9: MY OLLIE'S MISSING

My Ollie is missing. It can't be possible. He kissed me goodbye only a few hours ago... His excited, scruffy face, framed by his blond curls, melted my heart as he gleefully left for the first day of his second co-op term. The first day leaving from *our* house, not from Dad and Ted's. We may have fallen in love quickly by any standard, but our love is as deep and strong as any that's ever existed. Ollie's my world.

But now... now my world was threatening to come crashing down around me. All because of Ted's unexpected texts. My phone call with him didn't help at all. He simply reiterated "Ollie never showed up at the office. And his phone is either broken or he's just not answering." I quickly confirmed Ted's findings - twice.

I was fighting to not just shut down, but I was already barely able to function. The break room felt claustrophobic; my heart was in my throat. Patients were waiting for me, but all I could think about was

Ollie. I was failing to keep my panic from rising as my Dad, Chris, rushed in. His face was serious but calm.

He gently stated, "From your face, I'm guessing you've heard something."

I blinked, trying to pull myself together. "I just talked to Ted. Ollie never showed up at work this morning. And... no one can get in touch with him."

Chris's expression softened, but his voice was steady. "I know, son. I just found out that Ollie's in the ER at John Peter Smith Hospital. He's being treated for a head wound, possibly a concussion." He hesitated before adding, "And... he's in police custody."

I felt like the floor was falling out from under me. My father saw it in my eyes and stepped forward to pull me into a tight hug. In a knowing voice only parents can muster, he said, "He'll be okay." Then added, "I've already called Alex, and he's going to meet us at JPS. He assured me that he'd be there in thirty. Corey, our pup's been hurt, and he's going to need you to be strong for him. We'll get through this together."

I let out a shuddering breath and broke down, crying into Dad's scrubs. I needed to let it all out before seeing Ollie. I knew we could handle whatever was happening. But I feared that our nightmare was only just beginning.

CHAPTER 10: PLEASE STEP OUT OF THE CAR

I was on top of the world. A new co-op term! More new friends to make, and the best part? I was leaving for work from *our* house. My life with my Norse God felt like a dream come true. I could still feel his kiss on my lips as I drove, humming along to my 90's alternative music playlist, completely lost in my happiness.

That was, until the flashing red and blue lights in my rearview mirror snapped me back to reality.

Frak. I wasn't usually the type of guy who got pulled over. Was I doing anything wrong? Maybe they just needed to pass? I signaled and eased my Bronco onto the shoulder, expecting the cruiser to keep on going. Instead, it pulled over right behind me.

My heart pounded in my chest. I wasn't speeding. Had I missed a sign? Before I could spin too far out of control, the officer approached my window, and...

holey carp. He looked like something out of a movie; six foot tall, dark haired, five o'clock shadow - before eight o'clock in the morning - imposing, with a stern look in his eyes, but yet still not... threatening. I rolled my window down as my inner monologue quickly practiced its most respectful 'Yes, sir's and 'No, sir's.

"Good morning officer. Can I help you?" I gambled that originality wasn't appropriate in a situation like this.

His stern face softened a little, and he looked at me with an expression that was something like a resigned anguish. "Morning. Can I see your license, son?"

I awkwardly wriggled and eventually freed my wallet from my khakis and handed him my Michigan driver's license. His eyes flicked between me and the card. His face flashed a momentary look of definite regret.

"Oliver, I'm going to need you to step out of the vehicle."

Wait, what? My stomach dropped. "Okay... did I... er, am I... I'm sorry. Is something wrong?" I was doing everything in my power not to freak out.

His face softened further. "Oliver, It's okay. I'm Officer Barrett. You're not in trouble - *according to me* - I think I know what's going on, but I need you to step out of the vehicle for a while. We'll need to wait for backup."

Backup? What the frak? Confused, I unbuckled and climbed out of my Bronco. The officer's eyes widened for a second, probably surprised at how big I was "Damn, son, you're a tall one!"

It almost made me smile. Nervous as I was, his words encouraged me to meekly reply, "I promise I'll go peacefully."

That earned me a chuckle. "I appreciate that," he said, clapping me on the shoulder almost like we were buddies. "You go by Oliver?"

"I prefer 'Ollie' if that's okay," I said, feeling a little more at ease.

"Alright, Ollie. I'm sorry, but we've got a bit of a situation here. We have to wait for another officer to be present, and then we'll explain everything. Just... hang tight, alright?"

"Officer Barrett? I was on my way to work. It's kind of an important day. Can I call my mentor, er boss, Ted and let him know I'm going to be late? I don't want him to worry." I wasn't sure why, but it felt like that might be asking too much.

Officer Barrett gave my question serious consideration. "Would you be okay with a compromise? How about you dial, hand me your phone, and I'll let Ted know you're alright, and that you'll call him later?"

I nodded and got my phone out. I quickly discovered that my request was pointless. I looked at my phone in shock. All I saw was an "SOS" where my cell signal strength bars should be. I looked up at Officer Barrett with disbelief on my face, "Um, I'm sorry sir, my phone has no service." Dark clouds of understanding started forming in the back of my mind.

Before I could piece any more together, a second cruiser pulled up and parked in front of my Bronco, blocking me in. A new officer stepped out and Officer Barrett walked over to greet him. From what I could see, it was obvious that their conversation was as serious as it gets. In the end, they exchanged a look that made my stomach churn. I watched as Officer Barrett returned, his face displaying a palpable burden of responsibility. He rested his hand on my shoulder. His touch was comforting, but his expression was serious.

"Ollie, I need to ask you something. Is Richard Carson your father?"

I started to get light headed. More dark clouds were forming. "Uh… yeah. Why?"

Officer Barrett let out a slow sigh. "Ollie, I get the feeling you're a good guy. I can see it from how you've handled yourself with me this morning. In fact, I'd be honored if you were my son. So, I cannot imagine what your father is thinking. Richard Carson reported this vehicle stolen last Friday. We don't have a choice; we're going to have to impound your vehicle and take you into custody."

My legs wobbled as I tried to process what he just

said. Everything around me started to lose its color; my dark clouds whirled into a maelstrom. Father had followed through with his intentions, unfortunately, three months before I expected.

"Stolen…" I barely managed to whisper before I suddenly felt I couldn't get enough air in my lungs. I desperately started gulping in as much as I could. I knew I was hyperventilating. Before I could calm myself, my Whataburger breakfast decided to turn against me.

I doubled over, and violently emptied my stomach onto the gravel-covered shoulder. My storm clouds started spinning faster, my heart was hammering away, blood screaming in my ears. I guess I raised my head too quickly, and the world dissolved into static. I whispered a faint "Corey" as consciousness left my body. The last thing I felt was a blinding pain at the back of my skull as I hit the ground. Everything immediately faded into black.

CHAPTER 11: PROTECTOR MODE ENGAGED

Dad canceled his midday appointments making sincere apologies to his waiting patients. I scrambled and called in every favor I had, to get my fellow nurses to cover for me for the rest of the day. They had my back. After an anxious hour, we made it to the waiting room of John Peter Smith's ER. It was apparently a bad day for a lot of people; the voices of dozens of worried family members echoed around us. Our scrubs helped us breeze past check-ins until we reached the ER nurse's station.

"Corey!" My old friend Paul called out when he saw us. "Y'all slumming it, or do you want to come back and start helping us out at county again? We could use some real RNs!"

I smiled, genuinely relieved to meet a familiar face, "Hey Paul!" I hugged him. "We're here on family business, what room is Ollie, er, Oliver Carson, in?"

Paul looked at his computer screen. "Woah, I'm

sorry, but I need to know exactly how he's a part of your family. The police are involved."

I know how stressed my face had to look, "He's my boyfriend and Chris and Ted are basically his fathers. Please?"

Paul's face radiated friendly sympathy, "Hey my man, you need to marry him ASAP." He winked. "You know protocol, but give me a sec, let me go talk to the officers and I'll be right back."

Paul left his desk, and I tracked him like a linebacker with his eye on the opposing team's quarterback, poised to break through if I had to. I caught the number on the room he stopped at, burning it into my mind. One way or another, I was getting into that room soon. No one was keeping me away from my Ollie.

Thankfully, after reaching the doorway and having a brief conversation, Paul looked back and smiled. Smiled?! And waved for me and Dad to join him. I didn't exactly run, but that's all I can say.

As Dad and I approached, we heard laughter - lots of it. Peering through the doorway, we saw two burly police officers seated on either side of Ollie's bed, grinning and chuckling. Recounting the morning's events to the third officer standing at the foot of bed. The most classic-looking police officer I had ever seen had his hand on Ollie's shoulder as he laughed out, "... And then my man Ollie here went pale as a ghost! Before I could grab him, he did a full-on faint, head-first into the only nasty piece of concrete in sight!"

I didn't think it was funny at all, but I noticed Ollie was laughing too as I burst into the room. And gave everyone a look that said I was Ollie's mate, protector, and that y'all had better explain exactly what the fuck was going on.

The man with his hand on Ollie's shoulder looked up seeing me barge in and immediately read my look. He held a friendly hand up. "I'm assuming that you're the 'Norse God' we've been hearing all about? Believe me sir, this boy loves you and I'm so sorry I allowed him to get hurt under my watch." His expression was absolutely sincere.

I managed a dazed but polite handshake with the officer, trying to keep my voice steady. "I'm Corey Rainer, nice to meet you. Mind filling me in on exactly what's going on here?"

Before Officer Barrett could answer, I realized that the man at the foot of the bed was Captain Alex Williams. He moved near me and gave my arm a reassuring pat. "Kevin here," he said, gesturing to the police officer poster boy, "will fill you in on everything. No need to worry. Stand down." He gave me a warm smile. "I'm going to take your dad out to the hall and catch him up. Your boy's a bit banged up, but he'll be alright. And now he's got an even bigger team fighting for him."

With that, he and Dad stepped out, leaving me

with the officers around Ollie's bed.

I remembered my goal and found my Ollie's eyes. He was beaming up at me, but as I moved to his side, I noticed his gauze-wrapped curls and IV. As he reached up and pulled me into a much-needed hug, my heart finally slowed. "Hey pup," I whispered, positioning my head to kiss him, unable to hold back a few tears of relief.

"Ollie, what happened? Are you okay? Why... why did any of this happen?"

Ollie chuckled hazily, "Corey, I think I'm a little buzzed... and I really like it. Oopsss, probably shouldn't say that in front of Ossifers Barrett and Calhoun here. He grinned up at them, adding, "But seriously, other than arresting me, they're the coolest cops on the planet. Can we invite them to the pool sometime?"

I let out a short laugh, shaking my head. "Alright, pup, let's save the party invites for later. For now, you just rest, and I'll get the full story from your new friends." I gave the officers a nod, motioning for them to join me outside the room.

I noticed Dad and Alex deep in conversation a few doors down as I turned to "Kevin" and Officer Calhoun. I kept my tone steady, even though my nerves were shot. "I don't know the story yet, but I appreciate you both looking out for my boyfriend. Thank you. Now, could you fill me in on what exactly happened?"

Kevin met my eyes, his expression sincere. "First off, Mr. Rainer, you're a lucky man. Everyone could use someone like Ollie in their lives. He's one engaging, resourceful guy. He's shared a lot about his situation and how you stepped up for him."

I exhaled, some tension easing out. "I know, and I'm grateful. Now, please, tell me what I don't know. It's... it's been a rough day."

Kevin continued, his gaze kind but direct. "I think it's been even rougher for Ollie."

I let out another breath, feeling a touch embarrassed. "You're right. I... I'm sorry." I took a moment to steady myself. "Thank you for that reminder. It means a lot." Officer Barrett gave my shoulder a reassuring squeeze and walked me through everything that had happened earlier. As he spoke, I found myself glancing at Dad and Alex down the hall. When he finished, I couldn't help it - I pulled both officers into a hug, genuinely grateful. "Thank you. Really."

They had no idea of my seething hatred toward Ollie's "father," but that would be addressed later.

****

Dad and Captain Williams - almost another "Uncle" - noticed our group hug and took it as their cue to join us. Before they arrived, I stole a quick glance into Ollie's room and found him completely out of it, drooling on his pillow. I smiled; I don't think I've ever felt more relieved or grateful in my life.

Alex started the conversation, "Hey, Corey, great to see you, son, though I wish it were under better circumstances. Let's start with the good news: we have a fair amount of leeway here. Ollie's father shouldn't have filed a stolen vehicle report. And by the way, these two..." he gestured to Officers Barrett and Calhoun, "are so impressed with your, uh, boyfriend?" - I nodded - "that they'd be willing to fly up to Michigan and testify on his behalf. You can't fake Ollie's reaction; the poor guy was completely blindsided. I'm really sorry about all this."

I took a deep breath. "But I'm guessing you're about to get to the bad news?"

Alex gave me a gentle smile. "Not quite yet. Damn, son, it's good to see you all grown up and handling things. I mean it." I felt a bit of pride as I nodded, and he continued. "Here's more of the good: we're not impounding Ollie's Bronco, and there's no way in hell we're taking him to the station. Once the doctor releases him, he's free to go home with his new family, and someone can drive his car home... for now. However, I can't let him or anyone else drive it again until we get the Michigan police to drop this."

Alex's expression turned more serious. "The not-so-good news is that the Bronco's title is in Ollie's father's name. Since Ollie was only 17 when he graduated high school, he couldn't legally own it then. While it was obviously intended as a gift, his father's good intentions seem to have soured, and unfortunately, we can't fix that overnight."

I nodded, absorbing the news. Alex continued, "While the Bronco's not technically Ollie's, we all know it should be. If Ollie has any documentation showing it was a gift, that could help us a lot. But for now, let's just get him home and settled. It's been a rough day for everyone. Hell, I might need to give our two emotionally traumatized officers a day off after this. And by the way, Kevin wouldn't say no to an invite to that pool of yours." Alex gave me a knowing wink.

As Alex gathered his men to leave, I quickly followed as they explained the situation to Paul and officially released Ollie into our care. I shook hands with Officer Barrett and Calhoun, offering them my most sincere thanks. Kevin mouthed, "Pool time," with a grin, and I chuckled. "Ask Alex for my dad's number. And yes - definitely, yes. Thank you."

CHAPTER 12: UNOFFICIALLY

Dad had to return to work, leaving me in the ER with Ollie, watching him sleep in his drug-induced bliss. My hand instinctively found its way to his soft curls, avoiding the gauze - just petting him, like he really was my pup. Damn, *petting*? I realized, with a quiet laugh. Maybe I do take this whole wolf/pup thing a little too seriously.

But then again, maybe it just works for us. Here we are, a little under eight weeks in, and he's already the most important part of me. *Eight weeks.* Sometimes, it's like I don't know whether to laugh or call a psychologist. But let's face it, love at first sight runs in my family's genes, for better or worse. And, damn, as it turns out, Dad and Ted practically engineered our first meeting because they knew we needed each other - even if neither of us had any idea.

Yeah, I get it - maybe it's a little edgy for a level-headed, 29-year-old RN to fall so hard for a 19-year-old co-op student. Someone who, honestly, is still growing into himself. But he's already been through more than most guys my age. His own father abandoned him to fend for himself, unprepared for the world he suddenly found himself having to navigate.

Yet somehow, Ollie had found what he needed to get by. For three months, he managed to survive on his own, starting a new life, alone, in a strange city, thousands of miles from everything he knew. Very few men of any age could handle that. But he did it. He was successfully living out of his Bronco, keeping it all secret, even from Ted. He was fighting his way through it, learning to make it work.

And since we've found him and he found us? He's thrived. We have our playful roles, me being his champion "Alpha Wolf" and him my sweet "pup," but he's anything but submissive when it matters. He's strong, quick-witted, and grounded - probably more than I am sometimes. I might be the older one, but he's definitely the older soul. And somehow, he brings out the playful kid in me, the kid I forgot I could be.

I'm all in, and I'm in it for life with him. I just hope he feels the same way.

****

I had just woken up from a brief nap, and I was holding Ollie's hand, brushing a few stray curls from his forehead, when the attending physician finally walked in. Damn, this is my profession, so I get why attendings are always late. But, lurd, I also understand why families of patients often feel like we're dropping the ball.

"Hi, I'm Dr. Holland. And you are?"

I looked up, deciding to go with a little creative introduction. "Hey, I'm Corey Rainer - Ollie's fiancé, unofficially. And I'm an RN who's done time here." I gave him my best professional smirk. "So, what's up with my soon-to-be husband?"

Dr. Holland's face registered a spark of recognition. "Corey! Of course. I remember you! You helped us out during a tough night shift a few years back. You're a great nurse! It's good to see you again, and congratulations on the unofficial engagement."

I smiled, shook his hand politely, and racked my brain, but came up with absolutely no clue to what "tough night shift" he was talking about. Still, I appreciated his warmth.

He continued, a bit scattered but clearly invested. "So, Oliver took a hard hit to the back of his head on a chunk of concrete. He bled more than we'd like, but he's young and very healthy, so no worries there. We closed his wound with sixteen stitches. It'll leave a scar, but with all his hair, no one will see it until he's eighty-five." He smiled wryly, clearly aiming to lighten the mood. "Though... he may need a bit of a trim now to even things out - it's a bit rough under the gauze."

Typical attending humor. But he continued, more seriously. "We've given him a couple doses of Versed to keep him calm. We're almost certain he fainted from a panic attack. He doesn't seem to have a history of them, so it could've been triggered by a sudden traumatic event." He glanced up at me, waiting.

"Oh, it was, no question." I nodded, already relieved to have a clearer picture. "But what about a possible concussion?"

"Yeah, it's definite," he replied. "Thankfully, it's not severe, but it's above 'mild.' And as you know, any concussion is still a concussion. He'll be fine, but he needs to take it easy the rest of the week. Lots of bed or couch time, with close monitoring, even if he doesn't need 24-hour supervision." He squeezed my shoulder. "You're one of the best nurses I know. You got this."

I assured my unremembered old friend that Ollie would get the best care possible. After a quick review, he gave us the green light to head home once Ollie was awake. With a fair amount of "big boy" painkillers in hand, we were finally allowed to leave the hospital late that evening.

Once home, I again had the honor of carrying my pup to our bed. Where I gently undressed him and tucked him in under the covers. He protested groggily, "I need to shower."

"Ollie," I chuckled, brushing a hand through his hair, "since when have I ever needed you to shower before getting in our bed?" He gave me a small, sleepy smile, took the pill I offered, and drifted off.

I, however, needed that shower. Alone, under the hot water, the stress and fear of the day finally broke through. I let the tears fall, mixing with the water flowing down the drain. I allowed my stress to slip away and whispered my gratitude that Ollie was home and safe; my whole body gradually calmed.

I finally slipped into bed beside him, curling around him protectively. As he slept soundly, I brushed a final kiss against the curls covering his ear. "Ollie," I whispered, "I can't lose you." With my arms wrapped around him, I held him close until sleep found me too.

CHAPTER 13: TEDDY BEAR

All the way home, a deep regret gnawed at me. I was the only one who couldn't be with Ollie in the ER, and a feeling of failure clung to me. But I really couldn't just leave. I couldn't walk out on the first day of a new co-op term. I'd been involved with this program since I helped save it back in the late '90s, bringing it back from the brink.

These kids need insight into the careers they've picked and the foundation that vision provides. They deserve a solid start in their chosen field. Even though I'd passed much of the torch on to a brilliant new co-op director and was now just overseeing my own group of kids, I still couldn't abandon my new students to find their own way on their first day.

Until, I finally realized, I'd abandoned my most important student. Exactly like his father had. Damn, am I any different? Not being there when he needed his new family most?

Fuck, it hurt. It hurt more than I could have imagined. Ollie had become so much a part of my heart, as though he's been with us far longer than these few months. He calls me "Dad" almost as often as "Ted," and I love it every time he does. Corey has always been like a son, of course, but Ollie - I feel like Ollie *is* my son. And I wasn't there for him today. I punched my steering wheel.

Corey had texted to reassure me that Ollie was okay and so out of it that he probably wouldn't even know if I was or wasn't there. But it didn't help. I still hated missing that chance to be by his side. As I walked through our back door, our home's silence hit me even harder. We were empty nesters again.

Chris texted to let me know he'd be a little late, needing to catch up on what he'd missed at the clinic during his hospital visit. I couldn't deny the envy I felt. He'd at least been there. And I... I had to be at work.

****

I set aside my guilt and started on dinner, eager for my man to get home. Nothing special tonight, no Ollie's-grandmother's-meatloaf, just a simple spaghetti with meat sauce. *Lurd* (Ollie's words playfully infected us all) At least I managed to bake garlic toast and toss a Caesar salad together. The house smelled like comfort by the time Chris came in from the garage.

I practically leapt into his arms as he walked in. After a rib-crushing hug, I held his shoulders, looked up into his eyes, and asked, "Is our Ollie really okay?"

Chris sighed, pulling me into another hug. "Yes, Sweet-Sweet, he's going to be fine. Corey will make sure of that. We'll probably need to back them up with some legal help, though. We've got plenty of friends with connections in law and I'm putting out feelers. Alex thinks it'll take a week or so for the Michigan authorities to get on the same page. But we may still have a battle with Ollie's 'father'."

Chris pulled back just a bit and gave me a look. "And I have an assignment for you too, my love. I need you to call in some favors with your TCU contacts. From your work with the co-op program and from your donations as an alum, I'm hoping you're still a big deal there."

I tilted my head, raising an eyebrow. "I'm not sure how 'big' I am, but. Okay... what are you plotting?"

"Hopefully," Chris said, "a brighter path forward for our future son-in-law."

"Oh, that's all? Well, in that case, I'll get on it as soon as I have the time." I couldn't help but smile, and he chuckled.

****

As we were sharing our completely mundane meal, I finally succumbed to my pre-destined meltdown. I couldn't hold my tears back. Chris jumped up from the table and rushed to my side, wrapping his arms around me. "Hey, hey. Ollie's fine, baby. We're all okay."

I wiped at my eyes, shaking my head. "I know. But I was the only one who wasn't there for him. I still haven't seen him, Chris. Corey told me he was asleep and there was no point in stopping by. But I *needed* to be there. I needed to see him and hold him."

Chris brushed a new tear from my cheek. "Sweet-Sweet, Alex told me a lot today. Did you know that you were the first person he tried to contact? Even while being arrested, his first instinct was to call you. The officers said he couldn't because his father had cut off his cell service. *You* were still his first thought."

I let out a watery chuckle. "Somehow, that's not making me feel any less guilty."

"He thought of you, Ted, the whole time. And when he gave the ER my name, do you know why? Because he knew you were busy on a day he knew was important, and he was too worried about upsetting Corey. Ted, that boy *gets it.* He loves you, and he knows you're here for him. Honestly, could we expect anything less from our Ollie?

"Listen, Ollie needs to be monitored this week. Corey's taking tomorrow and calling in lots of favors to do it. I have Wednesday. Is there any way you could take a four-day weekend and do Thursday and Friday?"

"Absolutely!" I was grateful to be able to redeem myself. "But I'm still taking breakfast to them in the morning." I looked into my lover's eyes, "So I feel a little better. But my love, could you help me out even more?" I gave him my version of the family smirk. "Believe me, I need it."

Chris growled as he moved in and surrounded me with his arms. We both had a lot of stress to work out.

****

I smiled and raised my face to meet my mate's animalistic kiss. I loved it when he was like this, wild and dominant. And I loved that he understood it was exactly what I needed right now. I took his hand and led him to our bedroom. I felt every emotion from the day still threatening to derail our coupling. I needed to get to our main event quickly.

After our twenty years together, we knew that we could undress ourselves quickest, but even with my current desperation, the act of having my partner unwrap me like a gift on Christmas morning was worth the delay. And I needed to feel special tonight. Thankfully, it was clear we were on the same page. I needed him close; I needed him to ground me like only he could.

We knew each other's bodies by heart, with our rhythms, our pauses, and the sparks that each made. We've done this dance many times, but tonight, it was more profound. The moment our lips met, I felt my tension begin to release, piece by piece. I was finally able to vocalize my need. Softly but insistently, "Chris, I need you to make love to me deep tonight. I need you to overwhelm me and push this day's fears, frustrations, and failings out of my mind."

I saw Chris raise his brow with a mix of concern and understanding in his eyes. I wasn't ashamed to say that I was the low dick on the totem pole in our house. When a 12-and-a-half-year-old Corey excitedly called us to his room to show us the results of his first foray into the joys of masturbation, I saw that even our son had me outclassed by good 2 or 3 inches. I never cared, and Chris reassured me it's the only reason I get to top him when I want that. I'm grateful.

Chris knew my limits. I could see that he was worried about breaching them tonight. But I didn't need limits right now. I needed to feel him in me as deeply as possible, to be reminded that nothing can separate us. He started to speak, but I cut him off, "I know babe, when you hit my second opening, you're either entering the Gates of Heaven or the Door to Hell. I'm willing to take the chance tonight."

"Yes sir, Muscle Boy, but let's give you a fighting chance." He moved behind me, and guided me to our bed, on my stomach, knowing it's the gentlest way to start. After the unavoidable awkward moment of finding the lube and making sure everything was in place, I finally felt exactly what I needed, the weight of his taller body on mine. He wasn't entering me yet, just covering me, comforting me, kissing my neck, letting his massive member slide over and gently wake its playmate up. With a low, breathy voice, "Do you want a little finger foreplay?"

I shook my head against his chest. "No, please. I need you to get me out of my head, NOW. Just go slow. I want to feel alive again, I need to experience the pain to make the pleasure that much deeper." Chris wrapped an arm under my shoulder and nudged my face to turn into his kiss. I felt the sharp burn as my opening was forced to accommodate his thickness.

The pain of entry accomplished exactly what I'd hoped. A wave of relief washed through my soul; its presence dissolving all my guilt, all my worry. I raised my hips, making Chris slide in deeper. He whispered a concerned "Shhh, we don't need to rush babe, we have plenty of time" into my ear. But it wasn't about time. It was about my desire to have his pain replace mine. Chris gave in to my needs and pushed in to the hilt. I let out a gasp as he held me and took my mouth into a deep kiss. His spare hand made its way under my chest to find a nipple in need of attention, and to provide yet another venue for my body to adjust to its invader.

I knew that this was going to be a heavenly event. The initial pain was subsiding almost too quickly, I almost longed for its return. My body had fully adjusted almost too soon. But I was opened in a way that only he could achieve. I motioned for Chris to start the next steps of our dance.

My brain was on fire. Every movement we shared drew me deeper into his lead. He was playing my body like only an experienced lover could, forcing all the pain and guilt out of my mind. Beautiful waves of lust and desire replacing it. I started bucking back into his thrusts, urging him to go harder, deeper, faster.

I knew we were both close, too close, and I wanted more tonight. I uttered a muffled, "Wait Chris, I need us to go deeper tonight." He stopped, but didn't withdraw. I turned to meet his look. "Please, I need to know which door we're going through." I knew he was so close that it was hard for him to withdraw. But he nodded, too lost in lust to speak.

I rolled over on my back and lifted my knees to my chest, inviting my stallion to mount me once again. A small inkling of reasoning returned to him, "Teddy, you know this only works maybe 1 time out of 10, and you got me really worked up. That... was intense."

I reassured my lifelong mate, "You're making me feel lucky tonight, I'll take those odds."

Chris is a protector just like his son, "I know what you think you need tonight, but Ted, you don't have to punish yourself. If I see pain in your eyes, we're stopping. Immediately, understand?" I nodded and once again presented myself.

"Trust me babe, you're exactly what I need."

Chris, placed his knees on either side of my upturned cheeks and positioned his erection at my entrance. Our eyes locked and mine begged him to enter and hit places only he could. He granted my wish and with a single, slow, unending thrust, he opened my deepest door. I cried out and he met my lips with a silencing passionate kiss. We stayed there, locked in the ultimate intimate embrace until my quivering stopped. The door opened and I was in heaven.

Still unsure of my state, Chris started his slow but deliberate, deep thrusts. Knowing he rarely got to perform this part of our dance. And. Oh god! Every gentle punch through my final barrier cleansed my soul. I needed this and its brilliance. I looked up into my lover's questioning eyes and let him know how ecstatic he was making me. I saw his dominant smirk as his urgency increased.

We again found our rhythm, and my soul brightened with an all-consuming ecstasy that washed away every ounce of the day's weight. Chris' deep, steady pulses inside me were bringing me back to my center. Each thrust stripping away my guilt and replacing it with pure, soul-filling joy.

The end appeared with an unwelcome suddenness. I was on the precipice of eternity and I let my lover know. He increased his speed and I was relieved to see he was as well. I felt his orgasm start at exactly the same moment as mine, triggered by nothing more than his internal presence. Our spasms were in perfect synchronicity. Each spurt he deposited deeply within me; I delivered to my furry torso.

As our bliss subsided, I started sobbing. I have a man who can do this for me. I have a son who can do this for his mate. We have a family that can support and protect each other through this nightmare. I let all my dark emotions wash away as my tears turned to a welcomed soft laughter.

Chris, still deeply impaled, let me gather my senses and looked down at me with an amazed expression. "So, was that a 1 in 10?"

I giggled, "No my love, tonight was a 1 in a million. We got this."

CHAPTER 14: DAD JOKES

I couldn't sleep any longer. I finally gave up after tossing and turning and just got out of bed. No matter how hard I tried, I couldn't shake the feeling that there was more I should have done yesterday. Instead, I let my panic get the better of me and acted like an ass to two of the kindest police officers I've ever met. 'Keven' called me out on it with the utmost gentleness and reminded me that Ollie was all that really mattered. I can't believe how out of control I felt. Just three hours of Ollie being missing, and I completely unraveled. That's not supposed to be me. I'm the steady one. The dependable one. But with Ollie, everything is different. He's my first and only real love - my equal in every way. And yet, deep down, he feels like my younger brother too, someone who needs my protection and guidance. It's double duty, and yesterday, I failed on both fronts.

And what about Ollie? He was completely out of it all day yesterday and didn't get to say much. I have no idea how he's going to feel about all this, but I know I'll be there for him no matter what. I keep reminding myself it's okay, he's safe. We can deal with anything we need to. His father might still have some power over him, but I'll make sure he never hurts Ollie again. That's my focus. That's my job.

It was just after 7:00 when I heard a knock on the door. I knew it had to be Ted. Sure enough, when I opened it, there was my "uncle" with a hopeful grin and a Whataburger bag in hand.

"Hey Corey," he said, stepping inside, "I just couldn't survive the whole workday without seeing my favorite co-op student. I brought breakfast." He raised the bag like it was a trophy.

"Hey Ted!" I pulled him into a bear hug, "Thanks for stopping by. Come on in. I know Ollie wants to see you. He's still asleep, but it's time to get him up for at least some water and a check on how he's feeling."

We dropped the food off in the kitchen and made our way to the bedroom. There was Ollie, sprawled out across the center of our bed, his curls forming a messy broken halo around his head, still completely dead to the world. The blanket draped over him rose into an impressive tent over his groin, a structure large enough to house a troop of Boy Scouts.

Ted raised an eyebrow and chuckled, "I knew it. Both my boys outclass me."

I objected earnestly, "No way, sir! You know you're my uncle and his dad." I motioned toward Ollie, sprawled in blissful oblivion. "We'll both always look up to you. And, come on, this just gives you more 'dad material' to give him a hard" - I smirked - "time about. Besides, Ollie was *top dog* the other night. I loved it, had no idea it could be that amazing. But honestly, I couldn't help thinking, 'Why couldn't I have found a boyfriend with a standard-sized *husband* dick?'"

Ted half-heartedly laughed, shaking his head. "For the last 20 years, Chris swears that's the only reason I get to be *top dog* every once in a while." He chuckled, but then his face brightened. "I'm glad you can handle Ollie. Don't share this, but... damn, he was happy the morning after that happened. Our pup is growing up."

I blinked, a little surprised. "Damn, he really must think of you as his father. I can't believe he told you that."

Ted grinned. "Hey, we've got to talk about something during our commutes. Frak... I'm really going to miss those."

I gave Ted quick side hug and moved over to my sleeping Ollie. Even though it had been weeks since he last flinched when I woke him, I kept my touch super gentle this morning. I rested my hand lightly on his chest, feeling its soft rhythmic rise and fall beneath his cute little island of blond fur. "Hey, Ollie boy," I said softly. "Time to wake up and tell us how you're feeling."

My pup stirred faster than I expected, probably

because of all the sleep he got yesterday. As he stretched, he did the move that never failed to ignite my desire - arms up above his head, body arching like a young lion waking in its den. His blond pit tufts fully exposed, perfectly matching his little chest patch, his scruffy beard, and the golden curls that weren't hidden beneath the bandages. God I wanted to immediately dive in and ravish my boy. But, he's hurt and, well, one of our dads is here, already getting a front row seat to Ollie's... morning *enthusiasm*.

Ollie's crystal blue eyes blinked open, squinting at the light before focusing on me. "Hey, pup," I said, grinning. "How do you feel?"

I noticed Ollie grimace slightly as he stirred, his face scrunching in discomfort. "Argh! Dang! Is this what a hangover feels like? If so, I'm never drinking. Wait, did I just say 'dang'? I might need to upgrade to actual swear words. This *hurts*."

I chuckled softly, brushing my hand through his curls. "It's not a hangover, pup. You've got a nasty concussion, sixteen stitches, and a lump the size of our great state of Texas. But don't worry, we've got pain pills if you need them. And as your devoted Norse God," I added with a playful smirk, "I'm prescribing you some breakfast first. Trust me, you'll want food before taking the meds. And you have a very concerned dad here waiting to see you."

Ollie instinctively leaned up to kiss me, his lips

brushing mine with a tenderness that melted my heart. But then his gaze dropped, and his eyes went wide as he looked down across the tented blanket and noticed Ted, smiling warmly from the foot of the bed. I've never seen a concussed patient get his wits together faster. In a blur of white cotton, Ollie yanked the pillow from behind his head and launched it over his, er, morning situation, creating a makeshift modesty shield.

"Hey, Dad! Er, Ted!" Ollie blurted, his cheeks flushing a brilliant shade of pink. "I'm so sorry about missing our big day yesterday."

Ted settled onto the edge of the bed near Ollie's waist, his chuckles slipping out despite his best efforts to stay serious. "Ollie, I don't think a co-op student has ever had a more legitimate excuse than you did. And before you start over-apologizing, don't worry, we'll survive without you this week. Just focus on healing up, Sport."

Ted saw Ollie's eyes open wider, so he softened his look, and switched to a comical voice to break the tension. "Hey now, 'Ollie, I am your father,'" he quipped in a cheesy Darth Vader impersonation. He gently placed his hand on Ollie's cheek, his eyes filled with warmth. "Ollie, you were just voted 'Co-op Student of the Term.' You were almost arrested, and you've got a more-than-mild concussion. You're good for a week off. In fact, I'll be spending Thursday and Friday with you. You have my permission to 'play hooky,' and hey, I get to play too. I love you, son.

Oh, and I brought breakfast."

I watched as Ollie's expression shifted. I wasn't sure if he fully grasped everything Ted had just said, but he could feel the sincerity. He leaned up and embraced Ted in an Ollie hug. I knew firsthand how therapeutic those could be, and the look on Ted's face told me how much he needed it.

Ollie pulled back slightly; his blue eyes locked onto Ted's. A soft, radiant smile spread across his face. "I'll survive my downtime with you," he said, his voice sincerely appreciative. And then, as naturally as breathing, he added, "Dad."

Damn, I love him. I love him so much it hurts. All Ollie ever wants is to return love to those who give it to him. He's so pure, so good. I swear, if I ever meet his real "father," it'll take every ounce of self-control I have not to throttle him on sight.

Ollie broke the moment with an innocent, slightly sheepish grin. "I'm really starving, um... well, I can't remember if I ate yesterday." He looked over at me, his face quizzical, as though he knew that I could fill in the blanks.

"Hey, pup. You were on a lot of meds yesterday, so it's normal for your memory to be a little hazy. Depending on how you're feeling, you might still need a few more today. They won't mess with your memory, but like I said, you'll need food before you take them. And yeah, you haven't eaten anything since breakfast yesterday. And according to your new friend, Officer Kevin, you lost that breakfast *way* too close to his shoes."

Ollie blinked for a moment, a vacant stare clouding his face. Then, his eyes widened. "Oh my lurd! I remember now. I was going to be arrested. My father... he reported my Bronco as stolen."

Ted and I both saw the darkness spread across Ollie's face, and it was like a reflex - both of us leaned in, surrounding him with our comfort. Ted's hand found his shoulder, while I cupped his face, pulling his gaze back to us.

"It's okay, Ollie," I said firmly. "We've got you. Don't worry about any of that right now. Let's focus on getting you up and fed."

I slipped into nurse mode as I added, "What's your pain level?"

Ollie blinked, confused. "Um, like... what?"

I smiled. "Sorry, occupational question. On a scale from 1 to 10 - except it's really more like, 'no big deal,' 'hurts pretty bad,' and 'holy crap, I'm dying.' So... which is it?"

Ollie scrunched his nose adorably as he pondered. "Um... I think it's a hard 6? Maybe a soft 7?" As he started to get out of bed, the covers slipped away and his not quite flaccid cock was suddenly on full display to the world.

Ted burst out laughing, clearly catching Ollie's choice of words and how they hilariously fit in with his current situation before I did. I smirked, shook my head, glanced at Ollie's pride and embarrassment, then joined in the laughter a second later. "Well, at least you're consistent, pup."

Ollie flushed, finally realizing what he'd said *and* that we always slept nude. "Frak me! I didn't mean... So, Corey, are you sure you couldn't give me the meds that mess with memory?" He gave Ted an apologetic look.

Ted waved him off, still grinning. "It's fine, son. I'm okay being the low dick on the family totem pole. And hey, Corey's the one who has to deal with your... *level*. I just get to laugh about it." He patted Ollie's shoulder and added with a wink, "This is definitely dad joke material for the next family dinner."

I chuckled, leaning down to kiss Ollie on the forehead. "Okay, enough jokes at the patient's expense. Ollie, let's get you up and moving so you can eat something. Food, pain meds, and then we'll get you showered. Sound good?"

Ollie smiled sheepishly, glancing between me and Ted. "Fine, but only if no one ever mentions this again."

Ted winked. "Sure thing, Sport. Unless it's at the most inappropriate time possible."

CHAPTER 15: ASSESSING THE DAMAGE

I tried my best to save what little was left of Ollie's modesty, positioning myself between him and Ted while steadying him as he slipped on a pair of tighty-whities. Once we had all his, uh, ample assets covered, we guided him down the hall and into the kitchen, where Ted's breakfast offering awaited.

Ollie's memory must have slowly started to come back, and he stopped cold in his tracks the moment his eyes landed on the big, unmistakable bag of Whataburger food sitting on the counter. His expression morphed into something between queasy and mortified. Ted caught the look and quickly said, "I thought you were a big fan now, Ollie."

Ollie's response was meek, almost sheepish. "Um... I was. Until it became the last thing I remembered from yesterday. At least I didn't get any of it on Officer Barrett's shoes." His eyes darted back to the bag as if it might betray him again at any moment.

Ted's face fell and he looked completely defeated. I quickly jumped in with my best attempt to lighten the mood. "Hey, Ollie, when in Texas..." I paused for dramatic effect. "When you get bucked off the 'Bronco' - sorry, bad choice of words - you gotta get right back in the saddle as soon as possible."

That earned a small laugh from both Ollie and Ted and the awkwardness in the room quickly faded. Ollie stepped forward, cautiously sniffing the contents of the bag, as if the food inside might jump out and attack at any moment. Finally, he simply said, "Thanks, Ted," his voice a little stronger now. "It smells wonderful. And yeah, I'm starving."

We each dug into a biscuit sandwich and a breakfast taco. Ollie's growing enthusiasm was infectious. By the time Ted left for work, his near defeat had been replaced with a big smile and a visibly relieved conscience.

****

I handed Ollie his morning pain pill and he gratefully swallowed it as we made the way to our bathroom. "Alright, pup, the pill shouldn't knock you out, but it'll probably make you a bit loopy. So, let's get the gauze out of your hair, assess the damage, and then get you into the shower."

"'Assess the damage?' My sweet Norse God, we need to work on your bedside word choice," Ollie quipped, flashing me *my* signature smirk. Lurd, how does he manage to be so adorable even when he's clearly in pain?

"Fair point," I chuckled, holding up my hands in surrender. "Let's just say that the attending doctor from yesterday mentioned that your golden curls *might* need a little overhaul." I hesitated and caught myself. "Wait. I mean... a simple haircut. Ugh, dang it. I thought *you* were the one who got flustered trying to explain things to me." I gave up and leaned down and kissed my wise old boy.

Ollie saved me and just grinned. "Good thing you're so handsome and hairy. Now, come on, you're good at pulling painful Band-Aids off, let's do this."

Taking his cue, I leaned down and kissed him softly before beginning the delicate task of unwrapping his curls. Layer by layer, the gauze gave way to the uneven tufts beneath, revealing the mess the medics had left behind. But the stitches were clean, and the wound looked surprisingly good. "Everything looks great, pup," I reassured him, catching his eye in the mirror.

His tentative smile was all the reply I needed. I continued, "The stitches are looking great. I'm honestly impressed," I said, stepping back to admire the doctor's handywork. "I think we can safely get you into the shower and I'll wash your hair for you. But, um... when was the last time you had a haircut?"

Before he could answer, I started stripping off my clothes, and then gently sliding his undies down his blond muscled thighs. I couldn't resist; as Ollie stepped out of his tighty-whities, I gently cupped his balls and leaned in for a kiss.

Ollie faintly blushed as we parted, despite the meds. "Honestly? Not since I've been here in Texas. Curly hair kinda gives you a long grace period, and, well, finding a barber never made it to the top of my 'critical things to do' list. Maybe I should've gotten it done after I moved in with the dads. Is it bad?"

I didn't have a hand mirror to show him the damage, so I grabbed my phone and snapped a couple of pics, holding it up for him to see. Ollie squinted at the screen before his eyes widened in mock horror. "Damn! I look like a shaved poodle in the rear!" His laugh was genuine, but I could tell the pill was starting to kick in.

"Don't worry, pup. Like with everything else, the dads already have you covered. We've got a trusted family barber. You'll be in good hands," I said with a wink, guiding him carefully into the shower. The warm spray enveloped us, and I wrapped my arms around him, holding him close as we lost ourselves in a slow, sensual kiss.

I carefully kept my pup's head away from the spray to keep the wound dry. My hands worked over the rest of his body, lathering up every inch of his beautiful form, each stroke a physical reminder of how much I loved him. The taut lines of his lean frame, the soft blond fur dusting his sternum, arms, legs and tummy; it all felt like a miracle under my fingertips. It was like touching him for the first time all over again, and my heart swelled with a joy that made the world outside the shower melt away.

The pill was definitely taking over. As much as Ollie's face told me he was loving our fun shower time, his body reflected the blissful haze he was slipping into - his amazing cock never got past a slight plump. Meanwhile, mine was hard as steel. I just ignored it, focusing entirely on him. I turned the dial, redirecting the water to the handheld shower wand, and gently started wetting his curls.

We began face-to-face, his dreamy, hero-worshiping gaze locking with mine as I carefully dampened his longest locks. I couldn't resist leaning in to boop his now definitely stoned nose, earning a soft, goofy smile in return. As I worked my way to the back of his head, I turned him around and I let my hard cock rest between his cheeks. I cradled him against my chest as I carefully washed the dried blood away from his curls. My hands were steady, my movements deliberate, taking care not to irritate his stitches. Thankfully, Ollie seemed way more interested in humping my hardon than being concerned about my ministrations in his curls.

After his curls were as washed as I could get them, We just stood together. Me holding him with my arms wrapped securely around his abdomen. It felt like pure heaven. The warm water flowed over us, reconnecting us as if the chaos of yesterday had never happened. I kissed his neck and shoulders, savoring the moment. He leaned into me, fully trusting, fully mine.

I could have stayed here forever, but I knew I had to let the moment end. With regret, I turned off the water and reached for a towel, carefully drying him off first, then myself. Ollie was clearly an absolute lightweight when it came to pain meds; his hazy, glassy eyes made me smile despite the worries still lingering in my head. Guiding him back to bed, I tucked him in beside me, wrapping him in my arms as we settled in for a morning nap.

There would be time to talk through all the ugly details later. For now, I was just grateful to hold him close.

CHAPTER 16: BLOCKED CALLS

Our nap lasted about 90 minutes, and as late morning settled in, we dressed and moved back to the kitchen table. Ollie was making up for yesterday's lack of food by polishing off a second biscuit and the last breakfast taco. It seemed his mistrust of Whataburger was officially over. While Ollie was focused on eating, I knew it was time to steer us toward the conversation we couldn't avoid.

"Ollie," I began gently, "are you feeling okay enough to talk about yesterday?"

He looked up at me through his extra frizzy soft curls, his expression serious but calm. "Sure. I've been trying not to think about it, but I guess it's time, right?"

I reached across the table and took his hand in mine. "So, why do you think your father reported your Bronco as stolen? Didn't he say you could have it while you were in Texas?"

Ollie dropped his gaze to the table, his shoulders slumping slightly. From our time together, I knew it was the look he gave when he thought he'd done something wrong - a look I'd grown to recognize and tried my best to dispel. "Yeah, he said that. But... Well, I swear I tried my best... It's just, well, he would never answer my calls. And I called a lot."

The weight in his voice broke my heart. I squeezed his hand tighter, fighting back my own emotions. "What do you mean, Ollie?"

"When I left Michigan, I was only supposed to be down here for the spring term," he explained, his voice barely above a whisper. "I didn't know I'd be staying longer until the summer and fall schedules came out. When that happened, I coordinated staying here for the summer with Ted and my advisor at UM. They both agreed it made the most sense. Like I said, I tried to tell my father, but... he never answered my calls." A single tear escaped, trailing down his cheek.

Before he could look away, I cupped his scruffy cheek, brushing the tear away with my thumb. "It's not your fault, pup. You did everything you could. You didn't do anything wrong."

I paused, trying to approach this as carefully as I could. "There's something else I need to ask. It's about what the police said yesterday, while you were sleeping. We know the Bronco is in your father's - Richard's - name because you were too young to own property when he gave it to you. Other than your insurance card showing you as the primary driver, do you have anything else that could prove it was intended to be a gift? Oh, and I'll need your phone's call history."

Ollie blinked, his face suddenly brightening like a switch had been flipped. Without a word, he jumped up, grabbed my hand, and pulled me toward the garage. He opened Bronco's passenger door and rummaged through the glovebox, his movements growing more eager by the second. Finally, he let out a triumphant, "Here it is!" and held up an envelope with a display of glee I hadn't seen since Monday's nightmare.

"What is it?" I asked, totally infected by his excitement.

He handed it to me with a proud smile. "It's a card. I've kept it with me all this time. It helped keep my confidence up through some really rough moments of doubt when I was living in Walmart parking lots."

I opened the envelope carefully, revealing a "Congratulations Graduate" card. My grin spread wide as I read the words inside. Yeah, this is going to make a huge difference.

****

We spent the rest of the afternoon and evening curled up on the couch, swapping stupid childhood and high school stories. Ollie's enthusiasm was contagious as he described his love for football. I couldn't help but imagine him on the field, all six-foot-three of him, dominating the game. He admitted, "If my father had shown a little more support, I maybe could've been going to college on a football scholarship instead of my academic one." His face saddened just a bit, the smallest shadow passing over his eyes before he smiled again. "But hey, no regrets. I love where I am now."

Hearing that felt like a kick to my gut. Ollie had every reason to carry some bitterness over his father's neglect, but instead, here he was, finding joy in the choices he'd made. Once again, I realized just how extraordinary my pup truly was.

"Ollie," I said after a moment, "I know this is kind of a big question, coming out of left field, but... if you had other college opportunities, would you be open to taking them?"

His head tilted in adorable way, exactly as if he really were my pup. His crystal-blue eyes caught the soft light of the room. "I mean, I appreciate UM. But, it's just where I was preordained to go. I've never really thought about anyplace else. Because let's be real - there's no way I could afford anything else without the scholarships they're giving me."

I smiled, giving his hand a reassuring squeeze. "That's all I needed to know. And I get it, completely."

****

We kept things simple and ordered pizza for dinner, from the same place we'd shared for our first night together in "my" house. The nostalgia wasn't lost on either of us, and as we ate, Ollie leaned against me, reminiscing about our memory from so long ago, er, or maybe just two months. I couldn't resist giving an internal amazed chuckle. As our day wound down, he took one last "big" pain pill and declared he'd switch to ibuprofen in the morning.

Once in bed, I pulled him close, my arms wrapping protectively around his healing body. My aching hardon nestled into his rapidly re-furring crack, my nose buried into his curls, breathing in his scent. "You make me so happy," I whispered against his neck.

Ollie murmured something I couldn't quite make out before sleep claimed him; his even breaths soft against my chest. I smiled into the dark, my heart full, knowing I'd get to wake up beside him all over again in another wonderful morning.

CHAPTER 17: OLLIE'S RETURN

I woke up bright and early, almost feeling like myself again - well, aside from a dull headache. But that didn't matter. I was in my happy place: wrapped in Corey's arms, being his little spoon. If I could freeze time, this would be my happily ever after. The real world though, had other plans. In just a few months, I'd have to return to Michigan. Still, I promised myself I'd savor every minute of the life I was building here, with Corey and the dads, before that time came.

I snuggled deeper into Corey's chest without thinking, and while I didn't mean to, I accidentally woke him. "Hey," he murmured sleepily, his voice a warm rumble. "Someone's feeling a lot better this morning. What time is it?"

I glanced at my Apple Watch and realized my alarm hadn't even gone off yet. "I'm sorry, Mr. Wolf. It's only five till six. I think I've just slept too much over the past couple of days." I shifted in his arms, rolling over to kiss my man. "I could go make breakfast and you could sleep in a little longer if you wanted to."

Corey's eyes softened, but the glint of his inner nurse, bursting at the seams was impossible to miss. "I'm glad you're feeling better," he said, stroking my curls. "But you know you're supposed to take it easy the *whole* week, right? My sweet, concussed boy." He leaned over to kiss my forehead before giving me his real good morning kiss - slow, tender, and all consuming. Damn. Two months in, and his kiss still made me feel like my world was suddenly spinning in reverse.

"Besides," Corey continued, grinning, "today's Dad's day to come over to Ollie-sit. I made sure to tell him we're on a Whataburger detox, so I'm sure he's bringing something special."

I furrowed my brow, puzzled again. "That's awesome, I know I'll have a great day with Chris, but... what's going on? I mean, Ted's spending tomorrow and Friday with me too. Did I miss something?"

Corey smiled, his nurse mode fully kicking in, "Pup, you have a serious concussion. Don't worry, you're going to be fine. But it's good to have someone around this week while you're recovering. Just in case you get dizzy or nauseated. Think of it as a well-deserved staycation with the dads."

I sighed, teasing him. "So basically, I'm being grounded to the couch?"

"Not grounded - *pampered*," he corrected, flashing

me his mischievous grin. "Enjoy it while it lasts. And guess what else? Today's your big haircut appointment! Dad worked his magic to get you in with Ricky. Trust me, you'll love him. He's a genius, and he'll get your curls looking sharp again."

I couldn't help but smile. "Okay, you've sold me. Let's get ready for Dad 2."

Corey's eyes sparkled as he reached for my hand. "Great. First stop: the shower."

I happily followed my wolf into our shower and patiently waited as the water finally got warm enough to get in. When steam finally began to fill the space, Corey pulled me into his arms. We kissed under the cascades and once again reveled in our mutual young love.

I didn't just feel cared for - I felt completely adored. Being with Corey wasn't just love; it was safety, passion, and home all wrapped together. His strong, furred chest pressed against my back as he spun me around and spooned me from behind. I let myself melt into him, his lips brushing against my neck, as he held me close. His hard monster nestled between my cheeks once again. Every moment reminded me just how lucky I was to have found him.

I was instantly hard as steel and I welcomed Corey's hand slowly jacking my cock as he teased my hole with his erection. This is one of our favorite morning positions when we can find the time. I took advantage of our situation and doused my palm with my favorite hair conditioner, slathered up Corey's masterpiece and then put the rest around my expectant hole. I aimed Corey's manhood at my entrance and he didn't disappoint.

It had only been since Sunday night, but hey, for a horny 19-year-old, that's a lifetime. I treasured the sweet burn as my wolf slid his unsheathed cock into my willing hole. He held me tight, with his bearded cheek against mine as he went balls deep and I relished in the feeling of once again being taken by my wolf. Damn my father, life doesn't get better than this.

I know he sensed my need, my desperation, to reconnect with him, short as our separation may have been. I arched my back into him, coaxing him to go as deep as he could. I still have issues taking him this deep in missionary, but when he takes me from behind, animalistic and raw, it's pure euphoria for both of us. And every thrust of his oversized cock across my prostate was driving me crazy.

It's hard to explain the goofy sounds you make when your lover's cock is rearranging your intestines, but I swear, every sound is true and representative of how you're feeling as it's happening. Corey is my world and he's in total control at the moment. I knew my wolf was getting close already. I guess you don't have to be a horny 19-year-old to feel deprived when you're used to almost daily incredible orgasms.

Corey started whispering into my ear in between sweet nibbles, "I'm really close pup, you ready?"

I suddenly realized that I wasn't, but I was so loving everything thing, that there was no way in heck I was going to ruin Corey's pleasure, so I simply replied, "Yeah, Corey, please make me yours again, I need it." Cheesy? definitely; true? even more definitely.

Three grunts and a rib crushing embrace later I could feel Corey's warmth filling my soul again. I wasn't kidding or being clever, I really needed that feeling of Corey breeding me. It made me realize that my life is wonderful despite my father's efforts to the contrary. I didn't cry, but I definitely let a sob-like shiver out as we kissed through Corey's climax.

As Corey recovered he quickly slipped back into Nurse Mode, and realized that, for the first time ever, I hadn't reached our mutual mountain top with him and he was instantly concerned. "Ollie, I'm sorry, I shouldn't have done that. It's too soon and you're not feeling right yet."

I spun around in his slippery embrace and kissed his worry away, "Corey that's absolutely exactly what I wanted - way more than those dang pain pills. I needed every second of that. But I don't know what's wrong with my dick. I mean, I can get hard - duh, but as soon as I thought I should be close, I realized my dick wasn't cooperating. At the risk of sounding like a teen public service announcement,

'Kid's, Drugs are Bad!'"

Corey hugged me and chuckled, "Give your body a day or so to get everything out of your system and I swear, you'll have the best orgasm of your life."

Just then, we heard a knock at the door followed by the sound of Chris walking in, giving an exploratory "Hello!?".

Corey hollered back, "Hey Dad! We're in the shower; we'll meet you in the kitchen in a sec!" I collapsed into my man's blond furry chest and hugged him while I felt his essence slip out of my well-used hole and down my leg. Corey helped me clean up - I mean, he is a nurse - then we dried off and got presentable for our other dad.

CHAPTER 18: RICKY'S MAGIC

I was the first to make it into the kitchen, immediately wrapping myself in Chris' arms. My emotions were bubbling over again, but I guess that's becoming my new normal. I said the first thing that came to mind, "I love you, Chris - er, Dad 2," as he kissed my forehead. "Thank you for coming over to spend the day with me."

Chris smiled, his arms tightening around me. "Ollie, you don't need to thank a dad for doing his job." He paused, his voice softening. "But I know you... you have to be our Ollie; you couldn't be any other way." Then, just to lighten the mood, he booped my nose, and I let out a surprised laugh.

From behind me, Corey chuckled. I turned to give him a side-eye, and he quickly looked away, pretending he didn't notice a thing.

But I wasn't letting it go. "So, are there any looks, smirks, or habits that y'all don't share?"

Chris laughed, shaking his head. "Pretty much 'nope.' You and your dad number one have effectively married the same man." He caught himself and quickly added, "Er, I mean, are in love with the same man." For the first time, I saw Chris stumble over his own words. It was endearing. He cleared his throat and smoothly pivoted, holding up a large paper bag. "Anyway, Ted said to lay off Whataburger for a while, so I brought La Madeleine."

Lurd! The smell was incredible. I peeked into the bag to find a small feast: two quiches, three "American" breakfast croissant sandwiches, and a couple of dessert croissants that looked way too decadent for breakfast. Definitely not Texan, but I wasn't complaining.

I couldn't help but blurt out my first thought, "Well, guess I'll have to skip the speedos at the pool after eating all this."

Chris laughed, "Well, damn, I brought my trunks. I thought we could just spend the afternoon at the pool after getting your hair cut at 9:30." He gently placed his hands on my shoulders, spinning me around to survey the damage. "Wow, Ricky's got his work cut out for him this morning."

I glanced back over my shoulder and gave Chris my best sad puppy look. It worked like a charm. "Don't worry, pup. Ricky will give you an amazing new look."

I resisted the urge to let out a playful "pant," chuckling to myself. This pup roleplay was getting out of hand - except it wasn't. I absolutely loved it.

We split the quiches and each had a breakfast croissant, savoring every bite. The meal was incredible. We decided to save the sweet stuff for an afternoon snack. Corey dressed and headed to the clinic, leaving me and Chris to get ready for the day.

As I dressed, Chris prepped me for my upcoming haircut adventure. "So, Ricky is fantastic," he began. "Maybe a bit over the top, but he's meticulous to a fault. He loves to take his time and make sure every hair is perfect. Oh, and don't be surprised if he asks you to take your shirt off for the cut." Chris caught my raised brow and smirked. "He says it's about seeing the man as a whole. Whatever. Just go with it - I swear you'll be thrilled with the result."

I won't lie, I was yet again experiencing a bit of a deer-in-the-headlights moment as Chris explained Ricky's methods. But any apprehension melted away the instant I saw Ricky's private studio, housed in an old mansion on an unbelieve, secluded little street named "Chase Court". "Cool" didn't even begin to describe this place, and "genius" didn't do Ricky justice either. He greeted me with a hug like we'd been lifelong friends, and from that moment on, I was putty in his talented, scissored hands.

Chris gave Ricky the rundown on my situation, and I swear, every few minutes Ricky would pause mid-trim to give me a reassuring hug. And yes, I was shirtless - per Ricky's insistence - but under a barber's cape, so it didn't feel like a big deal. Honestly, I wasn't entirely sure what the point was, but it seemed to help Ricky stay laser-focused, like it gave him a clear vision of his goal.

Ricky was nearly finished when he handed me a mirror to assess his progress. I braced myself to face the damage. I was a little stunned at first - seeing the rough spots up close wasn't easy - but before I could dwell on it, Chris and Ricky both wrapped me in quick, comforting hugs.

Deciding to ignore the bad, I focused on the good - the finished result.

Damn! I'd never had my hair this short, but it absolutely worked. My curls were now tamed into a sleek, more adult style. I still had bangs and curls flowing on top, but with short, almost shaved, sides and back. I couldn't stop staring. I loved it - it looked awesome.

That's when Ricky took it to the next level. "Ollie, would you trust me to trim up your beard?" he asked with a challenging twinkle in his eye.

I couldn't help but notice Chris sitting on the edge of his seat, silently willing me to say yes to Ricky's offer. Taking the hint - and maybe feeling a bit curious myself - I agreed. Once again, Ricky worked his magic, and I discovered just how intimate and soothing a beard trim and straight razor shave could be.

The precise movements, his fingers' light pressure on my neck, and the somehow masculine sounds of the razor scraping my stubble away - everything about it was mesmerizing, and damn, even erotic. In fact, I may have gotten a bit fluffed, but thankfully, the cape hid any evidence of my... enthusiasm. Or at least, I hoped it did.

When Ricky handed me the mirror for the last time, I was stunned. Forget "baby beard!" I was sporting a beautifully sculpted full blond beard that looked like it belonged on the cover of a men's fitness magazine.

Chris and I gave Ricky our final hugs as we left his magical lair, and I swear, I was floating two feet above the ground. Nothing boosts your confidence quite like a great haircut and beard trim. For the first time since my *almost* arrest, I felt genuinely good about myself.

CHAPTER 19: AGE IS A NUMBER

As soon as we returned to Corey's - er, our house - Chris and I changed into our trunks and headed out to the pool loungers. Chris glanced at me and pinked up once again as he caught sight of my nearly obscene trunks from Skivvies. He chuckled and said, "Yep, you could definitely be my son." I assumed that was a "dad joke" on how well I filled them out.

I laughed, unable to resist teasing him back. "Speaking of, remember, Corey's the one who convinced me to get these." I continued, "And, Dad... you aren't exactly being modest over there yourself." My new family's signature smirk seemed to come naturally to me now.

Just like his son, Chris raised his hands in mock surrender, chuckling. "Point taken. And I'm glad you got to meet Justin. He and his young husband are always a hit at pool parties. Plus, Corey said you held your own with him really well."

I couldn't let that go. "Yeah, Justin's great - *after* we got things straightened out. But, um, how young is his husband?"

Chris stretched in his lounger, relaxed but amused by my obvious curiosity. "Justin's 50, and his husband just turned 30. They're fantastic together, but I won't lie, they definitely turned some heads when they first declared their intentions."

I know my eyes glazed over as my thoughts focused on that age difference. Chris noticed and gently pulled me back into the moment. "Hey, Ollie, love doesn't always follow the rules we think it should. The heart knows what it wants, and when it finds it, the mind just has to accept that the unexpected has become reality."

I nodded slowly, letting his words settle. Then he added, almost as an afterthought, "You scared Corey on Monday. Badly. He felt so helpless when he realized he couldn't immediately fix everything for you, or possibly even get to you. I know my son; he loves you more than anyone he's ever known before. You are his world, Ollie. He's level-headed, but..." Chris hesitated, looking at me with a knowing glint. "Just be prepared if he has any big ideas he wants to share with you."

I couldn't help but return a quizzical look, but Chris just gave me his smirk - the one Corey had so obviously inherited.

With our unexpected serious moment behind us, the rest of the afternoon was pure bliss. We lounged in the sun, and dipped in the, er *heated*, pool when we needed to *cool* off. Even in Texas, May pool water isn't quite warm enough without a little help. Chris told me it was one of those paradoxical things Texans looked forward to every spring.

****

Corey got home just before six, long after Chris and I had traded our swimwear for more appropriate evening attire and were in the kitchen putting the final touches on a lasagna. The smell of garlic and baked cheese filled the kitchen, but it couldn't distract Corey from what he saw as he walked through the door.

I couldn't believe my wolf's face when he saw the updated me. He froze in his tracks and nearly dropped his keys. His reaction was priceless and completely unfiltered. "Ollie... um, fu - I mean, *damn*. Ollie, you look incredible. You *are* still my pup, right? You weren't replaced by some hot 25-year-old model while I was gone, were you?"

I couldn't suppress my joy as I wrapped myself around his scrub-covered chest. "I'm so happy you like it! I mean, it was scary AF seeing so much of my hair on Ricky's floor."

Corey's hands slid up to cup my newly-sculpted beard as he pulled back just enough to look into my eyes. "You're beautiful, Ollie. I mean, I already knew that, but dayam! You clean up *good*." His words made my butterflies take flight. Fluttering all around my heart.

Chris chuckled as he moved to the kitchen doorway, interrupting our moment. "Well, I'm glad our efforts today were a success. Now, I'll leave you two lovebirds to enjoy dinner. I've got to go meet Ted for ours."

He pulled us both into a quick hug before slipping out the door, leaving us wrapped up in each other's arms.

CHAPTER 20: NURSE COREY

As we were cleaning up the kitchen after the absolute best lasagna I've ever made, I finally had to confess something a little embarrassing to Corey. "My Norse God, I think I have a new problem."

"What's up, pup? Do you need another pain pill?"

"No!" I said quickly. "I've really loved feeling like myself again today. I don't wanna seem preachy, but I have no idea how people get addicted to those things. I hate how out of it they make me feel." I shook my head at the thought - unfortunately, that was a really stupid mistake that made my head throb.

Corey saw me wince and smiled sympathetically. "Okay, no more unnecessary head shaking. So, if it's not pain meds, what's up?"

I hesitated for a moment. "Well, um, I haven't... I haven't had to use the bathroom since Monday morning before I left for work. Is that bad?"

Corey's face relaxed, his concern melting into his

familiar playful smirk. "Aww, Ollie! It's a super common side effect from the meds they gave you at the hospital and the ones you've taken at home. It's no big deal, but I know it's uncomfortable. Lucky for you, you live with a nurse who loves seeing your cute little furry butt. Do you trust me pup?"

"Oh no," I giggled, "why do I get a little shiver every time you ask me that?"

Corey gave me a knowing grin and leaned in. "Remember our little awkward fun before I had to shave your hole and taint? Well, I think we need to do that again - for a completely different reason." He gently cupped my cheek, his thumb grazing the edge of my beard. "You trust me, right?"

"Of course I do," I murmured, my heart suddenly racing.

"Good. Then follow me to the bedroom," Corey said, in a very seductive voice, "because Nurse Corey is officially on duty and it's time for a little medically necessary fun."

This time, I didn't hold back. He knew I secretly wanted to do that again, so I shamelessly slipped into a playful puppy beg, panting with a grin that matched my enthusiasm. Corey just chuckled, ran his fingers through my shortened curls, and led me toward the bedroom exactly as if he were taking his favorite pup to the dog park.

He directed me to strip after we entered the bedroom, as he continued on to the bathroom. He finally returned, now also naked, carrying a big towel, two clear plastic liquid filled bottles with thin nozzles - just like the ones I'd been so embarrassed about all those weeks ago - and a larger black bulb with a thicker, longer wand attached. The sight of them made my face flush, but I couldn't deny my horny excitement bubbling just under the surface.

"Ollie," Corey began, "if you're okay with it, we need to do a deeper cleaning to help your system get back on track. The opiates have slowed things down, and this will help get everything moving again." He set the items down gently and stepped closer to me, his hand brushing along my arm. "You told me before that you liked what we did the last time, even though you were embarrassed. This is a bit more involved, but it's similar." His gaze intensified, and he tilted his head with a small, mischievous smile. "So... do you want to play pup?"

My dick had already responded. And Corey took notice. "Good boy! Here's the game, I know you're also concerned about what you weren't able to accomplish this morning." He sat down on the spread towel and scooted toward the center of the bed, once again, presenting his furry lap to me. "So, pup, I know you haven't been bad, but why don't you lie down across my lap, let your hardon squeeze between my thighs and allow me restart both your systems."

My cheeks could not get any redder, and my dick couldn't get any harder. This was nasty. Kinky. And

I was absolutely quaking with excitement. I jumped on the bed and kneeled beside Corey, My dripping cock pointing across his lap. Before I could lower myself across his thighs, he whipped out our lube bottle and coated my aching hardness. When I made contact with his furry quads, I was able to squeeze my dick between them with just the right amount of friction.

Corey played his role with expertise. He parted my cheeks and started massaging my happy hole with a lubed finger. I started whimpering, and it wasn't role playing. "Okay pup, let's make this as fun as possible, we're not in a clinic now." He smacked my cheek for emphasis, I moaned. "Here we go baby." And his finger suddenly got my undivided attention.

I was lost in ecstasy, slowly humping between Corey's muscled quads while enjoying his finger dancing with my hole and prostate. As usual, I nearly protested when his finger finally had to leave. "Okay pup, unlike last time, we do want this liquid to go deep. Here's the first bottle." I felt the thin nozzle easily slip past my barrier. As Corey squeezed, I felt the warmed solution enter my gut. It's such an interesting sensation, and all my feelings were amped up due to my submissive position and the fact that Corey was going all erotic nurse on my ass.

I felt the nozzle pull out and the second enter as Corey explained, "You're a big boy, here's the second part. Just relax and let it flow in." And I did, as I once again restarted my humping between Corey's thighs. I was rewarded with another sharp slap while I felt more warm liquid entering my body. Unlike this morning, I knew I was going to easily crest my summit. In fact, I was getting close already.

Corey again interrupted my inner monologue, "Okay pup, here's the hard part - timing!" I uttered a confused 'huh?' "I have one more bottle of just saline to make sure the first two doses go as deep as they can. I'm going to administer it slowly and hopefully time your big finish just as the bulb empties. How are you feeling my boy?"

"Damn I love kinky nurse Corey, I'm really close. I'm ready."

There was zero professionality here, only naughty pleasure. Corey started, I'm sorry - fucking me - with the much larger nozzle and it was absolutely mind blowing. Every stroke was hitting my prostate perfectly, giving me jolts of erotic pleasure. My humps between Corey's thighs were already getting dangerously erratic.

After maybe 10 more strokes, I was barely able to utter a completely overstimulated "Corey, I'm cumming!" before I let lose one of my all-time biggest loads. Corey continued his part and shoved the nozzle in deep, causing a final rope of cum to coat his thighs. I probably made some all-new embarrassing noises. But, hey, it was a whole new level I hadn't even known could exist.

Corey slowly removed the final nozzle and gently

rubbed my reddened cheeks as I came down from the summit I was so grateful to have returned to. "Damn Corey! That was kinda mind blowing. Please don't make me have another concussion before we get to do that again."

Corey laughed, "Deal pup, but there are other more appropriate toys we can use. In about 10 minutes, you're not going to think this little episode was all that fun." I looked back over my shoulder to see his apologetic face mouth "sorry". And dang, Corey knows his stuff, 10 minutes later, I didn't want anyone near my bottom. But hey, both problems solved.

CHAPTER 21:
TED'S OLLEY-DAY

I think I'd said this before - right before catastrophe struck... Dang, I felt good! Once again, I woke up in Corey's arms on a beautiful, sunny morning. His soft, contented purr filled the room as the first rays of light crept through the curtains. Our song, so obvious and perfect, played through my mind - the *No Rain* lyrics reassuring me that I'd always have someone with me when I woke.

This time, I managed to slip out of Corey's arms and bed without waking him. I caught my reflection in the mirror and instinctively reached up to tame my curls, only to stop and smile. *Oh right, there's not much left to tame.* Dang, Ricky. You're a genius. Grinning to myself, I padded off to the kitchen, already planning my morning masterpiece.

I texted Ted, knowing he'd be up as early as I was, and told him I had breakfast under control. Giddy with purpose, I got to work on my favorite meal of the day. The kitchen soon filled with the enticing smell of sizzling bacon, sautéed peppers, and onions for our omelets. It wasn't my fault the wonderful aroma woke my wolf up just a little earlier than normal.

Corey stumbled into the kitchen, his hair tussled and his tighty-whities bulging in all the right places. He growled sleepily, "Dang, Ollie. I could really get used to waking up to this every morning. Love you pup."

My own mostly naked body wrapped itself around his, and I melted into his chest before nuzzling my face into his pit, breathing him in. "Love you too, Wolf." I tilted my head back to offer him a proper good morning kiss.

Right on cue, Ted's familiar chuckle interrupted us. "Get a room, you two. Oh wait, this is your house... Ah, do I need to step outside?"

Corey and I broke apart with matching grins, only to immediately engulf Ted in a tight, warm hug. His initial surprise melted into acceptance as he laughed. "Okay, okay, I get it. Dads need hugs too, I'm not complaining."

I backed up just enough to look into Ted's eyes. "Love you Dad." His misty-eyed smile told me that those words meant just as much to him as they did to me.

My omelets were a huge hit, and for a while, we simply enjoyed each other's company, laughing and talking as if the last few days had been nothing but a bad dream. It wasn't until Corey was about to leave for work that Ted suddenly jumped up, clearly remembering something.

"Wait! Don't go yet!" Ted hurried out to his car and returned with a small, neatly wrapped box. He handed it to me, stopping Corey in his tracks.

"Ted! What did you do?" I asked, feeling a little overwhelmed. I know it's silly, but I've never been comfortable with unexpected gifts, especially when I don't feel like I've done anything to deserve them.

"Ollie, son," Ted said, his grin infectious, "consider this another step in becoming a full-fledged Texan." Over my shoulder, Corey chuckled knowingly. Once again, it seemed like everyone but me was in on the secret.

I *did not* cry. At least not immediately. Inside the box was a brand-new iPhone 16 Pro. Ted must have noticed my wobbly expression because he quickly added, "Hey Sport, you needed an upgrade, *and* a dad who will never cut off your service."

That did it. I was in his arms, letting maybe a couple tears soak into his shirt. Ted held me tightly, his hand rubbing reassuring circles on my back, but he wasn't finished. He gently pulled back, grinning from ear to ear.

"And Ollie, you may not understand this, but I managed to get you an 817 number."

I blinked, utterly confused. "Um... thank you? Wait, is this another Whataburger thing?"

Corey smirked knowingly, but it was Ted who explained. "Ollie, back in the day, the Dallas area code was '214' and Fort Worth was '817' then things got complicated with '972' and '469' and a few other ones I don't even know. But, my boy, '817' means you're a *real* citizen of Fort Worth, Texas!"

Suddenly, I got it. Ted wasn't just giving me a phone; he was giving me a place to belong, a home I could call mine. My face broke into a smile as I threw my arms around him again. "Thank you, Dad."

His simple, thoughtful, meaningful gift may have put my omelets to shame, but I was okay with that.

****

After spending some time setting up my new - and service activated - iPhone, I found myself just marveling at the thought of it. It felt liberating to have something that my father couldn't take away, a symbol of security I hadn't known in a long time.

As the excitement turned into contentment, Ted and I settled in for a day that mirrored my afternoon with Chris. Of course, he couldn't stop gushing about my haircut and beard trim. "Dang, Ollie, I thought you looked great before, but Ricky really leveled you up."

I chuckled, brushing a hand through my freshly styled hair. "Um, I guess I was a bit of a scruffy stray when we met?"

Ted laughed and shook his head, "Nah, you've always been a showstopper, son. This just makes it certified."

The warm sunshine and the lazy ripples on the pool were mesmerizing, and I couldn't keep my emotions in check. "Ted, when I call you 'dad,' you know I mean it, right? Like, it's not just something I say for fun. I felt it the moment you became my mentor, but now... after everything that's happened..." my eyes glistened. "I love you, sir. And thank you - for all of this. I don't even want to imagine what would've happened if I'd been arrested for living in a stolen vehicle."

Ted's eyes mirrored mine, his voice soft but steady, "Ollie, I've told you before, I feel guilty for not stepping in sooner. But I never want you to forget this: you have two fathers, and a boyfriend, that you've always deserved. Don't you ever doubt that for a second Sport."

The sincerity of his words hit me, and I couldn't help but beam. "Yes, sir!"

I decided to press my luck. I wish I could still blame it on the meds, but I think it's just another part of decompressing my emotions. "Ted - *Dad* - this might not be what you want to hear, but you kept me brave enough to live in my Bronco."

Ted looked at me with an unreadable expression, a mix of curiosity and concern. I rushed to continue before I lost my nerve. "I mean, this is probably stupid, but from day one, I knew you had me. Even if I didn't really understand it, I felt it. Even when I was too scared to let you know what was really going on." I took a deep breath. "The thought of you made me feel safe every night I was alone in that Bronco. You gave me something to hold onto when I didn't have anything else."

Ted's eyes flashed, and I saw his lips press into a firm line, as if he were fighting back tears. He moved over and pulled me into another one of his rib-crushing hugs, his voice thick with emotion as he whispered, "You're safe now, son. You'll never have to worry about that again."

The warmth of his embrace overwhelmed me, so I decided we didn't have to end it. Before I realized it, I was dozing off wrapped in my muscle dad's big arms. In that moment, I wasn't worried about whether or not my Bronco stayed mine. It didn't matter. I was in the right place - surrounded with love, safety, and family.

CHAPTER 22: FOUNDATIONS AND FRACTURES

Last night was the first time since my arrest that we were completely in sync again. I know we're "young" lovers, but Corey knows exactly how to stretch my limits in the most amazing ways. We finished our coupling in our current favorite position: me on my side, right leg bent up to my chest, Corey straddling my left leg, leaning over my torso, passionately kissing me. All while thrusting deep across my blissed-out prostate. We found our rhythm effortlessly, finishing together - or at least close enough that it felt like we did. He has this way of making every moment feel perfect, even when life outside our bed is anything but.

I've been trying to accept what I've known deep down for a while: my father isn't the man I once believed he was. No more excuses, no more picking and choosing the right memories. My formerly beloved father is a total piece of shit. I'd use one of my non-swear words, but let's be honest, he doesn't deserve my consideration any more. I'm just grateful last night reassured me that I'm in the best hands possible - with a new family I never knew I deserved.

As usual, I woke up before Corey. We both gave it our all last night, but giving credit where it's due, he did more of the heavy lifting. He deserves a few extra minutes of sleep.

I decided to make a classic meal this morning: sausage, fried eggs, and - stealing from Corey's cookbook - pancakes. The smell of sizzling sausage worked its magic, waking my wolf just in time to greet Ted for his second day of *Ollie Duty.* But as soon as I saw Ted's face, I knew something was wrong. Ted wasn't himself. His usual warm presence had been replaced by a sorrow that threatened to fill the room.

"Dad, what's the matter?" I asked, stepping forward to give him his morning hug.

Ted returned the hug, but it felt hollow - like he was just going through the motions. His arms were there, but his heart wasn't in it. I pulled back to look into his eyes and felt a pit form in my stomach. Seeing him like this was chilling.

"Ted... Are you okay?"

His voice was low and strained, like he was dragging every word up from the depths of his soul. "Ollie, I don't know how to tell you this. I love you, pup, and I need you to believe me when I say that we all have you. Always."

I felt the ground shift beneath me as I watched his expression crumble. My stomach clenched, and I swallowed hard. "What's wrong?" I managed, though my voice sounded small even to me.

Ted hesitated, his eyes glistening as he searched for the right words. "This is going to be really hard, Ollie. Please, sit down."

I moved to the table on autopilot, my legs feeling like lead. The pit in my stomach was growing, but I wasn't about to lose my breakfast this time. Oh wait, I hadn't even eaten yet. Great. I sat down, numb and bracing myself for whatever was coming next.

"Ollie, son, we can turn this into a good thing..." He started; his voice steady but uncertain. He looked into my eyes, and I could see he realized he'd just said the absolute lamest thing possible. His usual calm, grounded demeanor cracked for a moment, but he continued. "Your father called the co-op coordinator at UM and... well, he was furious and a complete ass. He once again accused you of stealing the Bronco and lashed out about you not returning to Michigan as planned. He... wasn't exactly polite during the exchange."

The pit in my stomach threatened to swallow me whole as Ted kept going.

"Your coordinator tried to defend you, Ollie. He even told your father about the award you won. He tried to tell him what an incredible job you're doing here. But your father," Ted clenched his fists and looked away for a second, as if trying to contain his own anger, "your *father* wouldn't accept any of it. He threatened to involve the school in the legal charges he'd filed against you."

Ted moved to my chair and wrapped his arms around me, pulling me into his embrace. His solid chest, usually a bastion of comfort, felt unsteady. "Ollie, I'm so, so sorry. UM had no choice; they've removed you from their co-op program."

His arms tightened around me as if he could somehow shield me from what came next. He released me but then trapped me in his resigned gaze. "And, Ollie... as much as it kills me to say this, our company, we... we can't let you continue your summer co-op term either." His voice broke slightly at the last word, his grief for me palpable. "Ollie, you have to believe that this hurts me more than you can imagine. You don't deserve any of this."

Once again, my father had found a way to slap me from the darkness of my nightmare. My nose may be figuratively bloodied again, but I was done shedding tears over Richard Carson. I knew I was totally fucked, but having Corey, Ted, and Chris on my side made all the difference. They weren't just my safety net - they were my fortress.

As Corey joined us in our resumed hug, Chris made an unexpected appearance and noticed Ted's somber expression as he entered the kitchen. "Well, it looks like you gave Ollie the news, and um, unfortunately I have a more to add." He put a fatherly hand on my shoulder and continued, "Ollie, I want to stress that you basically have a whole city's police force behind you, but here's the news."

"First the good part, both the Fort Worth and Michigan police departments have agreed, no charges are being pursued or held against you. Your Bronco is no longer listed as stolen."

I felt the smallest flicker of relief before Chris continued, his face clouding with regret. "But your *father* is demanding you return the Bronco. He's given us two options: we pay to have it shipped back or you drive it to Michigan yourself. He's agreed to meet you in Ann Arbor instead of at the house."

Chris' voice softened as he added, "I'm so sorry, Sport. It's the best resolution our attorney could get out of him right now."

The weight of his words should have been crushing, but instead, I was filled with something else entirely, a kind of hardened resolve. "Chris... Dad 2," I said, my voice steady even as my emotions threatened to bubble over, "you've done more than enough. You're amazing, and I love you so much. Just tell me what we need to do. We've got this."

Corey finally broke his uncharacteristic silence and entered the conversation with a gentle but determined look. "Hey, pup," he said, his voice once again my steady anchor, "maybe it's time for us to take a cross-country road trip. We can make it a fun getaway, just you and me, while the dads and the attorneys work with your old cell phone logs and that graduation card, to build our case." His hopeful gaze locked onto mine, refusing to let go until I gave him a sincere smile and nodded.

This wasn't bravado; This was certainty. With my family behind me, I knew this wasn't an ending. It was just another chapter - sure, a totally frakked-up one - in a story I was going to give my all to win. And in that moment, I knew: it was Go Time again.

CHAPTER 23:
IF YOU ORDER NOW...

Lurd! If any scene ever needed to be lightened up, it was the one we just survived. I took it upon myself to do just that by pointing out the obvious. "Um, dads, Corey - did we just make it through our first unexpected family crisis without either me or Ted crying?"

Ted allowed his laugh to fill the room before he gave a small rebuke. "Hey now, Corey's a crier too! But yeah, I guess we did." His face brightened as he looked at me. "Believe it or not, before we found out about your father's latest antics last night, we were actually coming over with some good news to share this morning.

"But first, Sport, no one involved in your removal from the co-op program puts even the slightest blame you. In fact, they only have the highest praise for you. So, both your record at U of M and at our company will remain spotless. You're as much a superstar on paper as you are in our lives. Oh, and by the way, your U of M transcript? Immaculate. It's seriously impressive."

Ted gave his husband a subtle nod, as if passing the baton in a well-rehearsed relay.

Chris' face broke into a wide smile, one so unexpected and commanding I couldn't help but raise an eyebrow. Once again, I was wondering what family secrets I didn't know about. I was even really close to suspecting that they'd rehearsed this whole presentation. I looked at Corey suspiciously, and when he had to contain a chuckle and look away, those suspicions were confirmed. I simply gave up, leaned back, and decided to enjoy the show I knew was about to unfold.

Chris, Dad 2, started his speech, his tone strong and calm, yet brimming with excitement. "Ollie, ever since Monday's unexpected drama played out, Ted and I have been investigating new possibilities for you, and I think we've found a winner. Of course, it's entirely up to you. But tell me, have you noticed... what with all the purple and white everywhere and the giant stadium and sports fields just a few blocks away - that you and Corey live right next to a major university?"

I nodded but this wasn't going to be an easy sell, "Yeah, I've noticed dads. And, believe me, I've thought about it a lot. Also, don't think for a second that I even remotely know how to cope with leaving y'all and my new home and going back to a place I really don't want to be anymore." Hey! Still no tears! I'm holding it together. "But, even if you guys were willing to help a ton - and I mean a *ton* - there's no way I can afford a school like TCU without big scholarships."

Chris' grin only grew wider, a glint of triumph in his eyes. "Ah, Ollie, my sweet boy. Did you know that Ted, aside from being my greatest love; Corey's incredible uncle; and your number one dad, is also a TCU alum? And not just any alum, but a major mover and shaker and someone who was almost singularly responsible for building the tight bond between TCU's co-op program and your former employer? Our Ted here is a lot like you Ollie: Someone who's way too modest about their accomplishments." The proud smile Chris directed to both Ted and me was yet another bond tying us all closer together.

The baton was passed back to Ted, and he took it with his own proud gleam in his eyes. "Ollie, don't overthink it, this isn't nepotism. I just happen to know the right people to talk to, and I'm honored to be your sponsor. You, my boy, have already done all the heavy lifting; you just didn't realize it."

He leaned close and put his hand on my shoulder, his tone grew even more earnest. "You've got a perfect 4.0 GPA after your freshman year and your first sophomore semester, *and* the co-op award you just won? It's not just some line item on a résumé - it's a huge deal.

"I know it sounded lame as I said it, but what just happened with your job really can be turned into a huge opportunity. You're in a unique position now, especially with your summer suddenly freeing up. Sport, listen: the University of Michigan is one of the most respected schools in the world, but if you'd like to explore a new path, I'm *certain* that TCU would be thrilled to steal you away - *and* match nearly all of your scholarships."

Watching my two incredible dads deliver their tag-team pitch was like having a front row seat to a 3 a.m. infomercial. I half expected one of them to shout, "But wait, there's more!" Which I guess is kinda exactly what they were doing. I let a little chuckle escape; if I ordered now, I wondered if they'd throw in a set of steak knives.

Chris didn't let Ted keep the spotlight for long. With a playful yet determined energy, he metaphorically snatched the baton back from Ted's hand. "By '*certain*,'" he continued, getting more serious, "Ted means you're absolutely capable of making this happen. You're a superstar Ollie, but this won't be a lazy summer. You'll have a lot of work ahead of you; don't worry - we're here to make it as easy as possible. Ted will guide you through all the forms and applications, all you have to do is fill in the blanks with your amazing resume."

Chris couldn't stop, "Next, and this one will score

you some major bonus points, you need to get a Texas driver's license. Show the university you're committed to being a Texan - not just for now, but for the long haul. It'll send a strong message."

He paused and grinned. "And finally, here's the fun part. Ollie, you're going to write a killer introductory essay, just like every high school student applying to TCU has to do. Think of it as your chance to make a powerful first impression. Can you handle that?"

I hesitated, my euphoria fading while suddenly feeling the weight of the task. "I mean... I'll try. But I'm not the best writer, and schools can smell AI from a mile away. What if I mess it up?"

Corey took his opportunity to join the fray with gusto. "No, pup, you're not just going to 'try.' TCU is tossing you a softball here and you're going to knock it out of the park. Do you realize how much you've accomplished in the last nearly six months? It's honestly mind-blowing."

He looked into my eyes, his voice filled with admiration. "You moved across the country on your own, started a life in a brand-new city, without any help from your so-called family, and you didn't just survive - you thrived. You lived in your Bronco, worked two jobs, fought off thieves, got through an insanely 'intimate and exposed' medical exam." He snickered, "Okay, maybe don't include all the details on that one."

He flashed his mischievous smirk. "But the point is, you've excelled at everything you've set your mind to and you've been through more in half a year than most people face in a decade. You can't make this stuff up. You're amazing. You just need to let them see that."

Ted chimed in, reclaiming the baton. "Sport, what Corey's saying is, all you need to do is write *your* story. it's incredible because *you* are incredible. You'll have the admissions team at TCU in tears and throwing scholarships at you." He chuckled. "We could even workshop some titles. Um, 'Ollie's Tale,' or maybe 'Ollie's Trials,' ooh wait! 'Ollie's Test.' That has a nice ring to it, don't you think?"

I couldn't help but laugh, and shake my head. "Uh Dad, don't *you* think it's a bit, well, serial killer of me to include my name in any title that I might decide to use? But I do like 'Test.' It fits. And yeah, I think I get it. You all believe in me. Thank you."

Ted leaned back, clearly pleased with himself but couldn't resist one last jab. "Fine, you can leave out 'Ollie'. But you *have* to leave in the part about your, um, *little* 'morning blanket fort.' Just for me. It's a classic."

Ted and Corey both burst into laughter while I buried my face in my hands, happily defeated.

I love my Dad number 2; he's the sane one when I need him most. He just politely redirected the conversation. "And if you really want to seal the deal with TCU, let's sign you up for a couple of summer general ed courses at TCC." He noticed my confused face. "I'm sorry, Tarrant County College. That'll show them you're unstoppable, Ollie. Even when you had your world kicked out from under you, you got right back up and immediately started moving toward a new goal."

Ted stepped forward to deliver the closing argument, with a smile bright enough to chase all of his earlier gloom away. "Sport, there's one last thing you should know. The only reason we can't let you continue to be a co-op student right now is because your school dropped you from its program. If TCU becomes your new university, your old co-op position will be waiting for you. We'll take you back in a heartbeat."

Corey tried his best to seal the deal. "What do you say pup? Are you ready for a busy, fun-filled, productive summer? So that you can become a Purple Horned Frog in the fall?"

I just sat there, utterly stunned. Overwhelmed by the love and unwavering support of my new family. No one - and I mean no one - had ever done this much for me before. I was humbled, grateful, and so profoundly happy. On the same morning I'd received the worst news imaginable, my life had somehow made yet another 180 but this time, all for the better.

Instead of despair, I was filled with determination. I have lots of new assignments to complete and lots of opportunities to make the ones I love proud of me. I was back in my zone, in my element. I'm so freaking in love with Ted, Chris, and most importantly, my Corey, it was overwhelming. They weren't just presenting me with an opportunity; they were determined to gift me a whole new world.

"Daaaang! You guys don't make it easy to be depressed about a defeat," I beamed at my amazing family.

Corey moved in and wrapped me in his arms. "Pup, this morning wasn't a defeat. It it's a chance for you to live the rest of your life the way *you* want to."

I looked up and kissed him hard enough to make Chris and Ted blush - which was impressive, considering Ted's earlier 'morning blanket fort' joke.

CHAPTER 24: NO MORE SECRETS

Chris and Corey grabbed a few quick bites of the breakfast I'd prepared before rushing out the door. After all, their morning had suddenly been hijacked by our latest family crisis. Ted and I were left alone in the quiet aftermath, cleaning up the kitchen together, deep in contemplation. The clinking of dishes and running water were the only sounds between us, until Ted finally broke the silence.

"Ollie," he began tentatively, "are you really okay with becoming a full-time Texan? You know how much we all love you, but Michigan is a long way away. It's where you grew up. Leaving home is never easy, even when... well, even when you were kicked out of the nest."

He pulled me into a hug, as if anticipating a flood of emotions. And, okay, maybe my throat tightened just a little, but I stood firm. No tears - not today. Instead, I leaned into his hug, appreciating how secure he always made me feel, especially given the magnitude of the decisions I was being asked to make this morning.

"Dad," I replied, "I've been twisting myself into knots for weeks thinking about having to leave Corey - and you two - to go back to Michigan. Honestly? I'm dreading another long, dark, cold, lonely winter. I don't think I can handle that now." I paused, "Believe me, my recent mild winter stay here convinced me I'm just not cut out for northern winters anymore."

Ted chuckled, "Well, just wait, Sport. You're about to experience the other end of the spectrum. We call it 'the scorch,' and it's not for the faint of heart."

I wasn't letting him discourage me that easily. "I may be blond, but I promise, I tan just fine," I said, flashing a grin. "And anyway, I can't believe how much groundwork and effort you, Chris, and now that I think about it, Corey too, have put in for me. Y'all are my family. This is my home. I don't want to leave." A twisted chuckle bubbled up from the heaviness of the morning. "Plus, let's be real - I don't even want to deal with meeting my father when I return my poor Bronco to him. But I guess Corey and I have to plan that trip." I paused, becoming a bit more serious. "It seems like you and Chris know way more about all this than I do. How much time is my father giving us?"

Ted's expression shifted, maybe hinting at a new level of respect. "He wants it as soon as possible, but he's giving us no more than two weeks. I'm sorry

Sport. I swear, we never meant to keep you in the dark. We just thought you deserved some time to recover without having to deal with even more stress. But I understand now that you're no longer the stray pup we first took in. You've shown us you're ready to face life head-on." His voice wavered, but only filled with love. "That said, before you get all grown up on me, can I still tell you how proud I am of you? I may have only gotten to the 'Ollie Show' a few months ago, but I promise, I'll be your biggest fan for the rest of my life."

His words hit me straight in the heart, my voice steady but full of feeling. "Yes, Dad. Absolutely. I need it - and I appreciate your protection, your praise, all of it. But I'm about to be 20, and I'm also about to make some of the biggest decisions of my life. I think it's time y'all take the kid gloves off." I looked into his kind, caring eyes. "Damn, I wish I could've been your son from the start. But I'm so thankful I have you now, right when it counts the most."

I stood back and declared, "Alright, first step - let's get me a Texas driver's license." And we got down to business.

The rest of the day flew by in a whirlwind of productivity. We set up appointments, looked into TCC course offerings, and, since we lived so close, took an impromptu walking tour of Texas Christian University. I'll admit, I still have some reservations about the name, but the campus was beautiful.

After meeting some friendly faces and hearing more about what TCU had to offer, I couldn't help but get excited. In fact, I was getting pretty stoked about trading blue for purple come this fall.

CHAPTER 25: RISING

After our mandatory hardy breakfast and in between frequent, hot little make-out and cuddle sessions, Corey spent most of Saturday morning and early afternoon gleefully planning our road trip. Who knew that my often impetuous and almost always spontaneous high-school-class-clown-at-heart boyfriend could transform into such a laser-focused, hyper-organized trip planner? I couldn't complain, and he looked so happy, so deeply consumed by his task, that I decided to just let him be. Still, I couldn't stifle my growing curiosity. I was dying to know what had him so enthralled and euphoric in his scheming.

Eventually, I broke out my best puppy dog pleading eyes until I finally convinced him to take a break and join me at our local LA Fitness. We both needed to resume our workout routines, and thankfully, Chris had given me the green light for light exercise. Riding in my Bronco Sport as we made our way north to West 7th in our workout clothes, I couldn't help but notice, *damn, we look kinda hot in this car.* I let a chuckle escape before my thoughts were suddenly tinged with sadness. My Bronco wasn't gonna be mine much longer.

As we rode along, a *productive* thought finally hit me. "Hey Corey, what if I got my old job back at LA Fitness? Well, you know, I mean at the one we're heading to now. Do you think we could manage having just one car? I'd like to have something fun and productive to do this summer, aside from all the tasks the dads just gave me."

Corey glanced over with a knowing smile. "Sure, pup. Our house is right on Dad's way to our clinic. We'll make it work. Dang Ollie, you just can't sit still for long, can you?"

****

We walked in, flashed our cards, and Corey headed to pick up a couple of towels before making his way to the free weight area. Meanwhile, I decided there was no time like the present and walked back up to the front desk, introducing myself. When I asked to see the manager, I was completely surprised to be greeted by a familiar face, Jason, my former boss and friend. He extended his hand, giving me a firm shake, his smile surprised and wide.

"Ollie! It's great to see you my man! Love the haircut! Wow! You're growing up, buddy. What's been going on?"

"Jason! Dang, this is an unexpected surprise! It's a long story - I swear I'll catch you up on all of it later.

Right now, I'm here to work out with my boyfriend, Corey. You should stop by so I can introduce you. But first, my situation's changed again, and I could use a job. Is there any chance I could get my old janitor - junior grade - position back here?"

Jason's smile turned brighter. "Ollie, I'm sorry, but I don't think I can do that." Before I could work out the irony of his big smile and what he just told me, he continued, "This location's been underperforming for a while now. We're super focused on driving up new membership and keeping current members engaged. We need good trainers - motivated, passionate ones - to help people stay dedicated. I don't want you as a janitor, my man. But I would love you as a trainer."

My surprise was impossible to hide, and my enthusiasm bubbled over. "Jason! That's amazing, but... I'm not a trainer. I mean, at least I'm not *trained* to be a trainer."

Jason laughed and clapped my shoulder. "Ollie, I watched you work out for over three months, and I saw you helping out just about every New Years noob in the gym, expertly coaching them on how to do exercises properly. You're a natural. Your energy, your enthusiasm, and the way you connect with people. I know you'll be one of our most popular trainers. Don't panic, though, I'll start you off with a mentor to show you the ropes. But trust me, you've got this. So, whada ya say?"

Without hesitation, I grinned and replied, "Yes, sir!" Then, as quickly as my smile grew, it faltered a bit. "But, uh, Jason, I need a couple of weeks before I can start. It's complicated, but I've got some family stuff to deal with first. Is that okay?"

Jason playfully punched my shoulder and winked. "Ollie, I can see you're not just stalling for the fun of it. Whatever's going on, I'm sure you'll handle it like a pro. Let's go meet Corey, and I'll expect to see you back here in a couple of weeks, ready to crush it."

As I walked with Jason toward the free weights, I couldn't help but marvel at how my life seemed to quickly be getting back on track. Piece by piece, the puzzle that had felt so broken just yesterday was starting to come back together.

****

After our workout, we indulged in what had become one of our most grounding rituals - getting lost in each other's "post workout bliss" pit scent. The masculine mix of our fresh musk was more than comforting; it represented our bond, a reaffirmation of everything we were building together. Especially now when I need Corey most.

We moved our passion to the shower and once again made good use of my favorite conditioner. We should probably just stash a bottle of lube in the shower, but dangit, the conditioner smells so nice, and well, seems to stick around longer under the spray than traditional lube does.

After our explosive conclusion, Corey once again decided to clean up his impressive deposit that was slowly taking its usual path down my inner thigh. But his new cleaning method shocked me as much as his first rim job had. He knelt down behind me and started lapping his load from my furry hamstring. He slowly licked all the way up between my parted legs until his tongue gave my balls a quick tickle before moving on to directly confront my dripping hole.

The very moment my overloaded mind finally decided that this new activity was way hotter than I could have ever imagined, Corey's face suddenly blinked into a sour grimace. Before I could even ask, he jumped up with his mouth open, presenting his tongue to the shower's spray. My mind raced straight on to the place I didn't want it to go, and I was *this close* to never letting Corey's tongue anywhere near my rear again.

Seeing my expression fall from ecstasy and descend into horror, Corey quickly raised his hands in a universal gesture of "wait, don't panic." After the water had thoroughly rinsed his tongue, he let out a sheepish chuckle, "Sorry pup. Believe me, that's something we'll be exploring again. Um, maybe just not after using your conditioner as shower lube. While it works fine and smells great, it tastes like crap. The moment the words left his mouth, his eyes widened with realization, and we both totally lost it. One way or another, our lovemaking always seems to end in laughter.

****

I expected us to spend the rest of the afternoon and evening cuddling, but as soon as we were dry, Corey dove back into his self-appointed mission to craft the perfect road trip for us. I watched him for a while. His focus was so intense, I swear I could feel his love in every detail he planned. I'm pretty sure he believes that if he can make our voyage magical enough, I'll forget why we're going and what I have to face when we get there. That's probably not going to happen, but I appreciate his dedication more than I can say. And I swear, I'll try my best not to dread what's coming, if only for him.

He was still working on a few final reservations when I eventually gave up and went to bed, his laptop still glowing softly in his lap on the couch, his phone by his side. An hour or so later, I barely woke as he slid in beside me, wrapping me in his arms and once more making me his little spoon. Somewhere between waking and dreaming, I swear I heard him murmur that after our trip, he'd never have to worry about losing me again.

CHAPTER 26: HOTELS AND PROMISES

Sunday dawned a precious, dark and stormy late spring morning. We didn't waste the opportunity to have a romantic cuddle session in our warm and safe bed. The sound of rain tapping against the windows and the occasional rumble of thunder felt like the world outside was echoing the storm of emotions within me. It was as if nature itself was cocooning us in its embrace, urging us to lose ourselves in each other's arms.

Even though we just had some amazing, if bad tasting, shower fun the afternoon before, Corey was growling to go again. And once again, just like when I desperately needed him to reconnect with me after my little ER stay, there was very little foreplay. Just a lot of lube and a fury of fingers loosening my hole. All while our tongues were battling for dominance in their sensual dance.

There was no doubt; Corey's primal energy more

than made up for any sense of rushing. He entered me while still being my big spoon and then lifted my left leg over his hips. Satisfied with our position, he started thrusting into me with a feral urgency. All while kissing my neck, nibbling at my ear and jacking my dripping cock. I was instantly captive in his desire, once again under his spell.

He was in complete control and dictated our direction. He finally rolled me up and over him as he slid under me. Now my hips were on top of his as he thrusted up through my thoroughly stimulated hole and charged deep into my quivering tunnel of desire. Every stroke he made was pummeling my prostate to maximum effect. I realized that my chest was nestled beside his, so I lifted my arm, placing it behind his head, around his neck. Giving him convenient access to both my morning pit and my eager mouth. He scented his beard in one before deeply kissing the other.

After basking in our connected bliss for as long as we could keep our passion in check, Corey's upward thrusts eventually started getting stronger and more urgent. Each one was forcing my prostate to not just ooze precum, but to actually spurt a bit on every deep thrust. I knew I couldn't last much longer, and I let him know that he needed to keep his hand as far away from my ready-to-blow cock as possible. He complied and instead used it to rub, pinch and torture my erect nipple. I realized that I'd only traded one path to a quick orgasm for another.

Fortunately, our bodies were so in tune that Corey was rapidly approaching our summit together with me. His growls became more animalistic and his thrusts less controlled. He removed his lips from mine and used them to replace his hand at my nipple. His freed hand immediately returned to my cock. He bit my nipple as his orgasm took control of his actions. My lust-filled brain instantly converted the sharp pain into even sharper pleasure and an Old Faithful of cum erupted over both our torsos, while his orgasm warmly coated my insides.

As we slowly descended from Valhalla, my Norse God hugged me and chuckled into our shared post orgasmic kiss. Damn pup, I'm sorry, I guess I needed that after getting so excited about our road trip."

"I'm not complaining my wolf. That was amazing! And, um, well, isn't hotel sex supposed to be the best?"

"I guarantee you pup; it is."

I couldn't wait for Corey to back his words up with actions. But for right now, I just smiled and snuggled back his embrace, not caring about the orgasmic mess we'd just made. Luckily, we change the sheets on Sundays.

****

We had dinner with the dads Sunday evening. While we always enjoy our time together, this gathering felt unavoidably more business-like. As I expected, Chris dominated most of the conversa-

tion. He explained that our family attorney had engaged with a counterpart in Ann Arbor - an attorney
named Andrew Bowman. Andrew would arrange a
meeting location for us next Sunday just after noon.
Chris also reassured us that both attorneys were
working on a civil case against my father. "They'll
give you the full details once you arrive," he said in
his calm authoritative voice that almost soothed my
shaky nerves.

Corey took over, his much lighter and excited
demeanor a welcome contrast. With his trademark
high school boy enthusiasm, he laid out our itinerary. "We'll leave our house *early* Friday morning
for the longest leg," he began, his excitement radiating across the room. "We'll stop for lunch in Little
Rock, then we're pushing all the way up to St. Louis.
Hopefully arriving by late afternoon. We're staying
downtown at the Hyatt Regency at the Arch - I
swear, it's practically under the Gateway Arch."

I couldn't help but smile, caught up in his excitement. The weight of the upcoming meeting with my
father felt lighter for just a moment.

"With the longest part of the drive out of the way,
we'll have time Saturday morning for a leisurely
breakfast and a tour of the Arch," Corey continued.
"Then it's an easy four-and-a-half-hour drive to Indianapolis. With lunch somewhere along the way.
Once we get to Indy, we'll check into the downtown
Hilton... In a corner suite with floor-to-ceiling views
of Monument Circle." His grin widened, and I no-

ticed a twinkle in his eye as he added, "We've got reservations at a very special restaurant Saturday night."

Even as dread crept back into my mind at the thought of going back to Ann Arbor, Corey's excitement kept me calm. This wasn't just a trip - it was Corey's way of turning a forced march into an exciting new shared adventure. His effort didn't go unappreciated, and he had me feeling equal parts relieved and loved.

Corey finally presented the part of the trip I couldn't bring myself to get excited about: heading back up Interstate 69.

Sunday morning, we'd have to just grab a fast-food breakfast before making the four-hour trip up to Ann Arbor for the meeting with Andrew and my father. After the big event, we'd rent a car and drive to Detroit where we had reservations for a late flight back to DFW. That detail triggered the thought of losing my Bronco, dampening my spirit for a moment. But I pushed it aside. I wouldn't let that lone dark cloud ruin everything Corey had just worked so hard to plan.

After dinner, we exchanged our goodbye hugs. Chris reminded me about my morning doctor appointment. I promised him I wouldn't forget, though my mind was already racing ahead to our well-planned journey. For better or worse, it was time for me to move forward.

CHAPTER 27: DOCTORS KNOW BEST

Just like his son who will always be my protector and Norse God, Chris also does everything in his power to take care of me. He'd pulled some strings to get me a morning appointment with Dr. Foster, our family's general practitioner. I'd only met him once before, on my first Monday after moving into the dads' house. My bladder problem was Chris' concern at the time and he insisted on Corey taking me to the appointment, to keep from adding any more stress to my life. Little did he know how much Corey *wouldn't* help with that intention.

I couldn't stop a chuckle as I thought about that visit, my butterflies fluttering at the memory, even as my face still flushed at the awkwardness. As I started the short drive to Dr. Foster's office, I reflected on how far I'd come since that day. I wasn't the same scared, orphaned pup anymore - or at least, I was trying to convince myself I wasn't.

** 8 Weeks Ago **

Corey not only took me to Dr. Foster's office; he decided to follow me into the exam room. Dr. Foster had been Corey's doctor for as long as he could remember, so it was all just casual. Well, until the doctor decided he was going to give me a real, *complete,* physical. As he had me strip down to my brand new tighty-whities, I glared at Corey's smirking face. I did my best to keep my customary embarrassing erection under control. It wasn't my fault, medical professionals just get me excited; lol, which is why I scored so *hard* when I met Corey.

I was impressed with myself. I was mostly successful with my efforts to remain soft. Well, all the way up to the inevitable "Okay Oliver, please drop your underwear, we need to do a hernia check." I dropped my briefs and blushed a bit as he fondled my furry balls - at least it was in a very professional manner. I did my coughs and thought I was going to make it through with minimal embarrassment until I looked over at Corey's mischievous smirking face. Oh lurd no. I suddenly remembered what he had told me last Friday after he shaved around my hole and taint. I immediately knew what was coming next.

Sure enough, I heard Corey's voice, almost in a chuckle, "Hey Dr. Foster, can you do me a favor, from one medical professional to another?"

Dr. Foster had just finished examining my testicles and now had my penis in his hands, with my foreskin retracted, exposing my glans to his thorough inspection. Just as I was about to lose control, he straightened up, patted my shoulder and told me that everything looked good. He then glanced over to Corey and replied, "Sure son, how can I help?" I tried to pull my underwear up as fast as possible. But I already knew it was too late...

Corey earnestly looked at Dr. Foster and went exactly where I knew he would. "So, doc, I'm sure my Dad told you what's been going on with Ollie's bladder. I gave him a urodynamic flow study on Friday and unfortunately had to shave his anus and perineum. He's a very furry boy and I told him he'd need to see either me or another doctor today to make sure there were no ingrown hairs or signs of infection. Since he's here with his shorts down, could you check and maybe apply another round of topical antibiotic?"

I rolled my eyes at Dr. Foster's reply, "Absolutely Corey. Oliver, please remove your underwear again, face the table, lean over, rest your chest on the padding and grab the far side." I was all too familiar with those commands and with the position it dictated. I maybe let a little exasperated groan escape; I also maybe heard Corey let a little chuckle escape; but I still did as I was told.

Dr. Foster gently pulled my cheeks apart to get an initial overview. Exposing my hole to the cool exam room air immediately started working its unfortunate magic. Even worse, as soon as the doctor started using his left thumb and index finger to gently open specific parts of my trench, while his right fingers danced their way over my hole and slowly down my taint to my quickly rising testicles, I knew I was doomed and was already three quarters erect.

When he finally started applying a cool cream over the same area - I swear, giving my hole way more attention than necessary - I totally lost my battle and as per my usual, I had a full-blown erection. I let my forehead drop onto the table's padding in total defeat. I gave a resigned sigh. Dr. Foster allowed a warm chuckle to emerge as he gave my cheeks a reassuring pat before stating, "Everything looks fine back here, Oliver. Just lots of blond stubble emerging right where it belongs, no sign of ingrown hairs or any rash. You can turn around and get dressed."

I hesitated, just like Corey knew I would. Before I could utter any lame explanation for my hesitance, Dr. Foster let out a sincere laugh, tapped my cheeks again and spoke a hearty, "Don't worry son, it's nothing I haven't seen before. It's okay, just *turn around and be proud!*"

Upon hearing those words, my head shot up and I spun around before I could even worry about whether or not my hardon would sling precum across the room. The first thing I saw was Corey trying to stifle his laughter with his hand over his face in his typical admission of shame pose. I glared at him accusingly. He regained his composure and meekly replied, "Hey, so now you know who taught me that line." He shrugged, *almost* believably.

I marveled at the revelation until I finally realized I was standing there with a dripping erection in front of my doctor. I sheepishly apologized and tried my best to pull my underwear up and over my uncooperative dick. Dr. Foster took the opportunity to explain himself, "Ollie, I'm used to dealing with Corey. It's all good. You're a very healthy young man." He glanced down at my private little battle with my clothing and added, "Oh, and you really could be Corey's brother." He winked, gave me a fatherly side hug, and exited the room, allowing me keep a few shattered remnants of my dignity intact as I dressed.

I returned my glare to my so-called "protector," brushing off his endless string of apologies. I even committed to an exaggerated pout, holding it for the entirety of our ten-minute ride back home. The moment we stepped into the kitchen, Corey stopped me in my tracks. With a sincere tenderness that breached my defenses, he slid his hand under my chin and tilted my face up to meet his still mischievous, but irresistible gaze. His eyes held a spark of apology mixed with a knowing tease. Before I could protest, he leaned in to give me a kiss that was both apologetic and undeniably sensual. I wanted to stay mad, but my resolve crumbled as I gave in and returned it, letting his touch erase my lingering embarrassment.

As he finally pulled back, his mischievous smirk

returned, and his tone shifted seamlessly into Nurse Corey Mode. "Ollie, do you remember Friday morning? When I refused to let you leave for a very specific reason," he said, his voice was laced with mock seriousness. I nodded, my curiosity piqued by his tone and where this might be going. "Well, my sweet pup, that mean old doctor got you really excited," he continued, his hand slipping down to fondle my crotch. "And it feels like you're still in a dangerously erect state." His grin deepened as he teased, "Poor boy, you haven't had an orgasm since 9:30 last night."

I had enough of my wits about me to shake my head and utter, "That was our *first* one. Remember? You bred me again at 11:30 to make sure we'd have lots of puppies."

Corey chuckled, his lips brushing against mine. "How could I forget? But, Ollie, I'm afraid you're still at serious risk of DSB, which almost always leads to the nightmare of SRH. As your personal nurse, I feel it's my duty to help you out of this critical situation."

Totally mesmerized by his attention, I nodded and immediately stripped from the waist down, sending my shoes and pants flying across the kitchen floor. The spell Corey had me under broke for just a moment as I paused, confused. "Wait, what's, uh, DSB? And S...?"

Corey's smirk became more intense as he leaned in close, his voice dripping with seduction. "...

RH. Deadly Sperm Build-up and Sperm Retention Headache. They affect thousands of horny teenage boys worldwide." He reached down to wrap his fist around my cock, his grin turning downright devilish. "But lucky for you, I'm here to administer the cure."

I stood there chuckling until Corey moved me to the kitchen island, spun me around and commandingly pushed my chest down over it. As soon as I was in yet another submissive position, his fingers parted my cheeks and immediately started meticulously exploring my hole. I was instantly leaking and almost forgetting my recent embarrassment.

After much too short of a time, Corey rose up over me, pulled my chest up and spun me around again. He gave another kiss and said, "I'm sorry I can't give your hole the attention my tongue would love to provide, because, well, you're kinda covered in antibiotics." He grinned, "So let me do the next best thing."

He knelt on the floor before me and licked the trickle of precum flowing from my still mostly hooded head. I moaned as he retracted my foreskin and allowed his broad tongue to become my leaking cock's best friend once again. But that was just the beginning. After our only one intense weekend together, Corey had already mastered the art of making my body sing. With a mischievous glint in his eye, he quickly slicked his fingers and returned them to their favorite playground: my quivering hole.

With all of Dr. Foster's clinical attention and Corey's masterful buildup after, it didn't take long for me to reach my crescendo. With his fingers giving me yet another expert prostate massage and his tongue swirling around my head and shaft, it took my Norse God less than five minutes to expertly relieve my DSB and completely earn back my trust, forgiveness, and love - all while leaving me utterly blissed out.

** Present Day **

I shook my head, bringing myself back to the present - *again*, a painful mistake I should have known better than to make. Worse yet, lurd! I can be so stupid sometimes. Reliving one of my favorite steamy moments with Corey during a ten-minute drive to my doctor's office wasn't exactly my wisest move. So, now here I was, sitting in my Bronco, battling yet another inconvenient and completely unnecessary erection. Wonderful. Dr. Foster will *never* let me live this one down. Thankfully, by the time I checked in and sat down in the waiting room, I'd managed to will most of it away.

Dr. Foster appeared with a welcoming smile, ushering me into his exam room after a quick hug. "Oliver, it's great to see you again! I just wish it were under better circumstances. How are you feeling?"

"Hey, Dr. Foster! Thanks so much for squeezing me in on short notice. I feel pretty good, actually. My lump's gone, and my head only hurts if I shake it too hard." I hopped up onto the exam table as he directed.

He gave me a thoughtful look as he collected his tools. "Any dizziness, nausea, or trouble waking up in the morning?" he asked, leaning in to give my eyes a precursory look.

"Nope, I swear I'm feeling normal again. No issues at all."

He gently placed his hand under my chin, coaxing me to meet his steady gaze. As I did, he repeatedly flicked his penlight across my pupils, his focus sharp but reassuring. He nodded, seemingly pleased, before directing me to twist around on the exam table, bringing my right knee up so that I could turn sideways. "Let's take a look at your wound and stitches," he said, leaning in even closer, his hand gently coaxing my head to bow forward. Before commenting on their condition, he added with a smile, "By the way, that haircut really suits you. It looks great."

I felt a blush creeping up my neck. "Thanks, Dr. Foster," I mumbled, the compliment catching me a little off guard.

The exam wrapped up shortly after. "Oliver," he began, slipping back into his professional tone, "everything looks excellent. You're healing well from the concussion and the wound looks great. I think it's safe for you to ease back into your normal activities. Just be careful not to do anything too jarring - so no rollercoasters for a while," he quipped with a small grin. It was an earnest attempt at doctor humor - lame, but oddly endearing.

As I hopped off the table, expecting to say our goodbyes, Dr. Foster's eyes sparkled with a hint of mischief. "So, how's your perineum fur coming in? Any painful bumps or rashes? If you'd like, I can check it out and apply more antibiotic."

Before the familiar rush of heat could take over my face, I caught the playful tone in his voice and noticed the barely concealed grin tugging at his lips. He was just teasing me. He even allowed a chuckle to escaped before he could stop it. I met his eyes with an understanding grin. "It's growing back fine, Doc. And I think I'll keep my embarrassing erection to myself today, if that's alright with you."

He laughed and gave my back a hardy pat. "Hey, can't blame an earnest doctor for trying."

I shared his laugh as I headed out the door. I realized he wasn't just poking fun at me; he was reassuring me. Letting me know everything was good. It felt freeing to walk away without the weight of any awkwardness between us. Maybe that was his lesson. Life isn't about avoiding embarrassing moments; it's about surrounding yourself with people who can turn them into something better: funny, even endearing, reminders of how much they love and care about you.

CHAPTER 28: FAITHFUL STEED

The rest of the week flew by, exactly as I feared it would. The only snag in an otherwise productive few days was my attempt to get a Texas driver's license. Turns out, it's not as easy to get as I'd hoped. Well, or maybe just not as *quick to obtain* as I'd naively assumed. The earliest appointment I could get at any DPS office - in the entire DFW area - wasn't until mid-September. My frustration nearly boiled over, but I managed to keep my head from exploding. I reminded myself that intent and effort still count. Hopefully, TCU will see my commitment and give me credit for taking every step I could.

Otherwise, I accepted that my time had finally run out. On Thursday afternoon, in a solemn and almost sacred ceremony, I hand washed my bright blue Bronco in our driveway. If I had to give up my four-wheeled companion on Sunday, I was going to make sure he looked as pristine and sparkling as the day we first met. He wasn't just a car to me; my trusted steed was my shelter during cold winter nights and my refuge during bone-rattling thunderstorms. He'd silently cheered me on as I fought to defend our bond against would-be thieves. He even comforted me afterward, his radio soothing me with familiar 90's tunes as I nursed my blooming bruises and bloodied knuckles.

People say it's foolish to love an inanimate object, but I'd argue that no man has ever been more connected to his vehicle than I am to my beloved Bronco. I have my Corey and my incredible dads, who mean the world to me, but I couldn't shake the feeling that I was letting my closest, most loyal friend down. Giving my most precious possession up to the man who tormented me most, feels like the ultimate horror from my nightmare. I couldn't help it - I hugged my boy, pressing my cheek against his shining hood. I'm going to miss him. But before we part, we're going to have one heck of an adventure first.

CHAPTER 29: A SPECIAL SEND OFF

I heard Corey's gentle baritone, "Hey Pup, you up?" I mean I was technically awake - well, mainly because I hadn't been able to sleep all night. I rolled over in his arms and gave him an *almost* morning breath kiss. In my book, 4:00 a.m. is still nighttime.

"Yeah," I mumbled, "Just waiting for your alarm to go off. I'm not sure I really ever got to sleep last night."

Corey chuckled low in his throat. "Oh, you slept. I had to give you a nudge to stop your snoring." He playfully poked my ribs.

I scoffed, only half-amused. "Corey, I've told you before, I don't snore, it's more like a purr. There's a difference."

His eyes danced, and before I knew it, he launched into a surprise tickle attack. In seconds, the uneasy mix of dread and excitement simmering inside me dissolved into a fit of laughter. Still smiling, we jumped into the shower, letting the warm water and a slow, sensual make-out session, ease us into our long day. No conditioner fun this morning - my body and brain didn't want that kind of stimulation right now. But Corey's muscled arms and the press of his hard furry chest against my back was exactly what the doctor ordered.

Chris and Ted had made sure that we wouldn't start our new adventure on empty stomachs. They dropped off another La Madeleine care package last night while wishing us a safe trip and giving us their goodbye hugs. As they left, they promised that the attorneys would have plenty of news for us when we met them on Sunday.

Showered and dressed, we reheated our little French feast while brewing coffee. I made a lame joke that half of France must've just winced in unison at the sound of us crassly microwaving the food of their people. "Sacre Bleu!" indeed.

We'd packed efficiently - just two medium suitcases tucked neatly into the Bronco's cargo area and two dress shirts and jackets hanging from hooks on the sides. As we waited for the garage door to rise, I had my typical inner monologue moment and felt foolishly sentimental: this was my Bronco's last night beside his Mustang Mach E stablemate. I had no idea what my father had planned for my boy, but I hoped my trusted steed would eventually find a wonderful forever home.

We pulled out of the driveway at 5:00 am sharp. Corey, satisfied with our on-time departure, was happy to be our dedicated navigator until Little Rock. We began our epic voyage by heading toward University Drive. From there, we'd turn north and slip down the hill, over the river, and continue on to interstate 30.

The sky was still dark; the city was still asleep. My grandpa's "start of a long journey" mantra whispered through my mind: "Sit down, shut up, here we go!"

****

We'd barely crossed the Trinity River - just a few blocks shy of the freeway entrance ramp - when I regretted ever mocking the French. A sickening feeling of déjà vu washed over me as I caught sight of flashing red and blue lights in my rearview mirror. I couldn't believe it! That's twice now in my short Texas driving career. If this pace keeps up, there's no way they'll ever let me have a Texas driver's license.

Unlike my first episode, I somehow knew the lights were meant for me. I guided the Bronco into the empty Ol' South Pancake House parking lot, shooting Corey a helpless, wide-eyed look. Corey's expression wasn't any help. His face mirrored my confusion, but he quickly tried to reassure me. "Ollie, I swear Dad called Alex last night to let him know we'd be leaving at 5:00 this morning to return your Bronco. He made sure no one still had the vehicle flagged as stolen - anywhere between here and Michigan. I have no idea what this is about."

I glanced at my driver's side mirror to see the officer already heading toward my door. My stomach twisted as I rolled the window down. Corey reached over, took my clammy hand, and pressed a gentle kiss against it. His quiet show of solidarity steadied my nerves, reminding me I wasn't facing whatever happened next alone this time.

I looked out my window and instantly recognized the serious face leaning toward me. A big grin took over my own as I heard, "Good morning, son. I received a reliable tip that a known, curly blond-haired felon, was planning to flee the state with stolen property this morning." Seeing a friendly face more than made up for the little scare, and I nearly let my first tear of the trip slip out.

He stayed in character for just a moment longer, "Please step out of the car..." before breaking out in a big smile that matched mine. "...so I can give my favorite car thief a good luck hug."

My seatbelt was off in a heartbeat, and I jumped out to meet Officer Kevin Barrett's open arms. He pulled me into a bear hug that filled me with genuine warmth. "Ollie, Captain Williams told me at the start of my patrol last night that you'd be heading out early this morning to surrender your Bronco. I figured a show of support might help get you started on the right foot."

I laughed, my mood instantly brighter. "Thanks, Officer Barrett. But we might need to swing back by the house for an extra change of underwear after that stunt!"

Kevin cuffed my shoulder and let out a sincere belly laugh. I caught some motion to my right. By the time I turned, Corey had already circled around the front of Bronco to join us, pulling Kevin into a hug as well. "Ha ha, very funny, Officer Kevin. But truly, it's great to see you again. I just want to thank you once more for everything you did for Ollie. You're a good guy, and we'd love to have you and your..."

Kevin caught the hint and supplied, "Wife."

Corey managed not to blink at that revelation. "...over to the pool this summer as often as y'all would like. We owe you a lot, and it'd be great to get to know you both better."

Kevin noticed Corey's minor stumble and jumped right in. "Hey, you don't have to be gay to fall in love with Ollie. He's one of a kind. And Anna would love to meet both of you. Besides, the Captain can't stop bragging about your pool."

"Uh, Kevin," Corey said, chuckling softly, "Alex has only seen my Dad's pool, not ours. But I swear, we can host a fun afternoon pool party at our place too."

We all shared a semi-awkward laugh as Corey and Kevin exchanged numbers.

Kevin plowed through the situation, driving his final point home. "Ollie, I'm not the only one who wanted to see you off. I'm just the one crazy enough to hide and wait until you rolled by. Officer Calhoon and everyone else who's heard your story are all on your side. I'm pretty sure we could rustle up a decent cavalcade and head up to Michigan to help convince your father that the Bronco belongs with you."

I smiled, genuinely touched. "I appreciate that Kevin, but I think I need to handle this on my own." Realizing my small misstep, I quickly added, "I mean, Corey is definitely all the backup I need. Sir!"

I pulled Kevin into a final hug and asked him to pass it along. He let out another laugh. "You're pushing your luck, son. Not all big, burly officers are as cuddly as I am - but believe me, we'll all be thinking about you." He shot Corey a knowing look. "Take care of our boy, buddy." He gave us a polite parting salute before returning to his car. As he walked, he delivered his final words over his shoulder, "And you take care of him too, Ollie! Y'all are an amazing team."

Corey and I just stood there, a little stunned at this unexpected show of support. After a moment, we shared a reassuring hug of our own before climbing back into the Bronco. As we merged onto the freeway and headed east, I smiled to myself and couldn't help thinking that my father had absolutely no idea who he was meeting on Sunday.

CHAPTER 30: COREY'S NIGHTMARE

We rode along mostly in silence as we slipped out of Ft. Worth, sped through Arlington's concrete canyon, and even cleared Big D's downtown "horse shoe." All before the Friday morning rush had a chance to slow our progress. The plan was for Corey to take a nap early in the morning while I drove, so I could take mine in the early afternoon after we had lunch in Little Rock.

Corey had just about dozed off when I couldn't resist waking him, if only for a moment. "My wolf, I'm sorry, but we're in Rockwall. Look! See that Walmart on the right and the Buc-ee's up ahead on the left? That's where I slept and got ready for the morning of our test!"

I wasn't thrilled with Corey's less-than-enthusiastic response to my impromptu travelogue. He mumbled a way too casual, "That's cool pup," before rolling over in his reclined seat and drifting right back into slumber. I swallowed my disappointment and started toggling between the 80's on 8 and the 90's on 9, trying to find a song to comfort me, as we made our way east under a crystal-clear Texas morning sky.

I looked over at my sleeping wolf and consoled myself by thinking that, hey, at least once, in a very bass-ackwards way, I was able to have my boyfriend sleep over at my place. Well, if you can call a Bronco in a parking lot an official address. I finally just smiled and got over it.

My sleeping Norse God made it all the way to Mount Pleasant before rejoining me in our journey. But, he awoke with a jolt. He looked panicked, like he'd just surfaced from a bad dream. I watched him force a few steady breaths, trying to calm himself enough to speak. "Ollie! Damn... can we make a quick stop? I need to walk this off."

My concern flared instantly. "Are you okay?"

He shook his head slightly, still gathering himself. "Just give me a minute or two."

I eased the Bronco off I-30 and pulled into a McDonald's parking lot, rolling to a stop. I turned to him, worried and waiting.

Corey's still startled expression morphed into genuine remorse. "Ollie, I'm so sorry I blew off your comments about the Walmart parking lot and Buc-ee's. I was groggy, but that's no excuse." He looked me straight in the eye, his apology as real as the long road still looming ahead of us.

I saw his face darken, I think he was on the verge of tears, and I felt my chest constrict. Before I could say anything, he spoke, his voice shaky but determined. "Ollie, remember that thought you shared right before we fell asleep - the night after the dads told us to find our song? You were worried you might wake up alone again in some Walmart parking lot."

He took a trembling breath. "Well, karma just gave me a swift kick in the balls. Pup, in my dream, you had disappeared, and I had to search for you. And... well, I found you, um, dead in your Bronco, from a gunshot wound. All because I couldn't get you to trust me. You refused the dads' offer to stay with them. Fuck." He let his tears flow, no longer trying to hold them back.

Oh, my lurd! I understood, and pulled him into my arms. "Corey, my love, it's okay." I tried to calm him, "That didn't happen. I did trust you, remember? We had an amazing weekend getting to explore each other. And now here we are, together on a new journey, both of us safe." I tightened my embrace, feeling him gradually shake off the nightmare and return to the reality of the moment.

I could see Corey's face flushing with embarrassment, so I offered him a reassuring grin. "It's okay, my wolf." Now it was *my* line, "No more 'Twilight Zone' for you!" I smirked, "Or maybe just no more blowing me off when I share my important places with you." I raised an eyebrow, but my tone stayed caring. "Listen, no matter how much magic you've planned into this trip, it's still going to be the most stressful thing we've done as a couple. Heck, we might even have an argument, heaven forbid." I chuckled softly, hoping to lighten the mood. "But like Officer Kevin said, we are an amazing team."

This time, I was the one cupping his bearded cheek, comforting him. "So, what's it gonna be? A quick bathroom break and a couple of coffees, or do I need to drive all the way back to Rockwall so you can give my tour guide commentary all the respect it deserves?"

Corey finally managed a genuine chuckle and a tentative smile. We settled on kisses and McCafés.

CHAPTER 31: RHYME TYME

We'd been on the road for over 5 hours now - if you count Officer Kevin's surprise cameo and our quick McDonald's stop. Maybe it was the monotony of the highway or the lingering adrenaline from the early-morning police send off, but we were both getting a little punchy. The long drive out of Texas seems like it takes freaking forever and honestly, the countryside isn't all that pretty or interesting until you finally get close to Texarkana. Still, we were making decent time, cruising through the forests of southwestern Arkansas, in the middle of nowhere, about an hour away from our Little Rock lunch date.

Already tired of our two overplayed Sirius/XM channels, we decided to branch out into '80s alternative on First Wave. I recognized a few songs until the most bizarre track I'd ever heard started up with a simplistic, nearly juvenile, synth line and a hokey, repetitive drum machine beat. The lyrics were all just rhyming couplets, each one more outrageously misogynistic than the last.

I couldn't hide my shock and disbelief, which only made Corey light up. "Ollie! You've never heard '88 Lines About 44 Women'? It's a classic! My friends and I spent way too many high-school study halls making up our own lines. I guess we treated it like a teenage boy's rite of passage."

"Are you kidding? My father would have blown a gasket if he heard a song with a line like Jean thought guys weren't as fun as masturbating in the tub." Corey grinned and corrected me, "That's 'Joan.'" I rolled my eyes, but I still let a little giggle slip through.

I should have known Corey couldn't just let it drop. I saw the hamster wheel spinning in his head. Sure enough, after a few miles, he shot me a smug smirk and delivered:

"Ollie was a lone lost pup; his bladder made him sad. Corey was his big Norse God who brought him home to his new dads."

I groaned but couldn't stop a grin from spreading across my face. "Please, my Norse God, let's stop while you're ahead." Yeah, I knew it was a futile request.

Yep, absolutely futile. A few miles later: *"Corey loves his Ollie's curls. This pup's blond hair could charm the world."*

"How are you even doing that? And, oh, 'curls' and 'world' *barely* rhyme."

Corey smirked, "Hey, it was either that or 'girls'." I flashed him a sign of capitulation.

Two miles later, lurd, they're coming faster now. "Wait, this one's perfect: *'Corey begged: no bad lube today. Ollie blushed and turned away'*."

"Okay! One more, and I'm turning this car around right now and dropping you off at your Dad's house for grounding."

Corey grinned. "Last one, I promise. *'Corey met his Ollie in the very strangest way. And Ollie stole his heart away on that very day'*."

I couldn't help but beam at that one. "Sweet. But now you're squeezing way too many syllables in. That totally breaks the song's rules. But, love you too my wolf."

Of course he was unstoppable by this point. Not even two miles later, he delivered his magnum opus: *"We've traveled far and our love's on high. With dreams of purple frogs and Texas skies."*

I groaned dramatically and silently prayed for any earworm to rescue me. The XM gods apparently heard my plea, and the unmistakable synth line of "doot doot deet deet doot doot da de da deet" filled the car. Corey and I instantly abandoned the pursuit of bad rhymes for the sheer joy of chanting, "S-s-s-s, A-a-a-a, F-f-f-f, E-e-e-e..." We happily left our non-dancing friends, the real world, and any lingering tension, far behind.

CHAPTER 32: ARE WE THERE YET?

We were both getting pretty hungry as we rolled into Little Rock, and stretching our legs sounded like heaven. Corey broke the silence first. "Pup, I swear this road trip seemed way more fun in my head when I was planning it."

I couldn't help but chuckle. That sounded suspiciously like my Corey's version of *"Are we there yet?"* I kept that thought to myself.

"Corey, we just haven't made it to the fun parts yet. By the way, have you picked out a place for lunch?"

"Sure have!" Corey replied brightly, "But if you hate it, don't worry, it looks like we've got plenty of options."

We exited onto the frontage road, and turned under the freeway on 4th Street then headed toward the river on Cumberland. Corey read off his prepared list of restaurant choices as we passed through downtown. He'd originally pitched a place called the Copper Grill, but it looked a bit too upscale for my mood. I made a command decision and decided on Dizzy's Gypsy Bistro - a lot more approachable, and as it turned out, a perfect choice. The meal was fantastic.

After lunch, Corey led me back to the Bronco. To my surprise, he reached behind the passenger seat and pulled out a football. I blinked, caught off-guard. "Corey! What's going on?"

He flashed a goofy grin. "I figured we could get some exercise in and let you show off those mad football skills of yours. The riverfront's only a couple blocks away." He nodded a direction over his shoulder.

We indulged in an intense thirty minutes of tossing the ball around the park by the beautiful Arkansas River, working out some of our road-trip stiffness. Corey handled the ball better than I expected. I've missed throwing a football and I couldn't help feeling touched by his thoughtful gesture. It was so simple, yet so perfect for clearing our heads and reconnecting before hitting the road again.

As we settled back into the Bronco, flushed and laughing, I realized we were adding a new layer of memories to its interior. Our post exercise musk mixing with, and adding to, the scent of its leather. I couldn't help but wonder what my father would make of it all when he finally regained custody.

****

Corey took the driver's seat as we headed out on

I-40 toward Memphis. Dang! It felt totally wrong being in my Bronco's passenger seat. But also oddly special, like I was sharing my trusted steed with his new dad, if only for a day or two. I pushed that bad thought aside as I snuggled in for a nap on our 6-hour journey across I-40 and then up I-55. I just hoped I would have better dreams than Corey had.

As it turns out, you actually need to fall asleep before worrying about your dreams. By the time we'd reached Forest City, I finally gave up trying. It was kind of a good thing. From my lone drive down this way a few months ago, I knew this is where the pretty scenery ended and the broad, flat and featureless Mississippi river basin started. I just couldn't let Corey suffer through that dull stretch alone.

I decided to break the silence. "You know you should be honored, right?"

Corey glanced my way with a curious grin. "Why, pup? Wait, don't tell me - I'm the first person besides you to drive your Bronco?"

"Got it in one, my man. And honestly, I love seeing you drive him. It's the best I can do after you let me live in your house." I was sincere and just letting Corey know how much I appreciated him, but I don't think he took it the way I intended.

His smile slipped into something more serious. "Ollie, please don't ever say that again, okay?"

I tilted my head, confused. "Wait, what?"

He gave me a gentle, loving look. "Pup, it's not my house anymore. It's our house. For as long as you want it to be."

My heart soared. As we continued our journey, I couldn't hide my joy, and Corey's soft smile told me he felt it too.

****

The rest of the undeniably boring stretch flew by faster than I could've imagined. Believe me, you really should try sharing a ride with a 29-year-old man who can still channel his inner high school class clown. We invented ridiculous backstories for every annoying driver on the road, and he coaxed me into a rapid-fire round of weird favorites (and even weirder least favorites). I scored a victory by declaring Corey's scent to be my all-time top favorite.

Next, we tried our own version of "Name That Tune," which we failed at miserably. While we can both sing along just fine to songs on the radio, without actual music to guide us, our "doot doot dooting" attempts fell hilariously flat. But it didn't matter. Corey was doing his job, keeping my mind off the real purpose of our journey.

Just as the St. Louis metro area was coming into range, Corey accidentally brought up the subject of mothers. I realized I'd barely mentioned mine, and I wasn't even sure if his really existed. Unfortunately, the surge of traffic forced us to put that conversation on hold. We focused on wrangling our way through the stampede of cars, navigating our path toward the hotel, the topic of mothers left lingering for another day.

CHAPTER 33: GATEWAY ARCH

My man picks nice hotels. Granted, I hadn't traveled much beyond a few family trips, where Motel 6 and Days Inn were considered top-tier. Not that I'm trying to cut my father any slack for picking basic hotels, but my family mostly stayed local. The furthest we ever went might've been Cedar Point, which reminded me - Corey still owed me a visit to our own local Six Flags. Well, as soon as my concussion was completely gone.

All that to say, I was a bit overwhelmed as we checked into our "real" hotel, which, just as Corey had promised, was practically beneath the Gateway Arch. I'd never set foot in a place like this before. I couldn't stop a quiet "Wow" from slipping out. He really had managed to make this trip feel like a genuine vacation, one unlike anything I'd ever experienced. Walking into our room only deepened that feeling, leaving me all deer-in-the-headlights and speechless.

Corey caught my incredulous look and grinned.

"So, pup, is this the fun part now?"

I just nodded, setting my suitcase down and hurrying over to the window. The Arch was right there, it's silver sides gleaming in the late afternoon sun. The room itself was gorgeous, but that view? That was the money shot. It was just before six o'clock and Corey stepped up behind me, slipping his arms around my waist and pressing me gently into his chest. With a playful flourish, he lifted his watch into view for both of us. Mere seconds before six, he simply said, "Watch this pup."

From our vantage point, I could see straight through the Arch and across the river. Right as the clock struck six, a giant fountain burst skyward on the far shore, spraying a magnificent column of water for a full five minutes before retreating back into its circular pool. "Dang, my Wolf! How the heck did you time that so perfectly?" I asked, seriously impressed.

Corey chuckled; his arms still snug around me. "Actually, my Ollie, I kind of blew it. My little nightmare and our unexpected send-off from Officer Kevin put us just a little behind on our schedule. The real plan was to have you... shall we say, happily occupied in my arms at this exact moment, so that when the Gateway Geyser erupted, well, you'd be having your own little eruption too."

I giggled, leaning into his chest. "We might've missed that special moment, but I'm still beyond impressed. When you plan, you really plan big." Turning in his embrace, I gave him the kiss he'd more than earned, grateful for his thoughtfulness and creativity.

After narrowly missing his perfectly timed "fireworks" moment, Corey decided what we needed most was a relaxing shower before our 7:30 dinner reservation at an Italian spot just down the street. He began undressing me, and I tried to do the same for him - until he pulled one of my favorite tricks of his, trapping me in my shirt as he lifted it over my head. "Ollie," he teased, "I was wrong about waiting. We can't let this chance slip by. Your pits are absolutely on point, and while I wanted to save our first 'real hotel *experience*' - like you asked about - until after dinner... With your scent driving me wild, I just don't think I can hold off."

He pressed his nose and lips into my exposed pit, inhaling deeply and dragging his tongue in a slow, intoxicating line. I was instantly hard and ready to play after hours of being cooped up on the road. Still, I practiced patience, letting him indulge in my scent as I savored his attention. Once he finally freed me from my snare, I paid him back in kind, his end-of-day musk driving me just as wild as mine did him.

With both of us stripped down to our natural state, I started to head toward the king-sized bed. But Corey seductively caught my arm and pulled me into his embrace instead. "Oh no, pup," he growled, his voice low and warm. "The bed's for after dinner.

Right now, that cozy club chair between the window and the TV has our names written all over it." With a grin and a gentle nudge, he guided me toward our chosen playground for our pre-dinner performance.

I was a bit unsure, but Corey compensated by presenting his magically unpacked lube bottle and leading me to the waiting chair. He quickly turned it to face the view, then sat down with his commanding hardon pointing up to the Arch's apex. He motioned me to stand between his legs, facing him as he popped the container's top open and doused his fingers in the slippery liquid. He kissed me quickly, then motioned for me to spin around and lean onto the window sill as his slicked fingers found my exposed hole.

As always, he quickly had my complete attention, and my precum flowing. "Okay pup, kinda like we did in bed the other night when I rolled you over on top of me, just sit down on me and as soon as it feels right, lean back into me and let me start my part." I understood what Corey wanted and followed his commands. My pent-up desire made his entry as easy as possible and suddenly, I was literally locked into his embrace as his strong arms held my back to his chest and his 8-inch key locked my hole into his lap. Tab A wasn't going to leave Slot B until we were both satisfied.

My part in this new dance was all too obvious, I relaxed into him, slid slightly across his chest, and once again put my right arm around his neck. Us both being upright in the chair made our craved access easier and he even found a way to cup my exposed pit with his hand, allowing it, along with our faces, to form a private little bubble where we could both kiss and breathe in my testosterone-filled musk. It fueled us into a frenzy as he started pumping up into my hungry chute.

Sensing we were both getting close, Corey intentionally broke the spell by coaxing me to turn my head away from him and into the view outside our window. One of Corey's hands found my nip and the other my loaded cock. I marveled at the Arch suspended above our window. As they say, "supported only by math." I felt Corey's release heat my guts and mere moments later, my eruption created our own private arch shooting through the room. Supported only by our desire and love. Dang, I'm always going to have a special place in my heart for St. Louis.

CHAPTER 34:
ITALIAN DINNER

After our shower, we wandered the few blocks to the restaurant in a blissful daze. I felt spellbound by Corey and the city's nighttime energy. I'd never ventured much into Detroit, but now Corey's obvious love for downtown life - this time in St. Louis - was rubbing off on me. Hand in hand, I gawked unabashedly at the sights, marveling at how different this trip felt compared to my solitary journey six months ago. My man really had managed to plan something truly special.

The restaurant welcomed us with a warmth and the comforting scent of simmering sauces, roasted garlic, and fresh bread. I'd always thought that Italian food was something we could easily whip up at home, but the restaurant's menu shattered that notion. There was an entire universe of flavors and smells I'd never imagined. Once again, my wolf was expanding my horizons, showing me just how wide and wonderful the world could be.

Back in our hotel room, he expanded my sexual

horizons as well. We took a little more time for foreplay this time. Experimenting with perfecting our 69-ing. Believe me, with Corey's monster cock, I needed to be on top. But then, my almost as impressive dick threatened to suffocate him on bottom, so we wound up happily on our sides, each with a knee in the air, only taking what we could without choking.

Eventually, Corey's fingers stormed the field of their favorite playground and once again, I was open and begging him to unite us as only he could. I needed his comfort in this still-stressful trip, so I rolled on to my stomach with my arms tucked under my chest as I raised my hips to present my intention to my wolf. He immediately straddled my thighs and slid his way up them until I felt him drizzle lube on my hole. Shortly after, his cock's head was eagerly waiting at my once again furry entrance.

He teasingly pushed his head in and out of my hole, as if asking if I were still ready for another round. On his next entry, I answered by raising up and forcing him to go deep. After a few commanding strokes, he leaned his chest down to rest on my back as he started kissing my neck and nibbling my ear. I turned my head so that we could kiss as he simply and earnestly began humping into me.

It may have gone on for hours or maybe just a few minutes. Either way, we moved as one. No extravagant acrobatics, just full body contact - staying as connected as possible. And for the second time in a very few hours, I was lost in our bliss. Corey never even really faltered in his rhythm as he got close, I only knew he was about to breed me because I could feel his entire body tense until he finally humped as deep as possible and froze there, holding me tight through his release.

He eventually rose up from my back and gently rolled me over, immediately noticing that neither of us would be sleeping in a wet spot. His concern was jovial but genuine, "Pup! Am I losing my touch?"

"Absolutely not, I was in heaven the whole time. Your weight on top of me, making me feel all safe and loved? That's all I could ever want, but I couldn't get enough friction going to get me over the edge. I swear I'm good!"

Corey took that as a challenge, "No, no pup! Scoot over to the edge of the bed, pull those knees to your chest and let me take care of your sweet, over-loaded bottom."

I did as I was instructed, and suddenly Corey was kneeling on the floor and repeating the act that had scared, well, the crap out of me just a few days ago. This time, there was no mood-killing hair conditioner to ruin our fantasy. Once again, this insanely nasty act worked its magic and my libido was at a 10, which I imagined Nurse Corey would categorize as "Boy-Batter Geyser Imminent".

I started jacking my cock as Corey lapped his load out of my twice satisfied hole. His tongue was in perfect synchronicity with my strokes. Always wanting to go the extra mile, Corey reached a hand up to pinch a nipple and that's all it took for my second load to arch through the room - our second tribute to the monument outside our window. He finished our dance by working his tongue up my body collecting and mixing our cum in his mouth until he shared our combined mix in our kiss. Fuck! So many new levels.

CHAPTER 35: ANOTHER CURLY HAIRED HERO

Saturday morning arrived right on schedule and we were true to Corey's itinerary. We blissfully slept in until, well, all of 7:00 a.m. Lol. It was entirely my fault. I'd insisted on leaving the curtains open so I could enjoy the Arch-lit view if I woke up during the night. But I totally misjudged my exhaustion; I was so tired - and satisfied - I don't think I even rolled over during our contented slumber.

The sun's rays, shining through the Arch and straight into our room, made sleeping in impossible. Then again, I couldn't imagine a more incredibly beautiful alarm clock. After two amazing back-to-back rounds last night, we were perfectly content to just cuddle, tickle, kiss, and hold each other as the world woke up around us. Before things got too serious, we decided it was time to get dressed and hunt down some breakfast.

Fortunately, we didn't have to forage too far. The

hotel's restaurant offered a feast that easily competed with anything we could prepare at home. Don't get me wrong, I love it when Corey and I team up in the kitchen, but this was almost as good and we only had to leave a tip instead of washing the dishes on our own. I could definitely handle that.

We returned to our room to shower and started re-packing. Afterward, as promised, Corey guided us across the street to the Gateway Arch National Park and we began casually strolling around the amazing grounds and discussing the day's much simpler itinerary. Indy wasn't all that far away and we decided on an easy lunch in Terre Haute. We finally made our way to the Arch's underground entrance and I realized I'd seen all seen it all before - at least on screen.

I glanced at my wolf grinning, "This might be a little 'Y.A.' for you, but did you watch the 'Percy Jackson' series on Disney Plus? This place is like, well, exactly where they were."

Corey grinned, "Pup, you know that version's Percy almost has your curls, right?" He cradled my chin in his hand and gave me a sweet kiss. "Of course I've seen the series. I loved the movie back when I was in high school." He paused and gave me an accomplished look. "So, I believe that's now *two* famous filming locations I've taken you to." I let him enjoy his victorious smirk.

Corey bought our tickets and we squeezed into one of the little tube-like tram cars, marveling at the old technology that still seemed to work perfectly fine. Our little barreled car kept slowly tumbling as it adjusted to keep us upright while the train of cars navigated its path under and then up the curved arch. It was a bit claustrophobic, but definitely a one-of-a-kind experience. Thankfully, we had the cramped space all to ourselves.

We climbed out at the top, eager to stretch after being confined inside that tiny space. I guessed that most tourists probably weren't built like us. Again, as we walked up the final steps to the summit, I knew exactly where we were. Except I believe there was a manticore here waiting to ambush Percy, and I remarked as much to Corey as we made our way over to the observation windows.

He just grinned, but we weren't alone - other tourists were taking in the view - as he came up behind me while I was gazing out at the St. Louis skyline and whispered in my ear: "I've met the pup of my dreams, Oliver Aaron Carson. I want him to be mine forever."

The memory of our bike ride's storm sewer monolith climb sent chills up my spine and I softly returned our improvised vows, "My Norse God, Corey Allan Rainer, rescued me and gave me a new family! I want to be his forever!" Sure, we were paraphrasing a bit, but considering everything that had happened since that special spring afternoon moment, it felt just as perfect, and even more meaningful now.

After we shared a kiss that, thankfully, didn't seem to embarrass anyone around us, I felt the need to address the elephant in the room, or rather, in the monument. "So, as cool as this is, I can't help but feel a bit betrayed by Percy. That river water just looks nasty. There's no way he could have seen anything while he was submerged in that river."

Corey shuddered behind me. "I almost entered this into our contest in the car yesterday, but it's not just one of my least favorite things, it's a genuine phobia. I hate swimming in muddy water. And our home state? It's pretty much *all* muddy water." Corey nervously glanced at me, "Nice, clear, pools, I'm fine with. But Texas lakes and rivers are totally terrifying. My friends have tried to get me to kayak with them on the Trinity, and I just can't bring myself to do it."

He sighed, then continued softly. "When I was fifteen, Dad and Ted tried to help me overcome my fear. They took me to the U.S. Virgin Islands for a summer vacation. St. John is literally paradise on earth. There's even a little beach on the Caneel resort grounds named 'Paradise,' and it literally earns its name." He sighed, "I wasn't afraid at all there. I even did a few resort dives and decided to become a certified diver after we got home."

It was enthralling, discovering this new vulnerable layer of my big, strong, yet very human Norse God. "That's amazing," I said quietly. "I get it. The Great Lakes are the only 'beaches' I know, and they're usually pretty clear - and cold. Still, I'd never dip a toe in *that* river. And I can't even imagine what the beaches in the Virgin Islands must be like."

Corey flashed a wistful smile. "Hey, we just need a special reason to go back pup. I know you'd love it."

He gave me one last kiss before we squeezed back into the cramped tram for our return trip to earth. Then we headed back to our room, to finish the last of our packing. Upon leaving, I once again had to be me - I paused - preventing the door to our room from closing, to offer a sincere thanks and give a goodbye to our magical space before we checked out and re-loaded the Bronco.

It was time to keep moving forward.

CHAPTER 36: THE LITTLE ENGINE THAT COULD

** The Previous Evening **

I hate getting home late. Taking a four-day week-end was wonderful and I loved every moment with Ollie - barring the bad news I had to deliver. Even then, in true Ollie fashion, he picked himself right back up and started rebuilding his life, never letting his father's torments keep him down. I love my boy. But, after all of last week's unexpected time off, this week had been hectic. I was looking forward to a quiet weekend with Chris, hopefully with a little fun husband time included.

Happy to be home, I pulled into our garage and parked beside Chris's X5. Before I could help it, my eyes drifted to the empty spot where Ollie's Bronco used to sit. I felt a pang of melancholy, but I didn't have too much time to dwell on it - Chris came bounding out to meet me, wearing a grin so big it completely obliterated the memory of my busy week.

"Hey, Sweet-Sweet! What's got you all excited?" I asked, stepping out and melting in to his enthusiastic hug. "Have you heard anything from the boys?"

After stepping back, Chris gave me an animated look and replied, "Yeah, Corey just texted. They've finally checked into the Hyatt in St. Louis and are about to shower and grab some dinner." He gave me a deep welcome-home kiss, then lowered his voice slightly with excitement. "But that's not why I'm excited! We got some big news from the attorneys. Come on in and I'll explain."

I swear, like father like son. I followed my excited, fifty-year-old high school "boy" into the kitchen, where he was already cooking a dinner that smelled as incredible as his mood. I couldn't stand the suspense any longer. "Okay, Christopher, spill! What's the news?"

Chris flashed a sly grin, his eyes gleaming with a knowing spark. "So, I'm pretty sure Ollie won't be losing his Bronco..." He proceeded to outline everything the attorneys had discovered.

I was stunned - and apparently, there was more. Chris, ever the showman, presented the facts in a staged, almost theatrical manner that kept me on the edge of my seat. "It's not a slam dunk yet. There's one huge 'if' we need to clarify. I refuse to get Ollie's hopes up just to crush them again, so I haven't told the boys anything yet."

Before Chris could continue, I snickered and added, "You know, Ollie gave me a stern talking-to about us keeping secret plans from him. He insists he's a big boy now."

Only moderately deterred, Chris offered a good-natured shrug. "Alright, alright. I promise this will be the last - and most important - time. And I'll take the blame if Ollie's upset. Though, honestly, I doubt he will be." He leaned in, picking up his earlier momentum. "So, I think the best way to resolve that 'if' is for us to fly to Detroit tomorrow, drive to Lansing, and get to know a couple of very important people..."

He then revealed he'd emptied our Rapid Rewards account to get us tickets on Southwest to DTW tomorrow mid-morning. In typical Chris fashion, my detail-oriented man had made reservations for us in a cute boutique hotel in Ann Arbor, for Saturday and Sunday nights. He even went as far to reserve a room for Ollie and Corey on Sunday.

"You know they already have plane tickets back here for Sunday evening," I pointed out, giving my love a mildly judgmental smirk. "If you're really that confident this will work out, maybe you should tell Ollie and Corey now."

Chris brushed the suggestion aside with a confident grin. "Are you kidding? Ollie's birthday's in two weeks. First, I refuse to get him all excited only to be hurt again. And second, if this goes like I think it will, it'll be the best birthday surprise we could ever give him."

My man was on a mission. He had another son - if only honorary - to protect and make happy. That's what my love does. All I could do was sit back and enjoy the latest scene of my beautiful man's amazing performance.

****

The hopeful news along with Chris's unbridled excitement were downright infectious. Fine, so I'd lost my chill recovery weekend with my husband - but right now, I knew I was about to get some serious husband time. He'd been grabbing my butt every chance he got while we cleared the table. Finally, as I had to squat down to load the dishwasher, he eased up behind me. With a mischievous grin, he made me set the dishes aside and lifted my shirt off over my head as I rose up into his arms.

"Teddy Bear, you know what your pecs, lats, deltoids, triceps, and biceps do to me," he murmured seductively. Between lingering kisses - each one landing on the muscle group he'd just named. "Remember when I used to beg you to cook and clean shirtless? Pretending to be my hot, naked chef and muscle-bound house boy?" He chuckled softly, pressing himself closer. "I think it's time to reinstate that old tradition. Besides, Corey's not here to roll his eyes and barricade himself in his room to avoid our 'mushy stuff.'" To emphasize his point, he kissed his way up my neck, lifting my arm to sample my pit from behind.

A delicious shiver ran down my spine, even as reality barged in. "Careful there, big guy, you know I have to wear deodorant during the week."

"Damn, what a waste," Chris sighed, switching tactics to nibble my ear instead. "I wonder if Corey inherited my love of a manly pit..."

I couldn't help but laugh. "You should've been there when I brought them that Whataburger breakfast. Our Corey was practically drooling when Ollie stretched and presented his cute curly blond pits as he was waking up. I honestly thought Corey might pounce on our poor Ollie right there in front of me."

Chris shot me a crooked, satisfied grin. "Good to know. And here's something else good to know: I never wear deodorant on Fridays, just to make sure I'm ready for the weekend." I decided to return the favor by lifting his shirt over his head. One long, deep breath of my man's natural musk, and I already knew I'd be ditching deodorant on Fridays as well.

We may or may not have finished loading the dishwasher before giving in to the moment, leaving a trail of pants, shoes, socks, and finally two pairs of tighty-whities behind us as we headed for our bedroom.

****

We tumbled to the bed and rotated until we were

in a 69 position with me on top. I can do that with my standard sized 5.75" dick without worrying about suffocating my mate. I also couldn't help but give a little self-aware chuckle; only guys with dicks below 6" know their size to the second decimal. But tonight, it's not about size, it's about that little engine who could, pushing the train up that hill. And tonight, my little engine was ready to make a trip into Chris' tight train tunnel.

I telegraphed my intent by motioning Chris to raise his knees up so that I could lock them under my arms. And there it was, his musky, earthy, furry trench, perfectly presented to my salivating mouth, lips, and tongue. I dove in for my second feast of the night. The aroma was every bit as intoxicating as the first meal he had prepared me for the night.

Chris lowered his head and mouth away from my cock to deliver a low growl, "Damn Teddy Bear! I need to surprise you with a weekend trip to Detroit more often." Taking advantage of the comical moment, I pressed my face deep into his furriness so the vibrations of my chuckle could be translated into new moans from him.

Satisfied with my efforts so far, it was time. I rose up from my man, but not before giving him an upside down, Chris-musk flavored kiss. Then I started my kneel-walk across the bed to retrieve the lube from the nightstand. Chris stopped me, "You've already gotten me ready Teddy, just go slow." That significantly upped my heart rate, I swear I could see the beats pulse through my erection. I was nineteen-year-old hard, and I saw that Chris' giant pipe was already leaking over his belly button.

I made my course correction to shuffle around behind his still raised knees and quickly put them on my boulder shoulders. I spat on my little engine and watched him slowly do his disappearing act into my lover's quivering tunnel. Chris took it like a champ - the joys of having a party-sized dick.

I love having Chris inside me. I love being a bottom. But still, there's no denying the warm feeling of being inside your lover. Knowing that you can make him feel every bit as satisfied and fulfilled as he does you. As I started thrusting into him, I saw his eyes roll back and I knew I was giving him exactly what he needed; exactly what I usually needed from him. It was heady; it was the connection we didn't make as often as we should.

All too soon, I was all too close. I went in as deep as I could and leaned over his torso. My lips couldn't make it up to his without leaving his hole, so I settled on nibbling a nip instead. I rose up, "Baby, I know I wanted to start out on top tonight, and I think you're enjoying it too, but I'm in a selfish mood." And I gave him my most lusty grin.

He immediately understood and his own big grin told me he thought it was the perfect idea. I gently pulled out of his tunnel and made my way over to really get the lube this time. Chris assumed a sitting position against our headboard. This was happening! I frantically got as much lube in my hole as I could and then made sure his massive cock was equally well coated.

I straddled his lap, facing him. Slowly impaling myself on his girthy ass-destroyer. My heightened desire and our joint fever, made his entry as easy as it ever could be. I let his kisses and embrace sooth me through the uncomfortable adjustment period.

It was all so good; I almost didn't want to start our final act. I just wanted to sit here locked and bonded to my love. I knew at this point our fun would be over all too soon. But I still found myself leaning back on my arms, positioning my body so that his cock would give my prostate maximum stimulation. He bowed his head and was easily able to reach my cock with his mouth. We'd accidently discovered this position while making love in the car's back seat during a spontaneous intimate moment on a family vacation.

I started flexing my glutes, causing my stretched hole to work its way up and down his leaking cock while also fucking my little guy into his mouth. It really is a selfish position. I get my hole, butt-nut, and cock pleasured while letting Chris do most of the work. Well, I guess my bouncing counted for something. And as I feared, all that prostate mashing and tongue swirling rapidly took me over the top. I shot my after dinner treat into Chris' warm mouth. He eagerly swallowed it down.

Now it was his turn. His obligation fulfilled; he focused on his own pleasure, thrusting up into my still hungry hole with a new determination. God! I swore he was going to make me immediately cum again. My eyes were imitating his and rolling up into my head. I heard his low growling moans and felt a sudden deep thrust, and I knew he was delivering his payload. I looked down to realize that his effort may not have given me a second orgasm, but it had definitely added a stream of pre (wait! post?) cum to the fur on his tummy.

We finally collapsed into each other's arms, excited about our impromptu weekend voyage and the future it could hopefully give our Ollie.

CHAPTER 37: LANE CHANGES

** Saturday Afternoon **

I loved driving Ollie's Bronco - so much so that I was already thinking we could start saving up to get a new one for him. I wasn't about to share that thought just yet, not until I had a solid plan. As we crossed east over the muddy Mississippi and I shuddered at the murky water below, Ollie hit me with the most non sequitur question I'd heard from him.

"So, do you think Chris is maybe bisexual?"

I nearly choked on a surprised laugh. "Ollie! Where'd that come from? I'm pretty sure he's as gay as we are."

"Yeah, but, um, *you're* here and he was married for, well, I have no idea how long he was married to your mom. She is real? Right?" Ollie looked at me with a mischievous Rainer Family Smirk that he'd clearly perfected by now.

I couldn't help grinning back. "Yeah, pup, she's real, and yes, Dad was married. I hate to say it, but their marriage was a mistake." Ollie's earnestly inquisitive look told me he was after a lot more detail.

I softened my voice, taking on a more serious look. "So... is this my baby gay asking his more *practiced* gay lover for some insight?" I reached over and ruffled his neat curls, taking his nod as the go-ahead to explain.

"I think it goes something like this: everyone's heard of the Kinsey Sexuality Scale." I glanced over and saw Ollie's blank look, so I elaborated.

"Kinsey was a 'sexologist' who did most of his groundbreaking research at Indiana University back in the '40s and '50s. He proposed that sexuality wasn't strictly binary - it's more like a spectrum. His scale runs from 0 to 6. but, people say that being a total 0 - completely straight - or a total 6 - completely gay - almost never happens without some psychological quirks involved."

I caught Ollie's curious expression and pressed on, "So most straight people fall around a 1, meaning dads can love their sons, show affection, and have close male friendships without it being sexual. And most gays hover around a 5, still able to love and care for their mothers, sisters, and female friends in a non-romantic way."

"Personally, I'm a total 5. I'm pretty sure you are as well," I said, smiling at my pup. "I've never been with a girl, or even wanted to be. The moment I realized how much fun having a dick was - and that all my boy friends had the same cool toy - I knew that's where I wanted to give all my attention. Sure, most boys go through a curiosity phase, but by the time puberty finished and I realized how much pits and hairy chests drove me wild, I knew it wasn't just a phase for me, I was in it for life"

I smirked, "Here's another term: I'm a 'Gold Star' gay. Never even made out with a girl." I saw Ollie simply nod. "But believe it or not, both Dad *and* Ted probably fall closer to 4's. They've dated - and in Dad's case, even married - a woman. Still, I don't think they're anywhere near being truly bisexual. They prefer men; they're absolutely in love with each other."

I took a moment to organize my thoughts. "This is just my take - it's nothing scientific. The Kinsey scale measures something innate, like being left or right-handed. It's something that neither your brain or personality can change. But I believe there's another scale on top of that at play: rating how you *show* yourself. Maybe a better way to put it is, it's about how you 'present' your orientation to the world."

Ollie gave me a puzzled look. "Present as in acting straight or gay?"

"Not just that," I explained, "it's something deeper. You might be a 1 on the scale, but love things people stereotype as 'gay.' You might be totally straight, yet have no problem hugging or even kissing your male friends, showing affection without any hang-ups. And that's awesome - it means you're just a well-adjusted guy comfortable with expressing love."

I paused for a breath, then continued more seriously. "But there's an equivalent darker side. Someone who's a 4 or 5 might struggle to accept what their brain is telling them - that they love men. They can't handle it, so they try to 'present' as straight, often ridiculing openly gay people. They're what we usually call homophobes or 'closet-cases.'"

"Neither Dad nor Ted are remotely like that," I assured him, "but they're old enough to have felt pressure to live a straight life. Not like back in the '50s or anything, but still, there was encouragement to meet the right girl, fall in love, and, well, have me." I winked at my pup. "They were just close enough to the middle of the spectrum to make it happen for a while."

I glanced over and noticed Ollie looked a bit dazed by my info dump. I gave him a moment to let it all sink in. When he caught my inquisitive look to continue, his returned expression made it obvious that my lecture had gotten way too serious. With a clever grin, he decided to lighten the mood. "So, my wolf, I'll agree I'm a 5. But what do you think I present as?"

My inner monologue wrote admiringly: *Nice, pup! You always amaze me.* I gave him a smile I hoped he'd interpret as both impressed and loving. "Great question, my pup! And, forgive me for keeping our little role-play alive, but... I think you present as, well, a pup." I delivered it with *my* best interpretation of the Rainer Family Smirk.

Ollie giggled, but I could tell he was maybe a bit - what, offended? Slighted? So, I hurried on, "What I mean is, you're the best - like a puppy. A dog doesn't care if someone's a boy or a girl; they just love. If you give them affection, they give it right back. Ollie, when I look at you, I don't think about the terms gay or straight, I just see the most loving, caring man I've ever met."

Thankfully, that did the trick. His eyes flashed with emotion, and before I knew it, I was fending off an Ollie hug attack. I just tried to keep the Bronco in its lane while my pup showered me with affection.

****

After a few miles of shared, comfortable silence amid the beautiful green Illinois countryside, Ollie took a contemplative breath and picked up where we'd left off. "So, that's all cool - I like presenting as a pup - but I guess I should've been more, sorry - *straight* - forward from the start." He gave me a sincere look, placing his hand on my knee. "Corey, can you tell me more about your mother?"

I offered a gentle smile, finally realizing what he'd been aiming at. "Oh, Ollie, I'm sorry. I didn't catch that you wanted to head in that direction. My mother, Elisabeth, is a wonderful woman. She and Dad stayed married until I was in first grade. They made sure my early childhood was happy and, well, pretty 'normal.'" I paused, not wanting to take him down another rabbit hole. "What exactly are you wanting to know?"

Ollie kissed my hand, his voice quiet but curious. "That's awesome. I was mostly wondering what led to their divorce, and, well... where is she now?"

"Honestly, it wasn't any one thing. They both finally realized they needed to move on with their own lives, and everyone agreed I'd be fine staying with Dad. I was always a daddy's boy anyway. Mom moved to San Antonio and married a *genuinely* straight guy." I caught Ollie's curious look and raised my eyebrow. "Yep, that's right, pup - I've got a stepfather. No half-siblings, though. I guess I satisfied mom's need to be, well, a 'mom.'"

"I spent spring breaks and a few summer weeks with them every year, at least until I found my own circle of friends in junior high and high school. I still love her very much, and her husband Ben has always been wonderful to me. But I never thought of him as a father figure. Not even Captain Alex felt like a 'dad.' It took meeting 'Uncle Ted' before I bonded with a new parent figure."

Ollie seemed satisfied with my answer, so now it was my turn. "Quid pro quo, pup. I don't need to know too much about your father, but what about your mother?" I noticed Ollie hesitating, so I offered more clarity. "I mean, you've told me about your last night in their house, but what kind of person do you think she is?"

My little, okay big, pup took a thoughtful pause before answering. His reply, after all his earlier insight, felt surprisingly simple. "Honestly, I don't know." He gave me a sheepish look. "I mean I know my mother, but she always felt like two different people. One when it was just me and her, and an entirely different person when it was the three of us. I even kinda felt guilty that Father always dominated my attention whenever he was around, like mom wasn't really significant."

I decided to stop tiptoeing around my core question. "I get it. Your father's presence overshadowed your relationship with her a lot. But I have to ask: Ollie, what did your mother do when Richard slapped you to the floor and kicked you out of the house?"

My blunt question made Ollie blush and hesitate, and I instantly regretted putting him on the spot. Still, I needed to know. He took a slow deep breath, trying to gather himself. "Honestly, Corey, I haven't thought much about that night at all. I still don't think my brain wants to. Even now, I'm not sure how to piece it together for you. I apologize, I know I over-simplified the story before, and maybe I'm still not ready to say everything."

I caught his soulful gaze, but I still silently urged him to continue. "I love my mom," he managed, his voice trembling, "but I feel guilty. I don't think I ever gave her the attention she deserved. For some reason, my father always seemed to demand everything I could give, and I was willing to let him take it all." He looked close to tears, and I couldn't let him go there.

"Ollie, my love, it's okay," I said softly. "Your father sounds like a master manipulator. You didn't do anything wrong; you were just doing what your parents taught you to do." I held his eyes, hoping to steer him away from drowning in regret. "Let's get back to the question..." I offered a supportive look, silently urging him to focus on what happened that night.

"So, I remember telling them I was gay," Ollie began quietly. "I think mom looked a little shocked, but not disgusted. Upset, sure, but not mad. Then my father made her leave." I watched as Ollie's eyes flickered with a sort of distant understanding at the memory. "Yeah, mom left, just like she did when I told them I didn't believe in their religion. She stepped aside and let Father 'handle' it."

I saw my Ollie's expression darken. "But unlike that time, as soon as I tried to explain myself, that's when he backhanded me. Next thing I knew, I was on the floor with a bloody nose. I honestly don't remember much after that. But yeah, maybe I should've thought more about my mom. I'm sorry."

"Ollie," I said softly, "you're slipping back into

old habits, apologizing when you've done nothing wrong. You were the abandoned pup, just for being who you are. That's why I love you so much; my pup who presents as a pup - you simply want to love and be loved."

Taking a daring chance, I leaned over and kissed my man. He responded passionately, then quickly shot out a hand to help steady the wheel. "Corey," he chuckled, "I love you too, but we need to return my Bronco on Sunday - preferably undamaged."

CHAPTER 38: THE BATCHELOR LIFE

Aside from my beloved man-boy trying to steer us off the road with a kiss - a dangerously sweet move we thankfully survived - today felt way heavier than yesterday. Despite all of Corey's meticulous planning, the mood had shifted. It was as if the freeway itself had turned into a ticking timeline, each mile marking our approach toward something we couldn't avoid.

No silly song lyrics this time, no surprise football tosses. Instead, we found ourselves discussing deeper things: our sexuality, the roles our mothers had played in our lives, and the surprising admission that before meeting me, Corey had already resigned himself to a lifetime of bachelorhood.

It came up as we talked about dating. Of course I'd never really experienced it, but Corey had a long, frustrating track record. Plenty of guys were drawn to his looks, his height, or his success, but never just him as a person. And if someone did love him for the right reasons, it often backfired. His looks and outgoing nature made them paranoid, convinced he'd eventually cheat when he found someone "better."

He recalled thinking he'd finally found "the one," only for the guy to eventually insist, "You're too good-looking. You'll never be happy with just me. I know you'll cheat." Every past relationship seemed doomed by someone else's insecurities or superficial focus.

After hearing his horror stories, I was grateful that I'd somehow stumbled onto my true love without even realizing I was looking. We'd skipped all the exhausting guesswork, found each other, and learned to trust each other from the start.

*****

As we ventured deep into Indy, I was again enthralled and eager to explore another exciting downtown. After checking in to the hotel and confirming that yes, we really did have floor to ceiling views of Monument Circle from our 15th floor room, I showered my wolf with another flurry of sincere "wows." After that, exploring is exactly what we started to do. It was just at 4:30 when we left the hotel to venture out.

"Okay pup, our dinner reservation is at 7:00 tonight. I believe St. Elmo's is about two blocks that way," as he pointed over my shoulder. "And, according to my trusty Google Maps, there's also a Banana Republic somewhere around here. Serious question: Did you leave any room in your suitcase for a new shirt or two? I say we go shopping for tonight."

I still wasn't eager to spend money unnecessarily and I knew Corey had spent a lot on our hotels already. "Corey, I'm really fine with the shirts you got me at North Park back in Dallas."

"Ollie, let's have fun. We don't have to get matching outfits for tonight, I don't think we're that kind of couple, but let's at least each get a new shirt that *complements* the other. Something that makes us look like we're a couple.

To my surprise, we succeeded, with minimal arguing. We found the same shirt with different, yet *complementary*, colors. That both still managed to match our sport coats. I had to admit, shopping can be fun, and we're going to look great tonight.

We didn't walk straight back to the hotel, but took the time to explore our new city for the night. People may joke and refer to it as "Naptown" and "India-no-place," but I already loved Indy as much as St. Louis. And that's even before a hoped-for new round of hotel room fun.

****

After showering, primping, preening, and dressing in our new shirts. We donned our jackets and casually made our way to the restaurant. I was back in my new happy place, holding my man's hand while wandering through a brightly lit magical downtown. Gawking at the sights as he led us to our dinner reservation.

Walking into St. Elmo's, I braced for "fancy," but discovered something else: "legit" felt more fitting. This place had gravitas or at least an old soul. You could sense that big moments had played out here over the years.

We were shown to a two-person table in the middle of a long narrow brick-walled dining room. I fell in love with the place instantly - perfect for another special night with Corey. Speaking of, I'd seen my man in so many moods: upset, excited, goofy, sexy, caring, horny, and protective. But tonight, he seemed... different. Not exactly lacking confidence, but maybe just being a bit unsure of himself?

I decided not to dwell on it, especially since Corey had clearly known what this place had to offer, both in ambiance and with its menu. That explained our light lunch; I was starving now, and an old school steakhouse meal sounded perfect. As we ordered, Corey's confidence flickered back into place, though he channeled some of it into playful teasing at my expense. We both created our own version of surf and turf: I chose a 12-ounce fillet with a lobster tail, while Corey went for the bone-in fillet with king crab legs.

I probably shouldn't have mentioned my fear of bones in my food. Don't get me wrong, I know exactly where steak, chicken, and pork come from, but the moment I see a bone on my plate, my appetite bolts out the nearest exit. Corey almost - just barely - started to give me a hard time about it, until

I casually suggested a late-night dip in the murky White River that flows through downtown Indy. That shut him right up, and we both dissolved into a fit of laughter.

We made our way through appetizers, salads, and finally our entrées, each bite more incredible than the last. I loved being with Corey like this - no walls between us, no worries, just the two of us enjoying a perfect evening. The more time we spent together, the more I learned his quirks, strengths, phobias, and passions, the deeper I fell in love. Somehow, once again, he'd made me forget the weight of tomorrow's meeting. I couldn't wait to get back to our room and find out what new wonders awaited us there.

CHAPTER 39: COURSE CORRECTIONS

My pup, my love, my Ollie - I couldn't believe how perfect this evening felt. It was now or never; I knew I could do this. I'd set everything up just right, even arranged for him to have a flute of champagne if he said "yes." But first, I needed to lead him down a slightly different path. I wanted to playfully fake out his defensive line. I had a pre-proposal planned, something that was honestly more important than anything else until we could actually set a date. As we waited for our desserts, I began my speech.

"Ollie, I don't know how much Dad told you, but I completely fell apart the morning you disappeared. It's embarrassing to even think about. When you were almost taken into custody and ended up in the hospital," I took his hand across the table, determined to keep my voice steady, "even my old friend almost wouldn't let me and Dad see you. We weren't legally your family, and for the first time in my life, I think I considered doing something violent." I shook my head, trying to dismiss the thought.

Steeling myself, I stood from my chair and knelt before him, my heart pounding in my ears. Ollie's eyes went wide, like saucers - whether it was excitement or fear, I couldn't tell. But I had come this far, and I had to see it through.

** Ollie's Perspective **

Oh my fraking lurd! It had all been there, right in front of my face for weeks. Come on, Ollie, you're not an idiot! Chris practically told you to expect something big from your Norse God protector. Corey hinted at it himself - from whispering over your sleepy head that after this trip he'd never have to worry about losing you again, to mentioning we only needed a special occasion to visit St. John again. Oliver, you're smarter than this!

I love him - God, I love this man with everything I have. Do I want to spend the rest of my life with him? Abso-freaking-lutely! Yes! But do I want him to propose to me right here, right now, on the eve of what's likely be the worst day of my life? Please, my Norse God, no. I don't want the happiest, most important event of my life to be even remotely tainted by tomorrow's looming disaster.

I know my Corey. He's strong and loving, a brilliant man and nurse, but maybe his inner high school boy logic was getting the best of him tonight. Still, I won't disappoint him, or worse yet, embarrass him. No matter what, I'll say "yes" and hope for the best.

** Back to Corey **

While my love seemed to be torn between emotions, I decided it was time for my "fake-out." Reaching into my coat pocket, to retrieve my carefully prepared envelope, I continued, "My love, I never want to feel that powerless again, unable to protect you. And if our roles were reversed, I know you'd feel the same."

I retrieved and then held out the thick packet to my boy, who promptly abandoned the struggle of choosing an appropriate emotion and slipped back into his adorable deer-in-the-headlights look. "Ollie, my love, will you accept these legal documents as a sign of my love and dedication?"

Apparently, we'd drawn the attention of most nearby diners, who offered polite chuckles and even some applause. Ollie's face finally knew what emotion to choose and was absolutely radiant with love and amazement. He said "yes" before I could blink, and the crowd applauded in earnest. He leaned in, giving me a perfect kiss as the room cheered a bit louder.

Moving back into my seat, I began the explanation I'd rehearsed. "Ollie, my turn to apologize. I know this might not seem as romantic as I'd hoped, but these documents will help us defend and protect each other. They will even shield you from any future nonsense your father might try." I caught his puppy-dog, hero-worshipping gaze and I felt encouraged to continue.

"Before you get too happy," I said gently, "some of these documents are a bit heavy. But believe me, I mean every word you're about to hear." I allowed myself to enjoy the scene I'd scripted as Ollie began unfolding the papers, his curiosity palpable.

I watched him scan the pages. "The first three are the ones we'll likely use the most," I explained. "There's a medical power of attorney and a HIPAA authorization form." I caught Ollie's blank look and winked. "I know, I know - just believe me, medical red tape is my love language."

I tapped the pages. "This first document ensures hospital staff must treat us like family. They can't keep us apart if one of us is hospitalized. The second lets our doctors share information about us without hassle. Think of it this way: I won't need to physically be in the room and ask Dr. Foster to, um, help you get an embarrassing hardon again."

Ollie's face turned red, but his laughter was genuine. I grinned and continued, "And the durable power of attorney works the same way for our finances. More importantly, it means I have the power to protect your finances from your father. Ollie... And as for me, well, I'm giving you an equal share in my life."

That did it. I hadn't intended to make my pup cry,

but seeing those happy tears shimmer in my cherished Ollie's eyes was worth everything. "You okay, pup?" I asked softly.

"Corey, this is amazing," he said softly, his voice filled with awe. "I can't believe you thought of all this. And I can't tell you how much it means to me on the night before I have to give up my Bronco and face my father." As always, his face was an open book and if anything, his words were the abridged edition of his feelings.

"Okay, pup, the final documents are the big ones. You ready?" Ollie's eyes dazzled with anticipation. "So, the next one is important, but definitely a buzzkill. Pup, we'll never need it for decades and decades, but it's just how things work in this country." I met his gaze steadily. "It's a living will. It lets us make the hardest choices for each other if we ever face the unthinkable." His smile never faded, and I felt relieved he understood.

"And finally," I began, my voice wavering slightly, "here's the real biggie. Ollie, I love you. I will never stop loving you, never stop protecting you - even if the worst should ever happen." My eyes misted over. "This is my will. I'm making you my primary beneficiary. Dad and Ted have already agreed."

I knew my beautiful, tender, loving boy wouldn't make it through that without tears. He left his chair and fell into my arms, and we hugged so deeply that nothing in the world could tear us apart. I couldn't help feeling a bit proud of my little 'fake-out' strategy, knowing I'd just given him something truly important and unforgettable.

** Ollie's Perspective **

I should have never doubted my man, he was absolutely brilliant, and his grand gesture was perfectly timed. Presenting those legal documents, geeky as they were, gave me exactly what I needed to feel more secure about facing my father tomorrow. They felt like a big, comforting security blanket against my father's intimidation. Sure, we'd lose my Bronco, but that would be the last thing my father ever took from me. Damn!, Er, Dang, my Corey is amazing.

Well, at least he *was* - until he pushed further. "I love you, Oliver Aaron Carson. But I couldn't help noticing your face when I started this whole legal-document proposal. Were you... expecting something else?"

Oh, my wolf, I know you. You can be so wise in some ways and yet so clueless in others. It's part of your charm. My inner monologue's writer started furiously typing, and I did my best to keep an innocently amused expression.

I rushed to reply, "Ha! Dang, my wolf, you totally had me terrified. I mean, you know how bad tomorrow could get. It'll probably one of the worst days of my life." I paused, letting my gaze soften. "I thought, 'There's no way my wolf would ask me something so wonderful right before something so horrible.' Then I realized I was an idiot. You knew exactly what you were doing, giving me all the safety and protection I needed right at the perfect time. You amaze me my Corey."

At least that last part was one hundred percent true, and I hoped Corey could see it in my face. As fate would have it, I didn't have long to dwell on it. A tall blond man approached our table, looking vaguely familiar.

Before I could place him, he extended his hand first to Corey, then to me. "Hey, guys - sorry to interrupt. I'm here on a date night with my mom, and she said your 'proposal' was the sweetest thing she's ever seen. She insisted I come over and say hi." He paused, a bit awkward, giving us time to react.

Before he could continue his introduction, it hit me. "Wait a second! Are you... Eric Porter?"

The awkwardness eased as he broke into a modest smile. "Yes, sir."

I couldn't help a chuckle. "No! Um, I mean *no*, *you* can't call *me* sir! You're one of my favorite wide receivers! I learned so much from watching you. I never dreamed I'd meet an NFL player. Dang! Tonight is unreal!"

I glanced at Corey, who looked both confused and - wait, was that a hint of jealousy? "Mr. Porter, this is my boyfriend, Corey Rainer, the love of my life. Corey, this is Eric Porter, a wide receiver for the

Colts. One of my heroes."

Corey and Eric slowly re-shook hands, and I instantly slipped into fanboy mode. "Eric, sorry sir - is just Eric alright? I played wide receiver in high school and had dreams of playing in college until life got in the way. You really inspired me."

Eric, clearly used to such encounters, handled it like a pro. "Yes, just Eric and you're Ollie, right?" I nodded. "You've got the look of a natural. I don't know your story, but trust me, you should never deny a passion. If you ever get the chance, try out."

I beamed at Corey and felt my heart surge. "We're just visiting your city; we live in Ft. Worth and I'm hoping to transfer from U of M to TCU this fall. I'll keep that advice in mind!"

Eric pulled a business card from his pocket. "Then you definitely should. Here's my card. My mom would never forgive me if I didn't offer you two something special. The Colts play the Cowboys next season in Texas. Give me a call and I'll set you and Corey up with VIP tickets. But you gotta promise to root for the Colts." He flashed a dazzling smile.

I agreed in a heartbeat, thanking him profusely. With a final handshake to both of us, Eric turned to Corey. "Buddy, what you did tonight was magical. You've inspired me. You two are going to be unstoppable." We noticed a discreet wave from his booth - his beautiful mother smiling our way. He then slipped out of our spotlight as gracefully as he'd arrived.

I was on another planet, high on excitement and possibility. I couldn't wait to get back to our magical hotel room.

** Corey's Perspective **

In the eloquent words of Ted Lasso's Roy Kent: "FFFFUUUUUUUCCKKKK!!!!" What the hell just happened? I just went from the verge of proposing to the love of my life, to him thanking me for *not* proposing, to having some blond, buff, NFL god waltz over and steal Ollie's attention. Perfect. Just perfect.

To coin a phrase: "Corey, when you decide to fuck up, you go all out." Once again, FFFUUUCCKKK!

After Ollie's unexpected confession and Eric's "Special Guest Star" appearance, I needed to bail - fast. "Bathroom break" became code for "rush to intercept the waiter before he brings the champagne."

I caught up to our waiter and frantically waved him off from approaching our table. He took one look at my anguish and tried to reassure me. "My man, if you think what just happened was a 'failure,' you're dead wrong. I've never seen anything more perfect since I started working here. And trust me, this is *the* place for proposals in downtown Indy."

I managed a weak nod. "I know, that's why we're here."

He offered a sympathetic grin. "Listen, you big

blond superhero, you did exactly what you needed to do tonight. It might not match your plan, but it's exactly what your boyfriend needed. That boy told you he'll say yes - just not tonight. You both gotta get through whatever tomorrow is all about first. After that, believe me, he'll be begging you to propose. You two are an amazing team. I'm jealous, honestly. You got this; you did great!"

Damnit, and just like that, I was hugging a random waiter in a steakhouse in downtown Indianapolis. Afterward, I really did head to the restroom, splashed water on my face, looked in the mirror and pulled myself together. Ollie had given me a gift - I just needed to recognize it. I pulled my metaphorical big-boy pants up and returned to our table to finish this totally unexpected but still totally perfect night.

"So, Ollie. Who's cuter, me or Eric?" I asked, forcing my best smirk, adding every bit of bravado that I *didn't* currently have.

My boy lit up. "I can't believe you're even asking that on the night you've made me the happiest pup on the planet," he teased. "First off, Eric never rescued me, never gave me a new family, and never taught me the importance of using hair conditioner only for its on-label use." His crystal blue eyes met mine with his newly-mastered smirk. "Plus, I've seen his internet pics. He's smooth-chested and I'm pretty sure he trims his pits."

That was all I needed to hear: Ollie was mine.

Truthfully, he'd always been mine. Being stupid once tonight was enough - no need to go for twice. We finished our dessert with a few more public displays of affection and a handful of congratulatory nods from our fellow diners as we left.

CHAPTER 40: THE HOOSIER STATE

As soon as we stepped back into our room, I couldn't help but marvel again and I gave Corey another well deserved "wow." I elaborated, "Corey, look at this place! It may not have the Arch right outside, but this view is unreal." I stood there, soaking in the city lights and looking at the impressive Monument Circle below. "My wolf, how did you know it'd be this amazing?"

He gave me a warm grin. "That's easy, Ollie. I knew it would be perfect because you'd be here with me."

I snorted softly. "Lurd, those cheesy lines, my wolf…" I rewarded him with a playful kiss, the first of what I suspected would be many tonight. "Good answer, but seriously, two amazing hotels in a row? You're incredible." Corey just growled softly and wrapped himself around me, slowly guiding us back against the glass wall that separated us from the city spread out beneath us.

He teased, "It's just a bit of creative Google Mapping, some savvy Booking-dot-Com-ing, and a beautiful pup to inspire his lover's desire. Then voilà, *Magic in the Midwest*." And he started kissing me, all against our corner floor to ceiling view. I've never experienced Corey like this, it wasn't just kissing, it was more like his tongue was licking mine. Coaxing it to join with his in the most erotic dance we'd ever attempted. One more tender and yet, more animalist, than I'd ever known.

Corey broke our kiss unexpectedly, I tried not to look too confused as he stepped away, heading back toward the room's entrance. A moment later, the lights went dark, and I realized his plan. We were leaving the curtains wide open for our adventure, with only the glow of the city illuminating our private world.

And what an adventure it became. Corey moved with a purpose I hadn't seen since our first nights together, or for our reconnecting shower after my ER stay. When he returned to our vantage point, he captured my lips once more, and as we stood there bathed in city lights, he began to undress me - slowly, even reverently - making it clear that tonight, this room, and this view, were here for our enjoyment.

My jacket had long ago been abandoned to the closet, but Corey frantically lifted my new shirt over my head. Not trapping me this time, I could tell, he was way too amped up to play any games. He equally efficiently stripped me of my pants and tighty-whities. All I could take credit for, was proactively taking my shoes off as we entered our sky-high wolf den. I had a strong suspicion of what was in store.

I realized I was totally nude, except for my socks, while my sexually intoxicated beast was totally clothed. The inequity of the situation added to my excitement; I had no idea what was going to happen next. Corey didn't make me wait long. His growl was as authentic as it was demanding. He guided us to the bed and I was suddenly facing away from him on my hands and knees, as Corey's tongue made its way to my furry taint and awaiting hole. I let my own growl escape and dropped to my elbows as I felt the same tongue I'd been licking, start opening the entrance to my soul.

Corey's performance did not disappoint. But, knowing that spit and desire can only go so far, he gently added lube and his thick fingers to the mix. I can't be clever. That's all it takes for me to start my whines and begging. Which, to my total delight, is all it ever takes for my wolf to follow through on my wishes. Except this time, his chosen venue was once again, not our bed.

Even being completely under his spell, I was shocked and a bit anxious about where he led my compliant body. At his insistence, I suddenly found myself, totally nude, hard, and about to be bred, pressed against the glass corner of our floor to ceiling windowed room. Looking down on the center of Indy, I considered protesting, but realized it would be absolutely futile.

I heard Corey's zipper lower and I felt his still fully-clothed body press up against mine. Pushing my nakedness against the windows. My only hope was that the room's darkness and our elevation would keep our love private. But damn did the thrill ratchet my excitement up.

Finally, I heard the snap of the lube bottle opening again and I knew Corey was coating his shaft before applying another round to my willing hole. I braced myself for his frenzied thrusts, but I shouldn't have. As worked up as he was, he was still my protector and he kissed my neck as he raised my hands up the window to expose my pits to his delight.

As he was nuzzling my pits from behind, I finally felt his girth gently work its way into my anticipating pucker. It's so easy, all he has to do is make me want it so badly, then his entry becomes nearly pain free. But! I said, "nearly." Still, the burn quickly dissipated as I lost myself in the unprecedented view and reveled in the heat of my lover's body pressed against mine.

As he started to earnestly thrust into to me, I realized how much tonight must have meant to him. I understood what his intention was. I mean, it wasn't misplaced; he's always one hundred percent my loving Corey. Sometimes genius, other times, adorable clueless high school boy. At this special moment, I couldn't love him more either way. And he couldn't be making me feel any more amazing.

I tried my best to arch up toward his thrusting hips and that seemed to be what he needed. Suddenly my chest was pressed to the glass, my eyes trying not to roll back in my head so that they could appreciate the view. After way too short of a time, I heard a guttural, "Ollie, I love you. You're my world." And that was all it took. My DNA was running down the glass and Corey's was doing its best to finally give us a puppy. I swear we'll never stop trying.

He collapsed into my back and allowed himself to appreciate where we were. As he stared out the window, he softly said, "Ollie, I love you more than anyone else in this dazzling world."

I rotated and returned his sentiment. Our kiss lasted forever and I couldn't care less how many Hoosiers saw my satisfied butt dripping over Monument Circle. Well, I mean, it's a wonderful state and I hope no one took offense at my unexpected delight and appreciation of their state's capital.

CHAPTER 41: THE FINAL DAY DAWNS

Time continued its forward march, whether I wanted it to or not. We woke up at 7:00 again, but intentionally this time. We needed to get through the four-hour drive up Interstate 69 to Ann Arbor to make our planned meeting at 1:00. Corey said he'd text our Michigan attorney, Andrew Bowman, around 9:00 to confirm our exact meeting location. Dang, I was already so nervous I doubted I could stomach breakfast.

"Hey, pup," Corey growled softly as I rolled into him for our morning kiss and cuddle. He studied my face, his concern evident. "You're looking a little pale. Trust me, Ollie, it's going to be alright. I'll be with you every step of the way. No matter what happens, you won't be facing anything alone." He gave a playful nudge, "And come on, you love driving my Mach E. Besides," he booped my nose, "we'll figure out a way to get you back into another Bronco soon."

I smiled, gazing into his eyes. "I know, Corey, and if I get accepted at TCU, not having my own car won't matter nearly as much anyway. But the Bronco was supposed to be mine. I'm not going to say 'It's all I have' again." I saw Corey's smile falter slightly at that phrase - my emotional outburst on the day we met that I fear he still feels guilty about.

I cleared my throat, determined to explain. "It's a symbol of my accomplishments. I worked hard for it. And it was my reward for doing so well in high school and getting into U of M. It's something I'm proud of, and I know this sounds stupid, but it's something I love and cherish. And now my father gets to take it all away."

Corey pulled me close, hugging me in tight. "I know, pup. It's not fair. Let's hope the attorneys have made a strong case to present." He moved back across our pillow, trapping me in his protective gaze. "Ollie, I know it's a lame consolation, but I promise - this is the last time Richard Carson will ever take anything from you. After today, you're free."

I gave an accepting nod, absorbing his words. "In a weird way, I'm looking forward to showing off my big, beautiful, amazing Norse God to my parents. Like, see this, Father? Despite your efforts, I found the man of my dreams, and we already have a fantastic life - one you can't imagine and will never be a part of."

Corey moved back in for a second morning kiss.

"Ollie, when you put it that way, I almost feel sorry for them. Sure, we're losing a car, but he's losing an Ollie - the most amazing part of my life. That's a far bigger loss. Truly devastating." He gave me an unmistakable, early-morning, seductive gaze.

We allowed ourselves a few more luxurious moments of making out in bed before we headed, hand in hand, to the shower. I didn't expect to be up for any fun this morning, but our mutual attentions under the warm water calmed my nerves more than I could've imagined. Besides, I was getting really good at bringing my wolf the same joy he always brought me.

After drying off, we dressed in our best attire - our dress shirts and our best jeans - and then quickly repacked. I offered my silent, customary goodbye to our incredible room. Then we headed down to my Bronco for the last time. I felt steady, prepared, and most importantly, I had my wolf by my side.

****

We'd made good time on this final leg of our long journey, and Corey had received the information we needed; we'd meet Andrew in the Union's Michigan Room and have a few minutes alone to speak with him before my father was scheduled to arrive. I assumed that's when he'd brief us on what he planned to present.

I felt calmer than expected. It reminded me of taking a big test in school: you're nervous until it starts, but once you begin, you just hope you've prepared enough to work your way through it. I tried to convince myself I was prepared.

But then I saw it: the small bridges over the North Kalamazoo River. I felt the blood drain from my face, and the bile rise in my gut. "Corey, I need to pull over," I said, my voice shaky. He shot me a very concerned look. "I'll be fine," I barely managed. "I just need to stop for a few minutes."

As soon as the Bronco rolled to a stop, I jumped out, my hands on my knees. Corey hurried around the front to meet me. "Ollie, are you okay? Do I need to drive the rest of the way?" His worry was evident and genuine.

I couldn't answer immediately, so he pressed on. "Ollie, you're scaring me. What's wrong?"

I nodded, finally able to stand up again as I pointed across the freeway toward a cluster of trees near the river on the southbound side. "I'm sorry. I didn't expect this. Remember when I told you about the morning I left home? I just realized, that's where I pulled over to throw up. I'd never felt so lost, so alone, and so terrified in my life. The memory just hit me hard."

Corey wrapped his arms around me, holding me close. "I'm here now, Ollie. I've got you. We've got this." I melted into his embrace, the chill of old fears lingering. One way or another, my nightmare was finally coming to an end, just not before it managed to land a few more gut punches first.

CHAPTER 42: FILLING THE TANK

My pup nearly just had the second panic attack of his life, and in that moment, I completely understood why Ollie had so wisely and subtly insisted I hold off on proposing last night. No matter how carefully I'd planned every detail of our journey, and no matter how magical our time had felt, this still wasn't a vacation.

Sure, Ollie appreciated everything I'd done, and we'd shared some incredible moments, but it couldn't erase reality: despite all my best efforts, this wasn't a happy occasion. He was on his way to confront the man who should've been his greatest source of love and protection - yet instead, had become his biggest bully. This was Ollie being forced to return to the darkest corner of his nightmare.

My job wasn't to pile on more stress by asking a giant question he wasn't in the right place to answer. My job was to do whatever he needed, to get him through this horrifying day. For the first time on our journey, I wished Dad and Ted were here with us. We're a family, and we should all be here standing by Ollie's side as he faces his hardest test yet.

While we stood there, clinging to each other and struggling through the day's first challenge, our phones buzzed in unison. Somehow, the outside world barging into our little moment of recovery made us both chuckle - no rest for the weary. But when we read our screens, we broke out in wide smiles: Dad had texted me, and Ted had done the same for Ollie, sending us their love and best wishes. Even though they weren't with us physically, it felt like they were right here in our hearts and we knew we were in theirs.

We took a few more deep breaths and let those messages of love soak in. Then we hugged again, this time to celebrate how lucky we were to have our supportive dads. Finally, we remounted our faithful steed. Ollie decided to let me drive until we reached Ann Arbor - he knew the roads by heart from there and promised there would be no more breakdowns. If he couldn't keep that promise, I'd be ready help him through it. Go time had very definitely arrived once again.

** Ollie's Perspective **

I was so incredibly moved by our dads' perfectly timed texts. Selfishly, I wished they could be here in person, but I was grateful for their support from afar. I also appreciated Corey giving me the time to recover from my sudden wave of panic by taking over driving while I regrouped. We left I-69 for Highway 60, merged onto I-94 in Jackson, and then made the all-too-short final push into Ann Arbor. Each mile we covered brought memories of my pre-Corey life rushing back, drawing me closer to my inevitable confrontation.

As we neared my, hopefully former, college town, I asked Corey to pull into one of my old favorite gas stations - yeah, I'm the type of guy who has a "favorite" gas station. And fine, I'll admit I've already developed an affinity for a specific burner on our cooktop at home, too. The thought made me chuckle; maybe I really am a dog at heart. The first three months of this year were the most chaotic of my life. I was thankful for the stability and routine Corey and our dads had given me over the last three.

We got out of the Bronco - Corey headed for the restroom while I headed for the pump. I was edgy, punchy and full of nervous energy, so of course my brain decided now would be perfect for the most inappropriate inner monologue of all time: *Lovingly, I opened my boy up with probing fingers, reassuring him everything would be alright. Slowly, I inserted my nozzle into his waiting hole. With gentle yet firm pressure, I slid it deep into his chute. And as I pulled my trigger, I filled his guts with my life-giving fuel.* I couldn't stop the half-hysterical giggles that bubbled up.

I finished filling my mechanical "boy" up with gas

- I didn't want to upset my father by returning my Bronco on empty - as Corey returned from the restroom to find me in a fit of uncontrollable, nervous laughter. "Ollie?! You okay?" he asked, his concern obvious as he hugged me from behind.

I was a little surprised by his hug. I tried to speak between my maybe-too-manic chuckles. "Dang, Corey. I think I'm seriously losing it. You should've heard what my brain just wrote about me 'filling' the Bronco's tank." I met his worried eyes and let him calm me. "I'm so happy you're here. There's no way I could ever face this day alone. You're my wolf. But, you know what? Right now, I really wish Ted and Chris were here too."

Corey's face brightened, though I'm pretty sure he was still a little unsure about my mental state. "Funny you'd say that. I was thinking the same thing right before they texted us. Don't worry, pup - we'll get through this."

He gave me a fierce hug before I made my return to the driver's seat, heading toward the University of Michigan's sprawling yet beautiful campus. A place I once thought I'd eventually be graduating from. Now it was a place I simply hoped I'd soon be escaping from.

CHAPTER 43: DAD SURPRISES

Parking at U. M. was so much easier when you're a visitor and not a student! We quickly found a spot in the Thompson Street garage and made the short walk to the Union. This would be the first time I had ever used the stately old building for anything as serious as today's confrontation. As we entered, the familiar smell of its halls gave me yet another flood of memories - not bad ones, but overwhelming all the same. Especially in my heightened nervous state, making me constantly stop myself from over-reacting to everything.

Corey, my ever-vigilant nurse, immediately noticed my sudden pallor. "Ollie, just breathe, pup. We're here together. Even if all we do is hand your keys to Richard, grab our suitcases, and walk away, it'll all be over - and we'll be free. If he says anything mean, you know I'll make sure he's the one slapped to the floor with a bloody nose this time." He gave me a reassuring smile. "We got this, pup." We reveled in one final hug as we reached the door to our final destination.

We stepped into the stately Michigan Room. And much like the first time I entered Corey's house and failed to notice any details because I was too lost in his arms, I'd like to tell you how beautiful this dignified room was. I'd maybe even use the word "gravatas" again to describe its commanding presence. I'd hope to be able to describe the long stately wooden conference table at its heart, with its four high-back leather chairs on each side and one more at each end.

But I couldn't. In that moment, I barely even registered the man setting at the head of the table, who had to be our attorney Andrew. All because, my gaze was locked onto the two men sitting on the far side of the table - Ted and Chris. We were elated at the sight of them; Corey and I rushed straight to our dads. With grateful tears falling freely, I fell into Ted's arms first, then moved on to Chris, until we all ended up in a misty-eyed group hug.

Once we'd calmed down, and all tears were wiped away, we finally acknowledged Andrew, shaking his hand enthusiastically before taking our seats. Corey and I took the two center chairs - Chris on Corey's other side, and Ted between me and Andrew. As thrilled as I was, I couldn't help shooting Ted a reproachful look. "Um, Dad? I thought we discussed not having any more secret plans."

Ted started to offer a tentative smile while looking maybe just a little guilty. While Chris, sitting farther down the table, let out a soft chuckle. "Sorry,

Sport - this one's on me. Ted warned me we might get in trouble. Believe me Ollie, things happened so quickly, we barely had time to react ourselves. I didn't want to stress you out any more than necessary until we were sure everything would work out. Besides, we're your dads. We needed to be here for our boy." With that, Chris had just earned my next few tears of the meeting. At least they were also happy ones.

Before I could ask about Chris's cryptic mention of "being sure everything would work out," Andrew finally spoke up, his tone gentle yet firm. "You all really do make a beautiful family. I'm sorry any of you have to go through this, let alone all of you. But I think it's wonderful that you're all here together." He turned to me, his concern evident. "Oliver, things might get a little rough for your father. Will you be okay with that?"

I nodded, adding quietly, "I'm fine. I appreciate your help, Mr. Bowman - especially on a Sunday."

"Oliver, please, call me Andrew," he insisted. "Your father didn't leave us much of a choice. He refused to miss a workday over what he calls an 'overblown, simple transaction.'" Andrew glanced down at the papers he'd lined up meticulously, then said, "Richard and Susan should be here in a few minutes." I couldn't stop an unexpected shiver upon hearing my parent's names.

Ted and Corey immediately noticed and leaned in

from both sides, wrapping me in a double-sided hug. Not to be left out, Chris added softly, "Ollie, it's going to be okay. Let Andrew handle most of the talking - that's why he's here. If you *do* have to speak, just be straight-forward and honest. And I know it's not in your nature, but please don't get angry, no matter what happens. Finally..." He offered his own tentative smile. "I'm sorry pup, but be ready for a few more surprises."

CHAPTER 44: OLLIE'S NIGHTMARE

The door opened while Ted and Corey were still embracing me in their shield of comfort and protection. My nightmare appeared in front of us all, in the form of my father. He towered over the table, just as impressive as I'd remembered. Looking far less handsome than I recalled - his face pinched and sour, his demeanor cold and unapproachable. By contrast, my mother looked as lovely as ever, though every bit as subservient in his presence as I'd feared.

As they took the two seats nearest Andrew, my father spoke first, his voice as cold as his stare. "Who are these people, why are they here, and what deviant display did we just witness?" Even my mother seemed taken aback.

Despite Chris' instructions, I couldn't stay silent. "Father," I began, pausing to steady my voice, "these are the people who took me in and helped me when I was at my most lost and desperate." I summoned every ounce of courage and pressed on. "They're my family now: Dr. Chris Rainer and Mr. Ted Kern." I nodded toward them as I named them. "They're my - my new dads. And this," I added, proudly slipping my arm around my Norse God's shoulders, "this is Corey Rainer - my boyfriend, and the love of my life."

My mother's face registered mild horror, and she finally spoke. "Oh, Ollie. When your father told me how terribly you'd screamed at him before you stormed out - when he described all the horrible things you said and the degenerate life you had planned - I refused to believe my son could have had said any of it. Now, seeing you here in the arms of these strangers, I realize he was only trying to soften the truth to spare my feelings."

Stunned, I managed a tight reply. "Mom, I have no idea what you're talking about, but I'm sorry you can't see these men the way I do. They're the kindest, most loving people I've ever met."

Father pressed on, his voice dripping with contempt. "Did they convince you to do *that* to your hair? That's the gayest thing I've ever seen, Oliver. Honestly, how far are you willing to slide down this pit of sin?"

I couldn't hold back. "Well, Father, *you* inspired this haircut when I blacked out during your attempt to have me arrested. And what you call 'sliding down a pit of sin,' I call 'trying to figure out how to survive and continue on with my life' - the one you seem determined to ruin." I noticed a flicker of shock on my mother's face at the mention of my arrest.

Realizing my outburst, I sheepishly glanced over to Andrew, "Sorry sir, I'll do better."

Andrew stepped in calmly. "It's alright, Ollie. You're handling this well." Then, turning to my parents, he added, "This room demands both candor and civility. I expect the two of you to remember that. We're here to conduct our business as efficiently and politely as possible. Mr. and Mrs. Carson, you were encouraged to bring legal counsel with you. Before we proceed, I need to confirm you're willing to continue without representation. May we go on?"

My father scoffed. "We don't need a lawyer to sit here with us to witness my son being brainwashed by a deviant family of homosexuals. I have the legal title to that Bronco - plain and simple. Just hand over the keys so we can get out of here as quickly as possible. I can't believe how sickening this all is."

Andrew once again reinstated his control over the room with a confident and professional dominance, "Mr. Carson, I will again remind you to respect this room. But to your point, the title of the Bronco is not in question. That's not even why we're here. Still, since you decided to bring it up... While you may have the title, we know that the Bronco doesn't belong to you."

A weighted silence filled the room. My father's

confident posture seemed to falter, but not enough to make him concede anything. "What in our Lord's name are you talking about? I. Have. The. Title." He regained his sneer as he rested his case.

Andrew countered by standing up from his seat at the table's head and walking to the door. Opening it, he said simply, "We'd like you both to come in now." Two unexpected guests appeared at the door, their jovial demeanor cutting through the tension as they stepped into the room.

My grandparents! Well, depending on their current opinion of me, maybe just my mother's parents, stormed the room and immediately made a beeline for me. I guess I had no reason to doubt their love. I jumped up, gratefully accepting their crushing embrace. When they finally stepped back to take in my new look, Grandma Laura couldn't keep herself from reaching up and tousling my hair. "Ollie! Look at you! You're all grown up! And that haircut! You're so handsome!"

She dove in for a second hug, while Grandpa Joe patted my back gently. "Ollie, I'm so sorry we believed even a fraction of what your father told us about your abrupt disappearance from our lives. Please forgive us." His eyes shone with unshed tears, and that alone told me he was sincere. I just wish I knew what the heck he was sincerely apologizing for.

Before I could gather more details, my grandparents turned a hard glare on my father and shot my mother a look that was filled with equal parts sadness and disappointment. Grandpa settled into the lone chair opposite Andrew, while Grandma sat next to him, leaving a chair's gap between her and her daughter.

Once again, Andrew took the reins. "Mr. Carson, as I was saying, we're not disputing your possession of the Bronco's title. We're here to discuss the civil liability lawsuit we're bringing against you. We thought it would be appropriate for Ollie's grandparents to witness these charges."

He lifted his papers and stared down my father with a steady gaze. "Mr. Carson, I want to remind you that you and Mrs. Carson have waived counsel and agreed to proceed under those terms. Is that correct?"

I swear my father actually growled, but nothing like the way Corey or Chris ever would.

Andrew took that as an affirmative response and began his presentation, "Mr. Carson, our first count is *Gross Negligence.* You cut your son off from your support without warning. As a direct result, Oliver became homeless and was placed in grave danger."

Richard rebuffed instantly. "That's not true. We had an apartment set up for him weeks before he left. Everything was fine."

"Mr. Carson," Andrew said evenly, "This isn't a trial, you don't need to object, and it's meaningless if you do. However, Ollie, would you care to explain what happened?"

I directed my respectful explanation at my father, keeping my voice level. "Well, it's true we *had* an apartment lined-up. I was excited to live there. But those plans were made assuming I'd have an adult co-signer. I'm only nineteen, and most apartments won't let a minor sign a lease alone. Believe me, I tried looking around once the initial plan fell through, but the few places willing to rent to me were either way too sketchy or priced at more than double what I could afford."

Ted slipped a fatherly arm around my shoulders, his eyes glistening with moisture. "Sport, you know that's one of the co-op coordinator's responsibilities, right? The company would've co-signed your lease. That's part of why we're here."

Looking away from my father's continued scorn, I meekly met Ted's - my Dad's - devastated gaze; I offered a regretful shrug. "Ted... Dad... I'm sorry. By the time I found that out, I'd already spent more than a few nights sleeping in my Bronco. I figured if I'd made it that long, I could survive without an apartment." I lowered my eyes. "We all know how well *that* turned out."

Ted pulled me closer, pressing a kiss to my temple. "It's okay, son."

Our tender moment was cut short by my mother's quiet rebuke - I was shocked to see it wasn't aimed at us. "Richard," she said, her voice tinged with disapproval, "you told me Ollie had an apartment and would be fine."

Before my father could defend himself, Andrew laid a few sheets of paper in front of him. "We're also including a charge of *Intentional Infliction of Emotional Distress.* Mr. Carson, do you see this list of calls from Ollie's phone?" He pointed. "All of these, here in early January, were Ollie trying to reach you for help with housing. You chose to ignore them."

He pointed to another section. "And here in early February - these calls were Ollie trying to let you know he needed to stay in Texas until the fall. He had *no intention* of permanently keeping the Bronco, but he did need it while he was in Texas - like you assured him he was allowed to do."

Andrew paused; his accusing gaze firmly locked on my father. "Finally, Mr. Carson, do you see this group of calls here in early March? That's Ollie trying to reach you because he had been injured in a fight with people trying to steal his car - in the middle of the night. He urgently needed your help, and again, you chose to ignore every plea." Our attorney's tone was cold, etched with contempt.

But the person with the most appalled expression wasn't Andrew - it was my mother. She let out a sharp gasp, rose from her chair, and gave my father a slap to his shoulder before rising and moving to the chair next to her mother's, distancing herself both physically and emotionally from Father.

The silence around the table was deafening. All faces were aghast, save one. I realized that for the first time, everyone was finally hearing the complete details of my story; including the ones I'd kept to myself. Ted, Chris, and even my steadfast Norse God were wiping tears from their cheeks. Yet Andrew wasn't even close to being finished.

He pressed on, picking up speed as though he was compelled to keep everyone's undivided attention. "Next, we have *Defamation.* You had no right to report Ollie's Bronco as stolen. By doing so, you endangered him and slandered his reputation. We can dig deeper into that if needed. And be advised: two Texas officers and their captain are ready to testify on Oliver's behalf, as are members of the Ann Arbor police force who took your initial report."

My father's face had finally lost some of its defiance by now, but Andrew still forged ahead. "Mr. Carson, we also have *Pain and Suffering.* Ollie's arrest was so unexpected and traumatic that he blacked out, fell, and suffered significant blood loss and a concussion, from striking his head on a rock. He had to be admitted to a local ER and required multiple stitches and time away from work."

My mother, no longer holding back her tears, was visibly weeping. And still our attorney continued. "Finally, there's *Loss of Income and Employment.* Your angry call to the U of M co-op department directly resulted in Ollie's removal from their co-op program - and therefore, the loss of his job in Texas."

After reciting the final atrocity, Andrew concluded, his voice steady. "We're seeking a substantial sum in damages, Mr. Carson. The preponderance of evidence against you is significant. This is a civil case, and believe me, that's all it takes."

My father still appeared unmoved by the accusations that had just been leveled against him. In fact, his belligerent demeanor seemed to recover a spark of its earlier defiance. "Seriously? All of this is circumstantial and completely irrelevant. The Bronco's title is still in my name."

Andrew regarded him with an incredulous look. "Well, sir, if you insist on taking this to trial - and make no mistake, we are fully prepared to do so - you stand to lose considerably more than the Bronco's value." He paused, then added, "But I'm grateful you brought up the issue of the vehicle's title - *again*."

Flipping through a few of his pages, Andrew extracted my graduation card. "Do you recognize this card, Mr. Carson? It includes a handwritten note from you, explicitly stating the Bronco was a gift to Ollie. It meant so much to him that he kept it close during those long nights he spent sleeping in that very vehicle."

That final remark triggered fresh tears from nearly everyone in the room - at least everyone who *wasn't* my father; he sat emotionless, his face set like stone.

He refused to even glance at the card on the table. "It was a gift that was supposed to help Oliver on his journey to become a responsible young man. Not a vehicle to allow him to become a woke deviant who rebels against everything I believe in and tried to teach him." He glared directly at me, "Oliver, by staying in Texas longer than we'd agreed, you know you were taking advantage of me. That's not responsible behavior."

Before I could respond, Andrew took charge again. "Let's stay on topic. Mr. Carson, you must see what's coming next. I don't believe you're a stupid man. Do you notice who else signed the card in addition to you? Well, in addition to your wife who I see *you* decided to sign for..."

Andrew got no further; my grandmother spoke up, her gaze meeting mine with pride and affection. "Ollie, first, and most importantly, I'm so sorry. More than you can know. Until we met your... dads yesterday, we had no idea what was really going on. The story Richard told us was *drastically* different from what we understand now. We only kept our silence because - according to Richard - you needed your space." Her glare at my father was truly intimidating.

My grandfather picked up where his wife had left off. "Ollie, you know you're our only grandchild. We did well in life and we were able to set aside plenty of money for your future. I believe your loaded Bronco Sport cost, what, $45,000?" He shot my father a hard stare. "And *we* contributed $35,000 of that amount."

His glare intensified. "*Dick*, the Bronco isn't yours. It never was. We'll sue you into the ground unless you transfer the title to Ollie immediately. Hell, we'll even give you your precious $10,000 back - we made sure to bring our checkbook."

Before I could even begin to process what I'd just heard - let alone react - my grandmother Laura stepped in again. "Ollie, I'm so proud of you and so deeply impressed by everything you've accomplished." Her gaze shifted warmly to the dads. "Chris and Ted told us how incredible you've been in Texas. But tell me, sweetheart, why was it so important for you to save every penny possible?"

Once more, I found myself lost and confused, but I answered as politely as I could. "Grandma, Father completely cut me off from any financial support. I know I have a nearly full-ride scholarship, but I still have books and plenty of other expenses to cover. Even living as cheaply as I can, I still need at least three or four thousand a semester. I know that sounds like a lot, but... I would've been able to manage it if I hadn't lost my job." Staring down at the table, I could feel my cheeks burning.

Apparently, Grandma Laura still wasn't satisfied. "Ollie, my sweet boy, I understand that costs can add up, but you have more than enough money to cover your entire college career. I still can't see why you're so worried."

My face must have spelled *nonplussed* in neon letters, because I had no idea what she was talking about. Glancing up with an utterly baffled expression, I caught my grandparents shooting a fresh glare at my father.

Andrew appeared to be content with allowing the room's control to shift. My grandfather picked it up eagerly, fixing on my father with a pointed stare. "So, *Dick*, is there something you've *conveniently* forgotten to tell Ollie?"

My father's reply was sharp. "That money was placed under my control to give to Oliver *as I saw fit.* Don't forget, I contributed to it too. Since he earned his scholarships, it made more sense to keep the money safe and give it to him upon graduation - as a gift to start his new life." A smug look crept onto his face...

...Until my grandfather spoke again. "Yes! A *gift!*" He slammed his fists down on the table for an emphasis to match his tone, "Just like his Bronco was supposed to be! Well, now that Ollie has no financial support coming from you, we demand you give him *both* the funds *and* the Bronco. We donated another thirty thousand dollars to that account, and you added, what, another ten thousand? That brings your total loss up to twenty thousand. Trust me, *Dick*, we still have you covered. Hand over his money *NOW!*" I'd never heard Grandpa raise his voice before.

Wait. Had I heard that right and done the math correctly? "Forty *thousand* dollars?" My breathing accelerated, feeling like the world was suddenly spinning out of control around me. As always, my wolf was there, his hand pressed gently against my back, sneaking a calming kiss to my cheek. "You're doing great, pup," he whispered into my ear. "Just keep calm and let this play out."

My mother unexpectedly stood and spoke up. "No, Dad, it's not a twenty-thousand-dollar loss." As she turned to my father. "Half of that is legally mine, and I'm giving my half to my son." She leveled him with a look I'd never seen from her before, as though she was truly seeing him for the first time in years. "And unless you want me to claim my half of everything else we own, I suggest you hand over your ten thousand as well."

Her gaze solidified into a quiet confidence. "Richard, you're a good man when you aren't consumed by your religion and repulsed by anyone who doesn't share your views. I've watched you deeply love your son all his life - that's why I've put up with your extreme beliefs. You used to be a kind and caring father. But if you can't accept Ollie for the wonderful man he's become, that's your loss. Even so, I still believe you know you should give him what's rightfully his, and let him move on." Tears blurred her eyes as she returned to the seat beside her mother.

Andrew took that as his cue to intervene. "Mr. Carson, do we have a deal? Or should we proceed with filing our charges and moving toward a very public trial, one I'm certain won't end in your favor?"

I caught a look on my father's face I'd never seen there before. I recognized it because I'd worn it once myself: betrayal and sudden defeat. Even though he'd caused me so much pain, I felt no urge to gloat. I simply understood the place he now found himself in. I had been there too. I was lucky enough to accidently meet a whole new family who helped me through it. And I suddenly considered whether or not my father even wanted help.

He finally muttered a strained, "I agree. Oliver keeps the Bronco and gets the money."

Andrew nodded, concluding his role in our drama. "Thank you, Mr. Carson. Excellent. All that's left is signing a few documents and setting up the transfer of funds."

CHAPTER 45: THE WOUNDED ELEPHANT

I just sat there, surrounded by two dads, one boyfriend, two grandparents, and a surprisingly supportive mother, all celebrating on my behalf. Yet all I could manage to say was, "So... I get to keep my Bronco? And, um, I think I somehow now have forty thousand dollars?" My dads and Corey decided that was their cue to crush me in another joyous group hug, nearly squeezing me to within an inch of my currently very surprised life.

I noticed my mom tentatively edging closer to our side of the table. She offered a simple yet sincere apology and quietly asked if she could hug me. I couldn't refuse. We both cried until we remembered there was a very dangerous, angry, and wounded elephant in the room. Andrew's duties might be over, but mine weren't.

I took Corey's hand and glanced at Chris and Ted, silently confirming they were still here for me.

Squaring my shoulders, I turned to face that elephant. "Father, I really need to understand: what did I do that upset you so deeply?"

He answered in a tone heavy with misplaced privilege. "Oliver, you broke my heart. I... I love you so much. Yet you chose to reject God and expected me to be okay with it. Son, I swear I tried, only because of how much I love you. You were always a good son, but every time I looked at you, knowing we wouldn't share eternity together... it tore my heart out. There were so many nights I cried for you."

His remorseful expression battled against the harsh words I'd just heard before, and it was simply too much for me to accept. Still, I tried to respond calmly. "Father, I appreciate that. I really do take it as a sign of how much we once loved each other. But your faith isn't mine - it doesn't work for me. Once I realized my truth, I swear, I gave it to you out of respect, not defiance."

I held his conflicted gaze and continued. "If I'd have kept praying and worshipping with you, I honestly would've been disrespecting your beliefs, even bordering on blasphemy. I'm sorry, but it would've been a lie. You've never deserved that."

Father wasn't in a place that allowed him to grasp what I was trying to tell him, "Oliver, I understand you think you did right," He actually gave me a caring look of genuine concern, "but if you'd just keep praying, I swear you'd realize I'm correct. Son, your eternal soul is at stake."

I realized there was nothing else I could say. So, I simply spoke from my heart. "I'm sorry, Father. I can't do that."

Apparently that wasn't the response he was hoping for. His face darkened, and he pressed on with a renewed intensity. "Then you had to hurt me even more by choosing homosexuality - Oliver, how could you do that? It completed your betrayal, turning your back on God and on every value I ever hoped to teach you."

He forced himself to calm, but his voice was still taut with pain and anger. "I shouldn't have struck you, but you can't imagine how deeply you hurt me. Why, Son? How could you decide to live that lifestyle?"

At the mention of violence, both of my dads and my wolf moved in as close as possible. I felt surrounded by their love and protection. I knew I was supported so I chose to keep calmly explaining, "Father, it's not a 'lifestyle,' and it isn't a choice. I only told you the truth about who I am."

My father's scowl grew threatening. I knew that every one of my protectors were ready to jump across the table and take down my former father in an instant. I discreetly signaled my guardians that everything was under control.

And still, my misguided father pressed on. "Oliver, you here now, surrounded by these sick individuals, is exactly why I feared letting you stray so far from home. The moment you left my guidance - just as I worried - you lost every moral I tried to instill."

I smiled and kept my voice calm, anchored by the foundation around me. "Father, these men saved me. They didn't corrupt me. Being gay isn't something you get to choose; it's something you realize about yourself. The only real choice we get, is to decide to gracefully accept it and hope we find people to help guide us in living our truth."

Trying one last time to reach him, I added, "Father. Do you understand that I could be dead by now if not for their help? Meanwhile, you reported my car stolen and cost me my job. Why?"

He shook his head, unyielding. I finally understood that my father was truly unreachable. "Oliver, I had no choice. I knew God would protect you and that I was being taken advantage of. Yet somehow, every woke liberal idiot sided with you - the police, the university, your 'boyfriend' and his degenerate 'dads.' I was the only one trying to save you, to bring you back to your senses. It's never been about the Bronco or your job, it's about your eternity, your faith, your real family. You chose this mistaken path, and it kills me that I can't follow."

I was sadly stunned, his words stung. I couldn't believe that this was the caring man I'd grown up with. I found strength in the love on my side of the table but I still couldn't believe what I had just realized I needed to say: "Father," I paused, drawing resolve. "I understand that we're on divergent paths that we'll never reconcile. At least not today, and likely not ever. But I need you to listen closely, *Father*, because that was the last time I will ever call you that, Richard. And these may be the last words I ever speak to you.

"I don't hate you. No one is conspiring against you. No one is trying to hurt you. Those are all things you've done to me, whether you can ever understand that or not. Richard, unlike you, I'm not going to cut you out of my life. I'm not going to validate your fears of persecution. I'm not going to leave you alone and deserted. I'll give my new number to grandma, grandpa and it now seems, mom. But I warn you, do not use it until you understand that I have a new and wonderful life despite all the pain and suffering you've caused, not just to me but to my new family as well.

"Oh, and one final thing. The only people in my biological family tree who seem to care about me are grandma and grandpa *Douglas*. There don't seem to be any Carsons left who do. If Corey ever proposes to me, and I know he will, um soon, I will happily say yes and I'll be taking his last name. I don't need to be a Carson any longer."

I knew nothing I could say would ever appease my father's feelings or change his mind. The last thing I noticed as we left the room, was a tear making its way down his cheek. I knew how those felt and even

though he was my darkest nightmare, I felt no triumph in being the one who gave it to him.

CHAPTER 46: HOWLING IN HARMONY

Andrew and my parents stayed behind to handle the paperwork and sort out the money transfer, while the six of us stepped out of the Union into a suddenly beautiful radiant day. I realized I must have been mistaken earlier; I swear it had been so dark and gloomy when we'd parked. Now the sunshine felt perfectly celebratory.

The relief and elation at having aced my biggest test overwhelmed my senses. I tilted my face toward the brilliant blue sky and let out a joyful howl to the heavens, my spirit soaring. Before I could get too self-conscious, my wolf joined me. His deeper pitch blending with mine into a euphoric, harmonious duet.

Ted and Chris just laughed, while my grandparents wore bemused but charmed expressions. I chuckled at our antics, but quickly calmed my excitement to explain. "Grandma, Grandpa, sorry if that startled you. It's kinda one of our things. I call Corey my 'wolf,' and I'm his 'wolf pup.'" I paused, sheepishly. "Yeah, I know - it probably sounds weird without all the backstory."

Grandma saved me, "Ollie, it's cool as heck. Did you two practice that? You sound perfect together. Like two majestic wolves destined to be mates for life." She glanced over at her husband, giving him a mock rebuke, "Why didn't we ever learn to howl together in harmony Joe?"

Grandpa playfully shot back, "Hey, we're still pretty good at making our own music." I don't remember ever seeing my grandparents kiss before. Grampa saw my astonished face, "It's your fault Ollie. I think the love between you and Corey is affecting us all."

We lingered there, exchanging our congratulations until I noticed my mother walking toward us as my father stormed off in the direction of the parking garage.

Catching the sadness in her eyes, I asked softly, "Mom, are you alright?"

She managed a wan smile. "Yes, Ollie. Apparently, I'm a lot better off than you were six months ago. I'm so sorry, my baby. I still can't believe that my husband could have done any of this. I don't understand what's going through his head - he's let his beliefs twist him. I never realized how distorted and disturbed his thinking had become. I've been a blind fool."

Turning to my new family, she admitted, "I'm sorry, I don't recall all your names, but you're Corey, right?" He nodded. "Thank you, Corey, for taking care of my son when his own family deserted him. I can never repay you enough. Please believe me, I'm trying to work through my feelings," her expression said she was trying to acknowledge the love between me and Corey, "but I am truly happy for you and my son. I wish you both all the joy in the world."

Tears started tracing quiet paths down her cheeks. I stepped closer, wrapping her in a gentle hug. "Mom, will you be alright? Are you going home with Richard?"

She looked up at me. "Yes, Ollie, I am. But I won't keep following him blindly. We'll see if there's a way to work things out. I'm also getting my own phone number, so you can reach me whenever you want or need to. I promise I won't let you be shut out again. I love you, Oliver. And I'm so sorry."

We held each other one last time before she turned to face her own uncertain choices waiting in the parking garage. I could only hope this wasn't the start of her nightmare.

As Mom walked away, Chris guided the six of us toward the "the Cube," a giant kinetic art sculpture. The space was usually packed with students and tourists, but at this moment it stood alone, bathed in sunshine, the plaza was deserted - and, just the right spot for a quick debrief.

Ted spoke first. "Congratulations, Sport! We had no idea everything would turn out this well for you. And before you shoot me another side-eye, we only knew that your wonderful grandparents had contributed most of the money for your Bronco. That little forty grand bonus was as much a surprise to us as it was to you."

"Dad!" I exclaimed, throwing my arms around his broad shoulders. "The important thing is that you and Chris were here when I needed you most." I turned to embrace my other dad as well. "Chris, if all your secret plans work out *this* well, I can't be anything but happy - please, keep scheming. Thank you! I owe you both so much." I gave them an incredulous and grateful look, "I still just can't believe you're here!" Unable to contain my joy, I leapt into the air, arms raised above my head in joyful relief and unexpected victory over my nightmare.

Chris's eyes shone with the love every parent should have for their child. "Ollie, like I've told you: you don't need to thank a dad for doing his job. We love you Sport, and we'll always do anything for you."

After my heartfelt exchange with Dad and Chris, I looked over to see tears of happiness glistening in my grandparents' eyes. Moving over for another round of hugs, I murmured, "Grandma, Grandpa, I can't believe you contributed so much to my future.

I have no words other than just *thank you*."

Grandpa Joe responded with quiet pride. "Ollie, everything you've achieved in college, in Texas, and in that room today, is worth every penny we've given. You're our best investment. Just look how beautifully it's paid off. You're amazing, Oliver. We love you."

Grandma Laura added, "Oh, Ollie, you have no idea how happy you've made us. And your new family is wonderful. I'm beyond grateful you somehow found them." She turned to Corey with a fond look. "And you, young man - nothing would please me more than someday having you as my grandson-in-law. You two are perfect together."

A grin spread across my face as a thought bubbled up. "I love you too, Grandma. Oh, and by the way, you're famous around both our houses. Ted, Chris, Corey... this is the grandmother who taught me how to make my legendary meatloaf!"

CHAPTER 47: THE TRAGIC BALLAD OF OLLIE CARSON

Corey and I suddenly realized our original plans were now completely useless. We had no idea what was going to happen next. Only then did I understand why Chris had herded us over here: the plaza offered the perfect stage for him to deliver his next set of secret plans.

Turning to my grandparents, I tried to give them a few key points of my new family's dynamic. "Guys, Ted here is the warm, cuddly one - my new dad. His incredible husband, Chris, is the master planner of the family." I glanced at Corey with a smile. "And my love, Corey, well, he's the best of both of them." After a brief hug, I looked at Chris. "So, I'm guessing you have the rest of our day all figured out?"

I swear Chris looked half-tempted to take a bow. Instead, he just grinned and said, "Thanks for that introduction, Sport. But I'm afraid I don't have anything quite as clever this time around. I've only booked a hotel room for you and Corey tonight. I knew you hadn't planned on driving your Bronco back to Texas. I'm sorry we weren't sure how this would play out until Saturday afternoon, or we might've stopped you from driving all this way."

He went on, "So tonight, your room's on us. Corey, just get back to the clinic by Tuesday morning - and believe me, we've used up every favor possible. So, Ollie, no more unexpected drama from you. Okay, pup?"

Laughing, I gave him my hundredth hug of the afternoon, grateful for his plan, however simple and last-minute.

Corey jumped in to the conversation in full blown class clown mode - goofy smirk and all, "Actually Dad, I was thinking I'd just use some of our flight credit and fly back with y'all. I'm sure Ollie will do just fine driving home on his own, right?"

I tried to punch my so-called "protector" on the shoulder, but Ted beat me to it with his own punch - verbally. "Corey Allan Rainer," he scolded, "you know that would only end in a tragic country song, right? Are you crazy?"

Chris saw his opening and cleared his throat theatrically. "I feel the song should be called: 'The Tragic Ballad of Ollie Carson.'" He recited:

He left his man at sunrise, his Bronco rollin' free,
A blowout sealed young Ollie's fate - no more bright
plans would be.

Ted, not missing a beat, pitched in, addressing his older son:

Now Corey sobs in guilty haze, cussin' fate and mangled steel,
As angels pluck a mournful twang: love was lost to faulty wheels.

I couldn't stop laughing, "Dang! Please tell me that was rehearsed!"

Chris merely winked, "We're Texans Ollie, and you'd better practice up. Spontaneous sad county song writing is on the state's entrance exam. Oh, and we should get to the hotel. You two would probably appreciate a break and maybe a relaxing shower. We have early reservations at the Chop House - five o'clock. I wasn't sure you two got any lunch," he added. Then nodding to Joe and Laura, "and I know these two need to drive back to Lansing tonight."

We followed our little caravan to our hotel, suddenly buzzing with excitement about a dinner with my family - both new *and* old. Something that until just a few hours ago, felt forever impossible. Of all the ways this day could have gone, this outcome was nowhere close to being on my bingo card.

CHAPTER 48: I KNOW YOU

Corey and I kept trying to add a few more lines to my tragic ballad, but we were still riding so high on our celebratory wave that we couldn't stay focused for long before breaking down into fits of laughter. We finally agreed to just leave the lyric-writing to Chris and Ted for now.

Our little hotel for the night was a far cry from the grand high-rises of the past two evenings, but it was absolutely charming - and we thanked the dads again for their generosity.

I think our adrenaline had finally begun to ebb by the time we unlocked the door to our unexpected cozy home for the night. Corey set his suitcase on the provided rack and remarked, "Well, I might not have all the gay superpowers, but at least I always pack extra clothes for unexpected situations - just like this."

I shot him a mildly exasperated glance. "My more practiced gay - *so-called* - mentor, would it have killed you to share that little piece of wisdom with me back on Thursday night? You know, when it would've actually helped me?" I gave him a mock glare that, honestly, was more loving than reproachful.

Corey stepped over, wrapping me in a conciliatory embrace and planting a quick, loving kiss on my lips. "Pup, can you believe how this afternoon turned out? I still haven't wrapped my head around it. You've gotta be in some kind of happy state of shock."

I just nodded in his arms as he went on. "Well, my Ollie, now that you're a man of means, we could just go buy you a new shirt... *or*" - I looked into his eyes and caught sight of his most wolfish smirk - "you could just re-wear the one from last night. It already smells like perfectly-cooked steak mingled with an even more mouthwatering hint of Ollie musk."

I couldn't help but grin. Tilting my chin up, I waited, and he rewarded me with another sweet kiss.

Corey plopped down on the bed, his back against the headboard. He looked up at me with a twinkle in his eye. "So, seriously, now that you've got your Bronco and you don't have to worry about money anymore, are you planning on taking a well-deserved summer off? Or are you still going to train all the poor noobs who need your help at the gym?"

I attempted my best upper-crust affectation, but I mostly just wound up embarrassing myself, "Corey,

I may be loaded now, but I think I should stay humble and remain charitable to the unwashed masses." I let the act drop with more chuckles. "Besides, I think being a personal trainer for the summer looks way better on my TCU application than being some spoiled playboy by the pool." I paused, a mischievous thought sparking. "Actually... that pool-boy idea would make an awesome role-play scenario. We need to remember that one."

Corey only rolled his eyes good-naturedly, tapping my nose with another playful "boop" as I settled on the bed next to him. He still wasn't ready to move on from his appraisal of our afternoon. His face lit up with pride as he continued. "Ollie, the way you stood your ground in that room today - how you handled yourself while confronting your father. I couldn't be more proud. It was like watching my boy become a man... The man of my dreams. All right there, right in front of my eyes."

He let out a small, teasing laugh. "I mean, don't get me wrong, you've always been the *pup* of my dreams." Then his expression grew serious again. "Honestly, I've known it since the first minute I saw you. You're incredible, Ollie. I still can't believe you're *mine.* I love you, Oliver Aaron Carson."

It was my turn to speak. "Corey, you understand that the only way I was able to make it through all that happened today, is because of everything you, Ted and Chris have done for me. Right? Just as importantly, you were all right there with me the whole time. I could literally feel the love, support, and protection radiating from y'all, keeping me calm and confident."

My emotions bubbled up again, and I couldn't hold back. "But do you know what amazed me the most? After we left the Union and started howling." I smiled into my wolf's sky-blue eyes. "Sure, that howl was our best ever, but afterward, when I joked to Grandma Laura about not knowing our 'back-story,' I suddenly had the most amazing realization. Corey, I know we've only been together for barely three months, yet I feel like we have as much history as couples who've been together for years." I locked eyes with him. "I *know* you my wolf, and I love that you know me just as well."

I fought back the tears threatening to surface and took Corey's hand. "Even if today had gone as badly as I expected, it wouldn't have mattered. Our months together have been the best time of my life. In fact, it's kinda like my life really started the morning we met and it's only kept getting better every day since then. I love you Corey Allan Rainer."

I managed to keep my tears from spilling over, but Corey wasn't as lucky. He wiped his eyes and paraphrased one of our favorite lines: "Ollie, I swear - when you decide to deliver an emotional confession, you always go all out."

We showered, unfortunately separately, and then spent the next hour doing that thing that new lovers do... We took a much-needed nap.

CHAPTER 49: SAME SONG, NEW SINGERS

Since they'd just played such a big, 'secret,' and greatly appreciated role in it still being mine, Ted and Chris decided to hop in our Bronco for the short ride to the Chop House - a reviewer-described "glam" steakhouse on Main Street in downtown Ann Arbor. Honestly, I'd never been able to afford eating at a place like this as a student, so I had no idea it was all that fancy until I read the Google reviews while Corey was in the shower. Not that I'm complaining about another steak dinner; I just hope I don't start bulking up *too* much on celebratory meals instead of from actual workouts.

We stepped inside, and thankfully it wasn't as over-the-top "glam" as I'd feared. It had that same old-school steakhouse vibe I'd gotten last night, maybe just slightly fancier, but still warm and inviting. Our host led all six of us to a large table, and I couldn't help noticing the exposed brick walls, complete with gas-lit sconces. I guess I'm a sucker for that look. Oh, and the table settings? *Fabulous.* I'm definitely getting more comfortable in my skin.

I was about to laugh at my introspection, until I noticed Chris practically bursting at the seams about something. As soon as we'd settled into our seats, he couldn't hold it in any longer. "Ollie," he said, trying not to grin too widely, "what was all that business about you being sure Corey would propose *soon* - and you taking our last name? You know I'd be honored, but, is there something that we should maybe know about?"

I couldn't resist. Using my most innocently in- credulous tone, I teased, "Wait? What? Me and Corey keeping secret plans from y'all? I'd *never* think of doing anything like that!" I'm pretty sure it was the first time Chris had seen his trademark smirk mir- rored so perfectly on *my* face. It was a fun moment that neither one of us could hold a straight face through.

Before I could really continue, a stray giggle es- caped for a completely different reason - courtesy of last night's half-derailed moment. I glanced at Corey and immediately regretted it when I saw him blush and look a bit embarrassed. I gave his knee a gen- tle squeeze under the table, hoping to convey, *Don't worry, my wolf. I'm about to let you off the hook in the best way possible.*

Out loud, I said, "Sorry about that. Couldn't resist.

Anyway, Chris, no - there's no grand scheme that we've been hiding. But my Fearless Protector did make the most beautiful and thoughtful gesture last night."

I leaned over to give my man a quick kiss. "He presented me with some very important legal documents, so I'd feel safe no matter what happened today. We now have each other's medical and enduring power of attorney and a few other protections to ensure my father won't have any control over me ever again. Most importantly - and unbelievably - Corey made sure I'm taken care of in his will. It may not sound all that romantic, but the way he presented them brought me to tears, and got the whole dining room applauding."

Chris and Ted's faces lit up, bright enough to blind us all. Chris shot his son a proud grin. "Corey, that's fantastic - really beautiful. Good job son." Corey answered with a slightly shaky smile and still looked somewhat uneasy.

Deciding that Chris' praise was my cue; it was time for me to make my move. I reached for Corey's hand, gazing into his unsure sky-blue eyes. "That said..." I began, "...Corey, my wolf, I had a feeling you were about to ask me another very important question last night, *after* our 'document signing ceremony.'" His blush deepened, and his eyes darted around the table, giving me the impression that he desperately wanted to look anywhere other than into my eyes.

I refused to lose his gaze, and gently cupped his handsome bearded cheek. "My Wolf, I wasn't in the right place last night. I was so nervous about how bad today could have gone; I didn't want to risk having you asking me the most important question of my life right before what could have been the worst day of my life."

I gestured around our table, warm with family and love. "But now we know that's not how today went: I got to hug my mom and reconnect with my grandparents. And somehow I'm here in this beautiful restaurant with everyone I love - you, our dads, Grandma, Grandpa. Today has suddenly turned out to be beyond amazing."

Slipping my fingers through his, I felt a rush of joy and certainty. "So, Corey, my class clown, my Norse God, my Wolf, my Protector, my Love... I think this would be the perfect moment for you to turn *one* of my best days into the *absolute* best day of my life. That is...if you still have a question you'd like to ask me." I punctuated it with a kiss on his surprised, but smiling, face.

Corey started to regain his usual confidence and let out a half-laugh while slipping a hand into his jacket's breast pocket. "I was so rattled last night," he admitted, "I forgot to take *these* out of my pocket when we got back to the hotel. I guess that's actually a good thing?" He flashed me a hopeful grin, and I responded with an encouraging nod.

Standing up from his chair, he only remained upright for a moment before dropping to one knee. Opening the small ring box, he revealed two matching gold bands. Confidence finally radiated in his voice as he began, "Ollie, I started falling for you the moment I saw your brave but scared face in the waiting room. I knew I was head over heels in love after our first morning together. I knew I wanted to be with you for the rest of my life after our first weekend of exploring together. And when I lost you, even for just a few hours, I nearly died. When you came back to me, I knew I had to make our love official."

He looked up, eyes shining, "Oliver Aaron Carson, will you marry me?"

Everyone around the table already knew my answer. Ted must have felt safe to add his contribution to our special moment. He cleared his throat to get our attention before I could give my reply. "Um, Sport, as beautiful as this is, didn't we give you two a pretty important prerequisite before going this far?" He winked, and despite the timing, I could tell he was just enjoying a bit of fatherly fun with his boys. Oddly enough, he couldn't have given me a better way to answer Corey's proposal.

I wasn't sure if Ted realized just how perfect his reminder would be, but I met it with enthusiasm. "Yes, you did - and thank you for reminding us!" I turned back to Corey, still on one knee, and gazed into those sky-blue eyes that held my entire world. "Alright, my wolf - just like we did on the first Monday morning we woke up together..."

I took a breath and started our song, the melody that had become ours, the one that spoke of promises, of always being there, of finding joy even when the skies turned gray.

Corey's eyes widened in surprise before his lips curled into the smile I adored. He jumped in, his voice carrying the same hesitant, hopeful note he held that first time on that magic morning.

Encouraged, we continued together, the words flowing as naturally as our love - about staying through the storms, about never waking up alone, about knowing that together, we'd always have something real, something unshakable. Our voices blended, lifting into something greater than either of us alone, just like us.

And then, making it official, I ended with the words that mattered most. "Corey Allan Rainer, I will sooo-*oh, oh, oh, oh* marry you."

The table erupted into cheers, followed by applause from nearby diners as Corey and I stood and kissed - prompting an even louder ovation.

I wiped a few happy tears away as I glanced around. Grandma Laura's own tears flowed freely as she jumped up to join our embrace. Grandpa Joe moved around the table to shake Corey's hand and to clap my shoulder. "Congratulations, you two. I'm so happy for you both."

Just then, I noticed we were missing two very important characters from our happy scene. Corey and I must have realized it at the same moment, because we both turned toward our dads. Ted and Chris were equally teary-eyed, yet they seemed locked to their seats, more intent on sharing an astonished look with each other than on what we'd just committed to.

Corey ventured, "Dad? Ted? Are you two okay? I thought Ted was just joking. Did we actually upset you?" His question snapped them out of their trance, and they both started laughing.

Chris answered first, looking at us with eyes full of love and joy. "Oh no, Son *and Son*," he chuckled, addressing us both. "Not at all. You've made us incredibly proud; we're easily the happiest parents on the planet right now. But, Oliver, I do have a big question. Sport, how exactly did you come up with that song? Did Corey maybe start it first and you just followed his lead?"

I blinked, giving him my second nonplussed look for the day. "Um, no. Like I said, it happened on the Monday morning after my first night at Corey's house. There was a huge storm Sunday night but Monday was a beautiful, sunny morning. I woke up and rolled over to see Corey resting on his elbow; just watching me sleep.

"But the thing I remember most was that the sun lit his hair like a golden halo, and that song just...

burst into my mind. We sang it exactly the same way - me starting, then Corey jumping in like it was already in his head." I paused, feeling a bit sheepish. "I'm sorry - were there more, uh, rules we were supposed to follow?"

Chris beamed at me, chuckling softly before turning to meet Ted's gaze. Ted took over. "Well, Sport, Chris asked because there's a good chance Corey might've heard us singing that song around the house - a *lot* - when he was younger. Because, um...that's our song, too." Ted and Chris both glowed as they leaned in together for a tender kiss.

Though obviously delighted by our special moment, the two senior members of our group - my grandparents - wore bemused smiles. I decided it was up to me to explain yet another of my new family's endearing traditions.

"Grandma, Grandpa," I began, "I know this seems a little crazy. Please, let me fill in the blanks. During my first weekend with Corey - Ted and Chris could tell we were quickly falling in love - like, *two-days* quickly. Apparently, it's a Rainer-family trait." I gestured at our two obviously smitten dads before continuing. "Twenty years ago, they fell in love over a single weekend too."

I glanced at Corey, then back to Ted and Chris. "To slow us down and keep us from getting too carried away, they jokingly told us we couldn't get married until we found 'our song.' Turns out that, after Ted and Chris spent their first night together, they woke up singing the same tune. Totally sweet - and *ridiculously* romantic. But" - I flicked my gaze back to Corey exclusively - "what nobody expected was that *we* would do the exact same thing on the morning after *our* first weekend together."

I reclaimed Corey's hand, as well as taking Ted's before continuing. "And what no one at this table knew until right now, is that *our* song also happens to be *their* song." I said, unable to hold back a grin.

A fresh wave of congratulations swept the table. I turned to Chris. "Dad 2 - just so you know, you're *only* 'Dad two' because I met you second," I teased. Chris reached up to pull me close, planting a fatherly kiss on my curls and giving my shoulder a supportive squeeze.

I blushed but pushed on. "I love you too. But what I was about to say was, remember how, during our poolside 'recovery day,' you pointed out that Ted and I had both fallen in love with the same man, just twenty years apart? Well, I guess it makes sense we'd end up sharing the same song, too."

Chris chuckled, offering a playful salute. "Well said, Sport."

CHAPTER 50: GRANDPARENTAL ADVICE

We spent the first part of our impromptu family reunion dinner regaling the dads with tales from our trip, including meeting an Indianapolis Colts wide receiver after last night's 'document proposal.' We also couldn't resist bragging about the VIP tickets we scored for next season's Colts-Cowboys game in Arlington.

Once our waiter decided we'd settled down enough to order, the conversation pivoted to updating my grandparents about my life since January - when they'd lost contact with me. I skimmed over the details of my homeless situation before meeting Corey; they had already heard enough about that during today's confrontation with Richard. I was also pretty sure that any details of my "Intimate and Exposed" test would've been a bit too much. But I gleefully indulged, with plenty of enthusiasm, about everything that's happened since then. They were even excited about my likely transfer to TCU - to the point of making plans to visit us in the fall.

Our conversation shifted again as we dug into our meals - my second amazing steak dinner in a row. Grandma Laura took the opportunity to offer some engagement advice. "Ollie, Corey, I realize we've only known you two as a couple for a few hours, but I've never seen two people more in love. They say when you fall for someone, you literally *fall*, and you just hope the other person's there to catch you. Well, it looks like you two have done that perfectly."

She turned to me. "Ollie, I sensed a tiny bit of... maybe not embarrassment, but some uncertainty when you mentioned Corey's age. Sweetheart, you'll be twenty in two weeks. Did you know I was twenty when Grandpa Joe and I got married? And he's seven years older than me, just two short years shy of the gap between you and Corey. It only means he keeps me young, and I have to keep *him* in line!"

Ted let out a hearty laugh at the implied role reversal. "Well, that explains where Ollie gets it from. Trust us - he's by far the older soul between our two boys."

Grandma gave me a proud smile before leaning over to plant Grandpa with his second public kiss of the day. "By the way, that also means I'll be driving us back to Lansing tonight," she announced. "Joe hates driving after dark."

She gave Corey and me a soft laugh, then transitioned neatly into her final, and biggest, piece of advice. "You two wonderful boys, I'm not trying to rush you into anything. But from what I've seen today - this deep, beautiful love between you, the way you already seem to know each other's soul, and the amazing support you have from these two wonderful parents - I have to ask: Why would you ever want to delay your 50th wedding anniversary any longer than necessary?" And just like that, my sweet grandmother managed to coax yet another happy tear from me.

Before we could spontaneously exchange our vows on the spot, Grandpa Joe intervened with a gentle chuckle. "Not so fast, Laura. You forgot the most important advice." He pointed a friendly but stern finger at both of us. "Alright, you two lovebirds, you need to at least wait to tie the knot until you've had your first fight. You need to see how you handle being mad at each other before you settle into making googly eyes forever."

I genuinely appreciated my grandfather's wise advice, but I was far too giddy from all of today's events to let the conversation end on such a serious note.

Turning to my wolf, I suddenly blurted, "Corey, dang it!" The table went silent in surprise. "You literally *never* replace an empty toilet-paper roll. There's a new one right there under the sink. How hard can it be?"

I shot Corey a sly look, hoping he'd fire back in

kind - and he did. "Ollie, you *never* load the dish-washer's silverware basket right! Forks and spoons go handle down; knives go handle up. And you really do snore..." unable to stay too serious, he chuckled, "a little."

I feigned outrage, while trying not to start laughing myself. "Oh, come on! The silverware always ends up clean. And I've told you - I don't snore; I *purr!*"

Corey couldn't fake mock anger any longer and eased back into an affectionate tone. "Pup, you're right, it's a sweet purr. And from here on out, I promise to make sure you're always greeted with a full roll of TP when you enter the bathroom. My love, how could I have been so cruel and heartless?"

I followed suit with playful melodrama: "Oh, Corey, I'm sorry too. This is all so awful. Let's never fight again."

I thought I'd nailed it, but Corey delivered the master stroke: "Apology accepted, pup. So...does this mean we should head back to the hotel for our first round of hot make-up sex?"

Everyone roared with laughter. My slightly blushing grandfather glanced toward the dads. "Chris, Ted... are they *always* like this?"

Still laughing, both tried - and failed - *not* to encourage us too much. Between snickers, they simply answered in perfect unison, "Yep!" They knew when to just give up and love us.

Grandpa, apparently arriving at the same conclusion, brought the moment to a close: "Well, damn! Never mind. So...what does everyone's calendar look like for September?"

****

Much to my chagrin - and embarrassment - it turned out all four of our "elders" had one final secret plan in motion. Before the waiter could make his polite but usually fruitless attempt at convincing his table order dessert, a line of waitstaff approached our table with a cake blazing away under the glow of twenty candles that I assumed were meant for me. They were and I endured the entire restaurant's heart-felt - horrendous - rendition of "Happy Birthday." My cheeks burning brighter than the candles all the while.

Just when I thought the worst was behind us, Corey decided to bellow out an unexpected, yet admittedly perfect, coda:

> "Fooooor he's an Ollie good fellow,
> For he's an Ollie good fellow,
> For heeeee's an Oooooll-eeeey good fel-el-el-loooow,
> Which nobody can deny!"

I cut him off with a kiss before he could inflict anymore melodious damage. "Alright, Mr. Wolf, exactly how long have you been sitting on *that* little gem?"

He kissed me back and smiled, "Oh, let me see... I noticed your birthday on your medical charts right before your test. So, what - three months now?"

I figured he deserved another quick kiss before we dug into a sweet slice of cake to end our meal.

****

I knew it was time for my grandparents to head back to Lansing, but I had one last question. "Grandma, Grandpa... do you think mom will be okay? I mean, will she be safe with Richard? And do you think he'll ever accept everything that happened today?"

Grandpa rested a comforting hand on my back. "Ollie, we'll always be there for Susan - she knows that. I think she finally woke up to reality this afternoon. As for Richard, I can't say. None of us knew how extreme he'd gotten. But Susan will always be welcome in our home if things get that bad. Don't worry, son - she'll have support. She just has some big decisions to make.

After one more round of hugs and a few more Grandma kisses, the two people I feared I'd never see again climbed into their car. Before pulling away, Grandma rolled her window down. "We're looking forward to visiting your home in Texas, Ollie. I promise, we'll see you in the fall."

With that, they drove off. The four of us returned to the Bronco and headed back to the hotel.

CHAPTER 51: ENGAGEMENT NIGHT

I was still riding high on today's unexpected triumph - and on the loving promises to our future we'd made over dinner. I was pumped and all set to jump my new fiancé's bones. But he seemed to have something new in mind. "Hey Ollie, before we *consummate* our engagement, why don't we have some fun in the bathroom?"

I raised a suspicious eyebrow. Sure, Corey knew about my, well - let's call it what it was: a 'getting an enema from a nurse' kink. But I wasn't anticipating anything like that at the moment.

Sensing my confusion, Corey grinned. "Did you notice that we have a giant jetted bathtub, pup? Big enough for both of us. Believe me, I've got something new to show you."

As he started filling the huge tub, we stripped down, and once again, I got to marvel at my fiancé's body. It's still beyond me how such a perfect man could exist. He stood six feet, six inches of defined muscle and golden fur. Even his feet were picture-perfect. His calves and powerful thighs - covered in blond hair just a shade darker than mine - were equally flawless.

My "fantasy checklist" ticked on. His broad shoulders frame his rounded pecs, forming the top of his sculpted "V." Each pec, thickly dusted with dark-blond chest hair that will never stop making me get uncomfortable in my tighty-whities.

Adding to my euphoric discomfort, that wonderful chest fur abruptly stopped, right under his nipple line, somehow highlighting his pecs all the more. From there, the perfection continued with a pyramid of blond tummy fur that started at the base of his sternum, and guided the eye down into the lines of his abs - until, at last, it tapered off right as his deeper-colored bush and upper quad fur took over.

Damn I needed those pubes right now. While his pit musk never failed to drive me wild, the scent of those dark blond pubes grounded me and reassured me that this was my man. I couldn't stop myself; I knew we were about experience the joys of an intimate hot tub session. And I was absolutely thrilled, but I couldn't let the water wash my man's scent away before I was able to bury my nose in my wolf's crotch.

That's exactly what I did. He may have been a bit startled at first, but as soon as he realized my desire, his encouragement was exactly what I needed to hear. "That's right pup, you will always know the scent of your mate. Believe me Ollie, after today, we're never going to be apart again."

After reveling in the joy of simply breathing him in, I took Corey's already very fluffed cock in my mouth and knew that it was now or never. I slicked it up with as much spit as I could muster as I started taking its girthy length into my determined mouth. I let my tongue dance around his glans as his monster slowly sank in. By the time the first few inches were thoroughly wet and warm, my wolf was at his full hardness.

I kept going and refused to gag as his cock finally hit the back of my throat. Instead, I forced myself to start swallowing while I continued my drive forward. And for the day's next unexpected victory, I felt Corey's incredible shaft enter my throat. Once the inevitable had happened, just like the first time he breached my hole, I knew I was home free. Lol, well until I nearly asphyxiated. But I swear I had plenty of oxygen left as I tried to get my nose to reach its promised destination.

And I made it! I was thrilled to have actually pulled it off, even if only for a couple of seconds. As proud as I felt, I discovered that while every porn story I had ever read assured me that all I needed to do was "breathe through my nose." I quickly found out; that's a damn lie. Well, maybe at least until I could get some more practice in. But right now, as my watering eyes looked up to see my wolf's amazed face, I couldn't hold out any longer. I let my shaky little victory slip away as air finally rushed back into my lungs.

"Ollie! I can't believe you just did that! I don't know if I'll ever be able to return the favor, but dang! Is there anything you can't do?" He marveled. I soaked up his praise for a moment, before taking one last deep breath of his scent as we stepped into the hot, bubbling bath. We instantly started devouring each other's mouths while my tears finally cleared and we lowered our bodies into the tub.

Instinctively, we tried to cuddle together, with our heads at the same end, like we would on a bed. But the reality of our extra-large bodies gave us the first chuckle of our night's adventure. We quickly gave up and found that we could simply sit facing each other. My butt between his legs, my knees over his, my legs wrapped around his waist. The position allowed us to enjoy all the tongue dancing and nipple play that we needed as our steel swords passionately clashed against each other under the bubbling water.

Corey finally gave me one of his best sultry smirks - the best I'd ever seen. "Ollie, I know how much you like to mix water with you sweet little hole. Are you ready for some unexpected fun, pup?"

I could barely contain a happy pant, "Yes sir!" I had no idea where he was going, but after all our adventures, I knew I was in for a treat.

My commanding Corey took over, broke our embrace and moved so that he was now kneeling in the tub, his cock still every bit as hard as it was when it left my throat. "Okay pup, there's a swirling jacuzzi jet right behind you. It's meant to massage your lower back, but we're going to make it please a body part that's just a bit lower." He sat back on his calves and continued, "I want you to get on your knees, scooch back and lean toward me, lower your backside down and let the jet thrill your hole."

I followed Corey's instructions with an unbridled excitement. And suddenly, it was time for my first "Fuuuuck!" of the night. Believe me, it was justified. My eyes widened as Corey kept me in his gaze while I let an amazed moan escape my lips. I know there will never be anything that can match the feeling of Corey's tongue on my hole, but this was definitely a solid second.

My face couldn't hide my sudden rush of pleasure. I reached up, desperately grabbed the back of his head and brought his lips to mine. Our tongues dueled once more. I noticed that Corey had repositioned himself so that he was in the same pose I was.

While we were lost in our desire, slowly jacking each other's swords, Corey decided to make this moment of shared euphoria into an opportunity to deliver an unexpected revelation, "Ollie, my love, and soon to be husband, I have a confession."

With all the pleasure I was currently feeling, I was pretty sure nothing he could say could be all that important. Still, he continued, "So, when you took my virginity right before all this started? I maybe got a bit carried away in the heat of the moment."

Okay, that's not where I was expecting this to go, and maybe I did suddenly have a small look of concern on my still pleasure-overloaded face. He read my look and quickly continued, "Don't worry pup, you're still the only man who's ever put any part of his body into mine. Like I said, I just never felt close enough to anyone else to let that happen." I saw the honesty of his words and immediately returned to appreciating the feelings that the water rushing over my hole and the pumping of his hand were giving me.

Amped up by knowing Corey was feeling the same pleasure. I barely managed to utter, "Yes my wolf?"

Corey gave an embarrassed grin, "Well, you've seen *most* of my toys. I don't really have them to open up the tight confines of random one-night stands. I mean, you know that's not me." Locked into his eyes, I swear, my love truly looked embarrassed, but he continued. "I'm sorry I lied to you - just a little. I really wanted you to give you as much confidence as I could for the first time you took over as 'Top Dog.'"

I gave his overly large pole an extra tight stroke, but he managed to continue, "Believe me pup, every top needs know how amazing a well-directed prostate poke feels. I mean, otherwise, how can you claim to be a skilled lover? Ollie, those toys are for me. While I sincerely had no clue how incredible your real cock would feel, I've had plenty of experience of having my prostate mashed."

He gave me a playful smirk. And we both added a loving chuckle. But I suddenly felt like I had the advantage. So, I pressed on. "Um... My wolf, as amazing as this jacuzzi rim-job is, why did you decide to confess that little tidbit right now? More importantly, what are you willing to do for your penance?"

****

In response, Corey reluctantly led us out of the tub, promising he had something to make up for his little "fib." We quickly toweled ourselves dry. "Ollie," he began with a mischievous grin, "please don't get upset with my packing habits again, but an extra shirt and pair of underwear weren't the *only* things I overpacked."

He paused dramatically, rummaging through his suitcase. Finally rising up to present his buried treasure. "I thought we could maybe play with this in St. Louis or Indy, but both of those nights were perfect just as they were. Tonight is just as special, but I think it's time we explore a new level."

I could hardly believe what Corey was showing me. I mean, some of it looked pretty self-explanatory, but I was happy to let him explain. "So, pup, I picked this little piece of magic up right before we met. And now, it seems *everyone's* into it."

He held the complicated toy up as he started his excited explanation. He began by pointing to the main part that he was holding, something that looked like a perfectly reasonable 5-inch dildo. "This part is pretty clear - at least until you see all it can do - it goes up your butt."

I couldn't stop a little school-boy giggle. But he continued, "This wide, flat and bumpy, piece of silicon here..." He addressed the black material that was attached at a right angle to the base of the dildo, "Is a vibrator for your taint." He gave me a knowing raised eyebrow at the mention of my favorite furry body part.

"And finally, we have the trickiest parts. This first ring here, goes around your balls, to keep the plug snug in your ass. And this final loop at the end is a cock ring. I know you don't need anything to keep your soldier at attention, but believe me, the vibrations it delivers to the base of your cock are mind blowing. Any questions pup?"

I was prepared and immediately replied with two important ones. "Yes sir! First off, why does it need anything to stay snug in my butt? And secondly, as excited as I am to try this little beast out, well... If it's in my butt, where's your cock going to be?"

"Damn pup! I love your amazing mind every bit as much as your beautiful body! Those are the best questions you could have asked. So, first, it needs to be anchored around your balls, because it does this cool little trick." He performed yet another magic trick by suddenly producing a small remote-control fob in his hand. As he pressed a button, I could hear the whole apparatus start pulsing and vibrating. And my cock was happy to pulse right along.

To send my amazement over the top, Corey pressed the second button and the ribbed dildo suddenly began thrusting and expanding from its base. Once again, my brain broke. I may have even let a drop of drool slip out of the corner of my mouth. Hey, I am what I am, and that's usually a bottom. "Corey, I'm sorry, but *fuck*! That's amazing and I'm not even going to give you any frak for not showing me this fun little device before tonight." I playfully smirked, "But what about my second question?"

"Well pup, I figured with this animated silicone marvel satisfying your hole, you could maybe satisfy mine again with your real, hard, hot, massive, and eager cock. What do you say pup? Are you ready for another adventure to celebrate our most surprising and wonderful day?"

He didn't have to ask twice; I was ready and willing as he helped me first trap my testicles - something that was way harder than I'd expected. So much so that I'd almost gone soft before he helped me get my cock through the final ring. He encouraged me, "Don't worry pup, believe me, it's way easier to get into a cock ring when you're *not* hard as steel."

We finally got the tight ring around the base of my cock before he used the remote for the first time. Poof! All the vibrations ensured that there was suddenly no more softness, only an overstimulated erection.

"Okay pup, I know I didn't give you a chance to get me prepared, but believe me, I'm ready for this. So why don't you just lie back on the bed and let me deal with your big dick on my own, after all, I'm the guy who started this." I couldn't deny my wolf's hungry look.

I leaned back and raised my legs as Corey gently inserted the toy's vibrating business end into my quivering hole. After being accustomed to having his massive love gun squeeze its delightful way into my guts, this interesting little thing was an easy novelty to invite into my most private place. In fact, even with the vibrations running across my taint, I was skeptical about its ability to take our fun to the next level.

Then I suddenly couldn't care less. I watched as my wolf fingered a generous amount lube into his hole before applying even more to my vibrating cock. I knew I would reach the heavenly gates of our engagement night with or without the dildo's help.

Given my man's recently confessed anal expertise, I was only mildly amazed, but eternally grateful, for his ability to ease himself down on my aching, overinflated, hardon. Damn! Vibrating cock rings are definitely a new level. And, as I was soon to learn, this new level was only the first of many.

Corey slowly bottomed out on my pole and leaned down for more tongue play as he allowed himself to become reacquainted with my thickness and length. I reveled in the thought of making him just as happy and fulfilled as he normally makes me. My monologue sweetly wrote, "That's right my wolf, you will always be my benevolent alpha, through whatever tests we have to face, but always know that I will be here for you too, able to fulfill every need for comfort, protection and love you may have."

I knew he'd completely adjusted to my intrusion when his eyes rolled back. I was finally allowed to focus on just making sure I hit his prostate on every one of my solid strokes up into his accepting body. I was barely lucid enough to marvel at his powerful torso. Covered in its exquisite display of sweaty fur as I pleasured him, thrusting my cock into the core of his being.

Corey's look intensified, as if amazed at the power of our intimate act. He almost apologetically whispered, "Sorry pup, you got me to my peak way faster than I ever imagined." And he quickly pushed the remote's second button.

Sorry! But fuck, Fuck, FUCK! That's all it took for every firework I'd ever witnessed to explode in my brain all at once. I desperately thrusted up into my wolf as deeply as I could muster, before I nearly whited out. I managed to utter a sincere "I love you Corey, more than anyone else in the world," before that world erupted from my soul into to the accepting vessel of my fiancé. He returned the favor by drenching my almost furry chest with his own sincere display of love.

As our orgasmic high faded, we broke into our preordained round of euphoric chuckles. I couldn't help but tease, "Hey my wolf, I swear I could have lasted way longer - if you hadn't, you know, pushed all my buttons!"

He answered with a deep, lingering kiss, then admitted, "I know pup, you were amazing, but you had me too far past the point of no return; I needed you there with me."

Slowly rising off me, he added, "The good news is, we have our whole lives to figure out how to make our fun time last longer. It's like we have an erotic new assignment, pup." He winked as we headed to the bathroom to clean up.

We both winced when we noticed how late it had gotten - somehow time had slipped by faster than my quick-pull trigger. But as we settled into bed, I'd never been happier to be Corey's little spoon, tucked safely in the arms of my newly minted fiancé. I couldn't wait to wake up in those same arms tomorrow, ready to start our first full day together as an engaged couple.

CHAPTER 52: THE RETURN HOME

After our explosive first night as an engaged couple, we decided to face the consequences and sleep in - at least until 7:30. We showered and dressed in record time, no opportunity to determine if the hotel's conditioner tasted any better than ours back home. Suitcases in tow, we headed to meet Ted and Chris in the lobby.

I noticed a fatherly - if somewhat disapproving - spark in Chris's eyes. Corey spoke up, aiming to defend our late start. "Sorry, Dad. We just got engaged last night; did you really expect us to get to bed early and be up and ready to hit the road at 4:00?"

I sweetly added, "And I'm pretty sure we're both going to have puppies now." That was all Dad 2 could take; he rolled his eyes in defeat and gave me a goodbye hug.

Corey, shifted to a more serious note and continued: "I know this drive won't be fun, but we'll switch off. Ollie's taking the final leg from Texarkana so I can grab a nap. That should give me about three hours in the car, plus a few more at home. Tuesday won't be ideal, but I'll manage. Thanks for making sure I was covered at the clinic." Chris embraced his son.

I made my way over to Ted, wrapped him in a hug, and said, "Thank you so much for flying up here. You and Chris gave me the best surprise birthday gift I could ever imagine. I know y'all came here to ensure my grandparents were around to solidify our case against Richard, but having both of you by my side meant more than either my Bronco or my sudden cash flow. I couldn't have faced my former father without you."

That earned a final, bone-crushing goodbye hug.

Ted couldn't resist one last fatherly request. "Hey, Sport, I realize you two have a long drive ahead, but don't you dare finalize all your wedding plans on the way home. You gotta leave *something* for us to meddle in."

Chris offered his own, more practical advice, cupping my cheek with a gentle hand. "Oliver, here's a better plan: after yesterday, I believe you've got the perfect ending for your TCU introductory essay. How about getting it down on paper - or your iPhone - while you're on the road?"

I smiled, quietly marveling once again at how well they balance each other out. Just like Corey and me, they're a perfect couple - an unstoppable team. As we walked away, I remembered my initial thought upon seeing them together my first morning of no longer being homeless. Them in their tighty-whities, happily sipping coffee together. And I realized I had been given the same gift: twenty-five years of looking good and sharing mornings with *my* Norse God - and hopefully the next twenty-five after that.

I still can't believe the last three months have really happened. But I'm finally learning to just accept that I somehow get to be the luckiest pup on the planet.

CHAPTER 53: THE NEXT VERSE OF US

Our trip home was equal parts blessing and curse. Sure, Ollie getting to keep his Bronco was the best possible outcome, but damn this unplanned drive back was long and an absolute beat down. We'd been on the road for sixteen hours and were only just now about to cross back into Texas. I'd taken over driving at Little Rock, letting Ollie catch a few hours of sleep before his final turn at the wheel.

I gently woke him as we crossed the Red River and made our way into Texarkana. Ollie had just finished his Bronco-constrained stretching routine as I took the exit onto the frontage road and immediately veered into the Texas side of the Texarkana Travel Information Center rest stop. At this hour, there wasn't much else open, so it was going to be vending machines and a couple Red Bulls to help us make it home.

As we drove across the empty parking lot, making our way to the restrooms at the visitor center, Ollie shot upright in his seat and nearly shouted for me to stop. I slammed on the brakes. There was a fur-covered shape lying motionless on the asphalt ahead. Before I could react, Ollie bolted from the Bronco and ran to the mound of unmoving fur, prepared to help however he could.

I quickly stepped out and moved around to join Ollie in the beams of the Bronco's headlights. He knelt down beside the tragedy that was already too late to be averted: an obviously still nursing mother dog. We couldn't have been more than 30 minutes too late. His voice quavered as he looked up. "She's not a stray - she has a collar. Do you think she maybe got loose from her family?"

That's when I noticed a smaller form near her hind legs, just as still. "Ollie," I said softly, "I'm sorry." He followed my gaze and immediately darted over to pick up the unmoving puppy. Unlike the mother, the pup wasn't bleeding, but it too, wasn't breathing. Maybe it had been shielded from the worst of the impact by its mother's body, but whatever had happened, it hadn't survived. I could see Ollie composing his inner monologue: *As brave as the betrayed mother may have been, she couldn't save her deserted child from the inevitable.*

Tears began slipping down Ollie's cheeks as he brushed a gentle kiss across the little pup's forehead, then locked eyes with me, both of us on the verge of breaking down. "They were abandoned by their family," he whispered. "As heartless as they were, they must've thought leaving them here at the rest stop might give them a better chance - only it wound up killing them faster."

I caught the painful echoes in those words. There was little we could do, but Ollie found the only kindness left to give. "Let's move them over there by those trees. At least we can give them a final show of respect and make sure their bodies won't suffer any more until animal control can take them away in the morning."

Ollie quietly carried the tiny pup to the small grove of trees and softly laid it down. He returned to help me move the 40-pound mother as gently as possible. Together, we arranged them as peacefully as we could make them - the mother on her side, her pup curled safely into her paws. In a soft, trembling voice, Ollie offered a few final words, "I'm so sorry your family betrayed you when you needed them most. And I'm sorry you weren't given the chance to find the new family you deserved."

I couldn't keep my eyes dry through that simple, heartfelt eulogy. Wrapping my arms around Ollie, I whispered, "I'm so sorry. That was perfect." We stood there, holding each other, quietly weeping - reminded that not every abandoned pup gets to find a safe home.

Just as we parted and turned back to the Bronco, we spotted movement across the parking lot from where we'd placed the mother and pup, accompanied by the tiniest little whimper. Before I could stop him, Ollie tore off at a run toward the sound. I jumped in the Bronco and drove across the lot to meet him where he'd already knelt, once again ready to help.

"Corey! It's another puppy!"

I rushed over just as Ollie lifted the second little furball into his hands for a quick but careful inspection. The pup seemed frightened yet otherwise healthy - no obvious injuries or trauma. Ollie clutched him to his chest, and the tiny survivor wasted no time snuggling into the crook of Ollie's neck, tail wagging a mile a minute. Ollie giggled when the pup decided his earlobe simply had to be his new mom's milk dispenser.

There was no doubt: both puppy and pup had imprinted on each other. My pup finally had a puppy. I moved in to join them for a family hug, but not before Ollie could shoot me a pleading look. I chuckled. "Ollie, do you really think I could say 'no' to our new family member?" As he kissed me, the puppy joined in. Apparently I'd been imprinted on too.

We searched the surrounding area with our phone flashlights in case there were any other orphans, but it seemed our new boy was the sole survivor. We finally walked into the visitor center building, completely ignoring the "No Pets Allowed" sign on its door.

We took our new joy into the restroom to give him a better look and a more thorough inspection. He wasn't shy about showing his distress over leaving Ollie's arms - even for a minute - as we placed him on the bathroom sink countertop. But we had to make sure he was okay for the trip home.

Damn, leave it to my Ollie to stumble upon the world's cutest puppy. I don't know what breed he was - if any. I'd never seen anything like him before. He had a black muzzle, somewhere between a shepherd's and a Lab's. The black continued around his deep brown eyes and up his forehead where it gradually faded into a silvery blond fur on his head, temples and cheeks. His folded, squared ears shared the silvery-blond color, outlined in black along the edges.

The little guy had a medium length coat of the same silvery blond fur, but ticked with just enough black to outline the contours where his shoulders and haunches met his torso. All four paws were white until about halfway up his legs where a chevron of black kept it separated from the silver blond body fur. The white blaze on his chest with its own black border completed his amazing look. Aside from my Ollie, I'd never seen a more beautiful pup.

He couldn't be more than six weeks old. I only hoped he was weened enough to accept puppy food. I was sure the vet would let us know when we got home. Until then, he looked perfectly healthy, and well, obviously very happy to meet his two new dads.

We washed his face, paws and tummy in the sink before venturing out to the vending machines, hoping to find something he could eat. No such luck, but at least he happily drank a good amount of water from Ollie's cupped hands. With nothing more we could do, we returned to the Bronco and hoped to find a 24-hour fast food restaurant soon.

CHAPTER 54: A NEW SONG IN THE NIGHT

I knew tomorrow would be a beating beyond imagination, but I decided I needed drive this last leg home. There was simply no way I'd pry our new baby from Ollie's protective arms - especially since the pup had already dozed off, safe and warm against his new alpha. Nope! That wasn't how this story was going to end.

Once we were back on I-30, rolling toward home, I glanced over at Ollie. He was beaming down at our precious little bundle of fur, while he snoozed away in blissful contentment. A sudden epiphany struck me: after watching *my* pup turn into a grown man, we now had *another* "pup" in the house. Staring at that tiny, adorable black-furred face, I silently mused, *You've got some big puppy shoes to fill, little guy, but your alpha will make sure you grow into the best dog you can be.*

Ollie caught my gaze, and I swear I could read his

mind: before we'd even had time to process yesterday's whirlwind, we were suddenly parents - puppy parents, anyway. I voiced the only question that that could be said, the question of all questions: "So, Ollie... What are we gonna name him?"

Just then - almost as if the Sirius/XM gods had decided to stage their grand finale - an upbeat, infectiously cheery tune bubbled up out of the Bronco's speakers. We both froze the instant we saw the song's title flash across the screen. Judging by Ollie's amazed expression, he'd never heard the song before either. We locked eyes, smiling in stunned acceptance as the song began.

The melody was bursting with joy, the kind of song that made you want to roll down the windows and let the world in to share it. Everything about it felt right. The lyrics were perfect: about being lost in the universe, sailing blindly through life, and having no idea if anything was certain.

We turned to each other, stunned, smiling in unspoken understanding. The chorus started and built on the verse, filled with hope, with possibility - singing of new beginnings, of taking chances, of trusting the journey even when the path wasn't clear. All the while knowing one thing was true... In this crazy life we all need to take the time to appreciate the "Life of..."

And, in perfect harmony, we both shout-sang, **"Riley!"**

Our little guy stirred at the sound of his new name, blinking up at Ollie with sleepy, trusting eyes before giving a sweet puppy-breath yawn. Then, just as quickly, nestling back into the warmth of his family's protection - safe, loved, exactly where he belonged.

"So, Ollie... Did that really just happen?" I asked, staring down the dark freeway but sneaking glances at his incredulous smile. "Did that wonderful song neither of us has ever heard before, really just pop up on the radio right when we needed a puppy name?" I considered, "Does this mean we have a *new* song?"

Ollie's thoughtful chuckle sounded wiser than his nineteen - okay, soon to be twenty - years. "No, Corey, *we* still have *our* song - just you and me." He let out a more typical chuckle. "Okay, you, me, Ted, and Chris. But I think this is how it works: in addition to our song, we have a *new* one for the three of us - you, me, and *Riley*."

He gazed at me with the softest, most profound look in his beautiful eyes. "And someday, when another, less furry, baby boy or baby girl joins our family, the four of us will discover *another* new song. Each verse of our family will be unique and precious, but they'll all be connected by our past verses as we keep discovering new ones."

I stared back at my love, his wise face regarding my astonished one. And I wondered how on earth I could have ever gotten so lucky. Had the past three months really happened? I had resigned myself to a life of bachelorhood. And now here I am, suddenly presented with the man of my dreams and our new-found pup.

I'm the luckiest man on the planet.

www.ingramcontent.com/pod-product-compliance
Lightning Source LLC
Chambersburg PA
CBHW072346030726
47505CB00015B/2024